THE MAYOR AND THE MYSTERY MAN

A SINGLE DADS CLUB NOVEL

A.J. TRUMAN

TRUMAN BOOKS

Copyright © 2022 by A.J. Truman

All rights reserved.

No part of this book may be reproduced in any form or by any electronic or mechanical means, including information storage and retrieval systems, without written permission from the author, except for the use of brief quotations in a book review.

Cover illustration by Sierra Summit Designs

Cover title design by Robin at Wicked by Design

Chapter character busts by Michael T Art

Editing by Devon Vesper

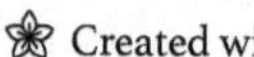 Created with Vellum

1

___

LEO

As mayor of Sourwood, I'd spent the past eight years dedicating my life to serving our community, making this town I've called home my entire life a wonderful place to live. But none of that will matter because any minute, my constituents were going to see my dick.

"How bad is it?" I asked Vernita Wallace, my chief of staff and campaign manager, who'd been with me since I first had the crazy idea to run for mayor. My favorite quality of hers was that she didn't sugarcoat.

"You tell me. They're your pictures."

Although maybe a dash of sugar on this horrific shitstorm wouldn't be so bad.

I whipped out my phone and tapped on the Milkman app icon, a sketch of a hunky guy in a way-too-tight 1950s milkman uniform. Boxes of naked and half-naked men with names like CumDumpster4u filled my screen.

For those living under a heterosexual rock, Milkman was a gay "dating" app. Allegedly, it was named after gay rights icon Harvey Milk and not because it was a conduit for men to meet and, uh, milk each other. Men got very revealing with the pictures they posted on their profiles. We were a visual species, after all.

"MisterWood?" Vernita read my profile handle aloud, and here was where I remembered that she was a mother and avid churchgoer.

"Y'know, because of Sourwood."

"Sure."

"Wood can have many different meanings."

"The beauty of the English language," she deadpanned.

"Just keep scrolling."

I bit into my piece of red velvet cake. After she broke the news to me, Vernita took me to For Goodness Cakes, the bakery in Sourwood. I tried to stay away from the sweets, but now was the ideal time to stress-eat.

I looked over her shoulder. It was quite a feeling getting an objective reaction to your profile pictures. I prided myself on staying in shape through daily runs. I was six-two and trim. My black hair was starting to gray at the edges, more so than I realized thanks to these pictures. At first, I breathed a sigh of relief. The pictures were tame. I was clothed and smiling.

"See, I'm not stupid enough to put naked pictures of myself on the internet."

"Some of these are pretty close." She scrolled to a pic of me shirtless on the beach (with my kids cropped out), and then one with me shirtless in my bathroom doing the classic mirror selfie.

"No dick pics."

"Gold star for you."

"And hey, I look pretty good for a forty-two-year-old father of teens." I managed a weak smile. "This might win me more voters."

She handed back my phone. "It's not about the pictures. We don't know what Damian's article is going to say."

Apparently, Damian, one of my former hookups, was penning a firsthand account of our time together for an LGBTQ-focused website that "sought to shine a light on important issues in the queer community," per their masthead. I wasn't sure how *this* advanced the cause. They reached out to Vernita to get a quote from me earlier today, mere hours before publishing. Woodward and Bernstein, they were not.

I preferred hookups with men around my age. Damian was my rare foray into fucking twentysomethings. It was slim pickings that night, and he had a good body and a background in gymnastics. I should've known that he would turn this around into a public story to spooge onto the internet. Fucking Gen Z.

"Is there anything I should be really worried about?" Vernita asked.

"Yeah. You're missing all the cake." I took another bite into red velvet goodness.

"Leo."

"And then, of course, I used my favorite sex toy on Damian: anal beads shaped like little swastikas."

"Thank you for putting that image in my head." Vernita blew out an exasperated breath, Grand Canyon-level creases carved into her forehead.

Probably not the best time for sarcasm.

I put a reassuring hand over hers. "All of my meetups were consensual with of-age adults, and we practiced safe sex. I didn't use a dime of taxpayer money to pay for supplies."

"Do I need to know what supplies entail?"

"Don't judge."

"Why go through the trouble of having one-night stands? I know three guys off the top of my head I'd love to set you up with."

"I'd rather have the swastika anal beads."

She rolled her eyes. Fortunately, we'd been through so much shit that there was pretty much nothing we could say that either of us would bail.

"Look, I like to blow off steam without the sticky entanglements a boyfriend brings, and I'm not going to feel bad about it. I have enough on my plate. I tried the marriage thing, and it didn't work. Not all of us are lucky enough to find Professor Charming and live happily ever after."

She chuckled at my nickname for her husband. He was an ethics professor at a local college, and it'd rubbed off on her. She could've been making a lot more money working for a lot more powerful political figures, but she turned down opportunities if candidates didn't abide by her ethical sniff test.

"Leo," she said with concern.

"I don't see why the people of Sourwood should care about any of this. It's personal. It's legal. Their property taxes aren't going up."

Before she could answer, her phone buzzed. "The article's live."

We navigated to the website. ONE HOT NIGHT WITH THE MAYOR, read the headline. My flesh crawled.

His essay detailed our "courtship" and then the night I met him at his apartment for sex. I breathed a sigh of relief because everything on the surface was above board. I couldn't help read the part where he praised my lovemaking skills and stamina.

"Stop smiling," Vernita said.

"Sorry."

I kept reading, and my stomach dropped. Damian talked about how I never contacted him again, how his heart was broken, and he felt used. Um, we met on a gay hookup app! He knew the rules.

He included screenshots of our texting, complete with–

"It's not a dick pic!" I shouted way too loud for a bakery in the middle of the day. "I'm wearing underwear."

A picture of me laying on my bed, grabbing my erection through my boxer briefs and smiling stared back at us. Vernita's eyes bulged open. After a career in politics, she thought she'd seen it all, and apparently, she had not.

"These types of pictures are common. Damian sent one, too. People want to see a picture of the merchandise before they make a purchase." I laughed to mask my terror at having the town of Sourwood see my junk on display.

"Why do guys always look so proud when they show off their genitals?"

I was giving the camera my best you-know-you-want-me face, which admittedly made me look kinda douchey. "You can't really see anything."

"I can see enough to know we'll have no problem landing the Jewish vote."

I crossed my legs under the table. "How bad is it?"

"Bad." She pursed her lips, but already the strategic gears behind her eyes were moving, which gave me hope. "True, you've committed no crimes. This is embarrassing but not illegal. We have a month until election day, and this image is what people will think about. We need to change the narrative."

I rubbed my temples. "Fucking Damian. Guy gave the worst blowjob of my life." He treated my dick like a teething ring, and his idea of dirty talk was asking me, *Do you like that?* every two seconds.

"He's not our only problem." Her eyes narrowed into slits. "Rita Buchanan entered the race."

"Rita?" I nearly spit out my dessert with laughter. "Are you serious?"

She nodded solemnly.

Rita's been a thorn in my side ever since she got elected to the city council. Her father owns a major real estate development corporation that's been trying to get their hands on Sourwood's riverfront property for years to build luxury mansions for the highest bidder. I've kept the land as a public park space so everyone can enjoy the view, not just a handful of rich people. To try and pressure me, he bankrolled Rita's city council campaign a few years ago, despite her having zero political experience and never being prepared for a single meeting. And now it seems the Buchanans are trying to remove me completely.

Well, too bad for them; I thrive on competition.

"Rita's an idiot. She's done fuck-all on city council. Nobody will take her seriously."

"Enough people do. She's been gaining in the polls, and this situation will only exacerbate that."

The world had officially gone mad. "What do people see in her?"

Vernita pulled up TikTok videos Rita did with her wife and young kids doing the latest online dance craze. They were the definition of wholesome and sweet, and I had CumDumpster4u, an angry ex-lover, and quasi-dick pics.

My confidence wobbled like it was walking on stilts.

"You think people would really vote for Rita?"

"If it's just on the issues and track records, no. But that's not how politics works. Image is a huge part of it. Even aside from this situation, you have some issues with your likeability."

Ugh. I hated that word. It was the moist of personality traits.

"People like me."

"They respect you. But you can come off a little..." She searched her brain for a proper adjective. "Stiff."

"Stiff?"

"I don't see you doing one of those videos or cutting loose."

I wasn't going to be one of those candidates flop sweating to make himself look cool. Watching old, nerdy politicians try to make TikToks and Instagrams was all kinds of cringe. My sense of humor skewed sarcastic, which I worried could alienate people not on that wavelength. But above all, I listened, I treated people with respect, and I cared about everyone in Sourwood. Sadly, the only thing speaking for me was my Milkman profile.

"Maybe I can set up a fun piece with a local blogger where you two go for a drink or bowling."

"Bowling?" I blew out a huge breath to the ceiling. "Yep, that'll save my campaign."

I thanked Marcy, the owner of For Goodness Cakes, and complimented her on the cake.

We strolled outside, where Maple Street was all decked out for fall. Decorations in the windows. Pumpkin-hay-and-wagon displays on street corners. Halloween cobwebs stretching across doorways. Sourwood had embraced fall more and more with each year, yet another example of this place feeling special and constantly filling me with warmth.

My heart beat in my chest as I watched my career, my passion slip away. I turned to Vernita.

"I love what I do. I love this town. I've lived here my whole life. I know more about every building, every park, every business, every street sign...I have worked so hard to make Sourwood a wonderful, inclusive community. We've been listed as one of the best places to live in the country for four years running, and there's so much more we can do."

When I first thought about running for mayor, I pictured famous ones who'd been with their towns for decades and had transformed them. They were like captains steering a ship with their steady hands. I wanted to be that steady hand for Sourwood.

"If you're telling me I'm cooked, then I guess I'm cooked. You don't bullshit me." I flitted my hands through a cornstalk decoration twined around a light post. "But if you think I still have a chance to win, then don't give up."

Vernita listened and took in what I said. Her face could be inscrutable one minute and then wildly expressive the next. It was a temperature check I relied on. But slowly, her stern, stoic expression broke into a reluctant grin.

"That's a smile. That means something positive is going to come out of your mouth." I smiled extra wide to keep her on the right path. "Repeat after me: We. Can. Win."

"I don't know if we can win, but I think we can try and stave off embarrassing defeat."

"There's that Vernita non-toxic positivity I love!" It was a sliver of hope, but I clung to that sucker. I wasn't ready to throw in the towel to a career I'd spent the past decade building.

We had a chance to turn this around. That was better than nothing.

2

LEO

When I stopped by my ex-wife Deirdre's house, we sat our thirteen-year-old twins Ari and Lucy down and had one of those Very Important Talks about this scandal. We talked through the article, what it meant, dad's personal life. We'd had several talks like this over the years: nine years ago when I decided to leave my law practice and run for office, then six years ago when Deidre and I got divorced, and I came out. And throughout the years, when people said mean things about me, we talked through them. Kids were smarter and more resilient than we gave them credit for, and being open with them was key to a great relationship.

The kids took it well. They had gay friends, and they'd grown up around my close-knit group of gay single dad friends. Fortunately, my kids were wise beyond their years, which made me nervous about the kinds of shit they were looking at online. They'd even heard of Milkman! Lucy told me she was sex-positive, something I wasn't ready to hear my thirteen-year-old daughter say.

But it was good news overall on what'd been a shitty day.

I drove back to my house, where I'd be spending the night alone. I deleted the Milkman app, refusing to get tempted.

I lived in an old colonial-style house from the late 1800s and had fixed it up over the years. It was spacious with unique built-ins, creaky wood floors, and a large fireplace. But being there alone, I felt the quiet. Not like I was angling for someone to move in. I meant what I'd told Vernita. My marriage flamed out, and I wasn't looking to try again. True, a big part of that flameout was because I liked dick. But even taking my sexuality out of the equation, I could never master the balance between career and family.

I spent the rest of the evening prepping for the upcoming city council meeting. My inbox was inundated with questions and comments about the article. People calling me a slut and a bad father, but then also ones supporting me against this intrusion into my personal life. It was only the first night. The article was less than twelve hours old. It would blow over.

It had to.

I worked in my office well past midnight, struggling to focus. I had to talk to someone about this. I texted my best friend Dusty.

Leo: How's the beach?

At first, I wondered if he was busy or even up, but this was Dusty. In no time, those three magical dots jiggled in the text chat.

Dusty: There are kids having a bonfire outside.

Leo: Kids?

Dusty: Early 20s. *shakes fist* Get off my beach!

He sent me a gif of an old man shaking his fist, then a video from his window of the kids in question partying around a beach bonfire. I used to envy him for living on the beach, but his neighborhood had the nonstop energy of a crowded college campus.

Dusty: I still can't get over people legally smoking weed. Remember how we used to have to sneak it?

Leo: Kids today will never know.

We could spiral into an unending discussion on nonsense like usual, conversations pinballing around different topics. But I had other things on my mind. I linked to Damian's article.

Leo: The state of my political career.

I waited for his reaction. This was a judgment-free text chain, but even still, I had that inkling of worry.

Dusty: Your dick is front-page news.

Leo: Unfortunately.

Dusty: Slow news day?

Dusty: Good Lord, this article is horribly written. Rufus could write better essays.

Leo: Rufus is getting his piece published in *The New Yorker*.

Rufus was the name of Dusty's imaginary dog. Whenever we saw a crappy movie or show, or he noticed a shoddy carpentry job, he loved to say, "My dog could do a better job than that." He said it so much that one day I asked what his dog's name was, and Rufus was born. Rufus could do anything.

Dusty: This is not journalism. Even I know the difference between they're, their, and there.

Leo: They wanted to get it up fast since the election is coming up.

Dusty: You okay?

Leo: I'm embarrassed.

Dusty: Don't be. Sounds like once guys go Leonardo, they don't go Backonardo.

Leo: That was terrible.

But I still laughed out loud in the comfort of my office, adding life to this silent house.

Dusty: You're a heartbreaker.

Dusty: Wait.

Leo: What?

Dusty: MisterWood?

I slumped down at my desk, but I could feel his eyes on me from the screen.

Leo: I needed a name.

Dusty: How you ever got play with a handle like that… you must have really good pics.

Leo: Please don't look.

We didn't have boundaries. We were best friends. But I didn't want him to look at those Milkman pictures. My privacy had been punctured in so many ways today; I didn't need one more from someone I cared about.

Dusty: Do you wanna talk?

Leo: It's late by you.

Dusty: I'm up.

"Hello from the future," I said into the phone moments later.

"What is the future like?"

"Shitty so far."

Dusty lived in Los Angeles, where it was eleven-thirty at night on Wednesday, as opposed to two-thirty in the morning on Thursday here in Sourwood.

"Don't you sleep, man?" Dusty asked me.

"You always ask me that. Sleep is optional for me." Getting more than five hours was a miracle. In fact, when I've gotten the rare eight hours of sleep, usually when sick, it just makes me feel more tired. "And it's late by you, too."

"I just got home from work."

Dusty worked for popular teen soap *Ocean City* as a carpenter. Their hours were nuts since they constantly had to build new sets for upcoming episodes. But no matter how late I called, he was always around.

"How are you doing?" he asked in his calm voice. I breathed out a relaxed breath for the first time today. It was like my whole body exhaled.

"I had a root canal last month, and I'd much rather go back to that than have to deal with this crisis." I walked around my office, earbuds firmly in my ears. My wall was filled with framed pictures of me out and about in Sourwood. "Would you say I'm likable?"

"I'm biased, but yeah."

I could hear a split-second of hesitation. "You didn't sound too confident in your answer."

"Where is this coming from?"

"I'd have a better chance of weathering this shitstorm if I were likable, whatever the hell that means. I'm not a talk show host, Dust."

"I like you." His voice had the slightest twang. He moved around a lot as a kid, his accent an amalgamation of different states. Yet when he got into carpentry, it brought out the southern man's man in him. "But you don't let people in right away. They have to work a little to get to know you. Once they're in, though, they've got a friend for life. I speak from experience."

"Damn. Thanks, Dust." I found myself at a loss for words, comforted by the insight into myself.

"Just calling it like I've seen it for twenty-plus years."

"Fuck. Has it been that long?" I found myself wandering through the house, his voice and our conversation lighting up the halls like he was beside me. "Where does the time go?"

"You have a beautiful family and an awesome career to show for it. Unlike some of us."

I didn't take the bait. Dusty bounced around careers his entire adult life, never finding the right fit. Perhaps after a childhood of moving, he was one of those people who constantly had to be in motion. Unlike me, who lived in the same town since birth. Carpentry seemed to be working out for him, and even though he took a roundabout way to get there, the important fact was that he was there.

"You have a great life, Dust. A place on the beach, working on a hit TV show."

Dusty didn't respond right away. Silence hung between us.

"You're a good guy, Leo. You love that town. This will blow over."

"I hope so. Vernita says I'm stiff."

"You're not," he said with full confidence. "I have the anecdotes to prove it."

"What if I lose re-election?" I strolled into my empty living room, adjusting books on the built-in bookcases by the fireplace, which were drooping under the weight.

"You can run again."

"It's not that easy. If I lose re-election, then this scandal will follow me around. The albatross around my neck." I picked up a picture on the mantle. It was me at my first ribbon-cutting ceremony for a new playground. I had practiced holding the big scissors so I didn't mess up in public. "If my opponent wins, she's going to destroy the soul of this town, turn it into some indistinguishable suburb with the same chain stores, the same sterile-looking condos. And that will be on me because I couldn't keep it in my pants."

I flopped onto my couch and stared into the empty fireplace. I was met with silence.

"This is the part where you say something inspiring and uplifting."

"Sorry. I was grabbing a beer from the fridge."

"Sam Adams. Bottle, not can."

"You know it."

I pictured Dusty's wide smile and his eyes crinkling at the corners as he shook his blond hair out of his eyes. He'd always had a surfer look and zen mentality to him.

Dusty exhaled in a low thoughtful groan. "I remember when you called me up scared. 'Does this sound batshit crazy,' you said."

I closed my eyes and laughed, the memory coming alive.

"You said you were thinking of running for mayor and leaving your law practice behind."

It sounded nuts when I first had the idea, but I couldn't let it go.

"A guy with no political experience? Going up against Mr. Three-Term–"

"Four-term"

"You were a long shot. You had me on the phone for two fucking hours, doing your pros and cons bullshit, and I kept telling you to pull the trigger."

It was like it was yesterday. Those small decisions that have big ripple effects. Dusty had complete confidence in me that never wavered over that epic conversation.

"But even though you were scared, you knew in your heart you could do it. Deep down, you wanted the challenge. You like challenges. Hell, I remember when I first met you. You were always driven to win." Dusty let out a raspy laugh, and he still had the bountiful cheer that echoed throughout college.

Freshman year of college. My political science seminar. I got into it with this guy in the back of class with a puka shell necklace and ripped jeans over the legality of the Clinton impeachment. After a while of going back and forth, I got the feeling he didn't care about Bill Clinton so much as he enjoyed getting a rise out of me.

But from there, somehow, a friendship was born.

Wasn't it strange how you met your friends? The most random moments could be monumental. There were guys I thought I'd be lifelong friends with—frat brothers and debate teammates and internship co-workers—but none of those friendships lasted like the one with the laid-back, pot-smoking student in the back of the class.

"You thrive on challenge, Leo. Deep down, you love this. Because now you're the underdog again."

I kicked up my heels on the ottoman, loving the sound of that. "I'm the underdog."

"The Leo McCaslin I know doesn't throw in the towel." Dusty yawned through the phone.

"First yawn. You know the rules."

"Whoever yawns first..." He yawned again. "Get some damn sleep, Leo. You sound exhausted."

"I will," I lied. My whole body smiled like I knew a call with Dusty would do. "Good night, buddy. Love you."

"Love you, too."

We clicked off, and the house felt empty all over again.

"This will all blow over," I said aloud.

Too bad I was very, very wrong.

3

DUSTY

Every morning, I woke up to the same sounds: explosions and gunshots at full volume from the TV, my roommates shouting insults at each other as they played, and my third roommate jerking off in the bedroom next to mine. And every morning, I told myself I needed a new fucking place to live.

My clock read a few minutes before eight.

I stood up, yanked open the curtain of my small window, and gazed at the Pacific Ocean. The view was the sole benefit of this shitastic living situation.

Morning. See you soon :) I texted Audrey, then scrolled through her IMDB profile. She had creamy skin and wild red hair that flowed like wildfire. Five months of dating, I was as much a goner as the first time I saw her walk onto set.

I watched my phone for a response, but none came. She probably had an early call time.

I thumbed down to my text conversation with Leo, which brought a smile to my face as it always did. It was like an epic poem at this point, going back years and years, a catalog of inside jokes and daily highlights and lowlights. A part of me was tempted to look at those Milkman pictures that were leaked out of sheer curiosity to see if Leo still kept it tight, but I held back out of respect.

The shouting of roommates one and two snapped me back to my present. I blinked away from the clear blue ocean to my tiny bedroom. The closet was stuffed tight with clothes. My bed and dresser left only a sliver of walking space across the raggedy carpet.

On the other side of my wall, roommate number three let out a high-pitched moan, and his bed stopped squeaking.

I had to get the hell out of here.

———

AFTER SHOWERING in our one bathroom that had an assortment of their trimmed pubic hair bunched at the drain, despite my roommates promising to clean, I got dressed and poured myself a bowl of Cheerios in an attempt to be heart-healthy now that I was in my early forties. These little golden circles drenched in milk were the only things keeping my heart rate down while gazing upon the shitshow of this apartment—junk everywhere, couches covered in burns and stains that my roommates proudly ignored.

Leo believed I lived in a swank apartment on the beach, a lie I had kept up through selective photos I'd shared in texts. I didn't want him to know the truth.

"Dude, you almost made it to the next level."

"I would have if you didn't cockblock me."

"Fuck off. No way you were going to make it to that level. You didn't pick up those machine guns."

"I would have, assbox."

"Fuck off, dickblanket."

And on and on it went as they discussed *Roman's Choice*, their current video game obsession. Their insults usually consisted of the words ass or dick combined with a random object. Seeing as I roomed with struggling actors and writers, they were generally in the apartment at all hours. The TV never turned off.

"Hey guys," I called from the kitchen. They paused the game and looked my way, their heads slowly turning like the girl from *The Exorcist*. "Can you try and clean up sometime today? The place is getting pretty messy, and I cleaned last week. Even though it wasn't my turn."

I had made a schedule for cleaning, which had gone ignored.

"Uh, yeah, sure," said Roommate One, greasy hair shoved under a beanie. I refused to call them by their names. "But like, uh, yeah, I have an audition today. So I gotta focus on that."

"So you can't clean today?"

"Uh, yeah."

"Then why did you say yeah, sure?"

He shrugged and scratched his nuts. I shifted my vision to Roommate Two.

"I have a shift today," he said of his waitstaff job. Considering how little he listened to me, I wouldn't want to be one of his tables.

They turned back to the TV and resumed their game. Roommate Three rooted through the fridge. I doubt he'd washed his hands.

I took the bold move of stepping in front of the TV. Roommate One considered trying to play around me for a second.

"Guys, this is not a way to live." I tried to sound cool and diplomatic. I used to be one of them, the chill guy who thought it was cool not to care about things. But part of being an adult was admitting that you *did* care about *a lot* of things. "We have a nice apartment. We should treat it well."

"The place is fine," Roommate Two said. "We'll pick up later."

"The thing is, you always say that, and yet when I come back from work, nothing's been picked up." I pointed to a beer can on the coffee table. "I know for a fact this empty can has been on the coffee table for five days."

"Then why haven't you picked it up?" Roommate One asked with a shit-eating gotcha grin. He hi-fived Roommate Two.

"Things have to change." I shakily put my foot down.

Roommate Two readjusted himself, which made me wonder if he had gotten crabs from Roommate One. "If you don't like it, you're welcome to move. You're on a month-to-month."

His eyes narrowed at me in victory. It was his name on the lease. His name, and his dad's.

"This is a nice place. You have a view of the damn ocean. It wouldn't hurt to keep things clean. And maybe respect each other's stuff more." I snatched my box of Cheerios out of Roommate Three's post-jerkoff hand. "I'm not opposed to sharing, but it's a two-way street. And right now, it feels like a one-way street."

"We wanted to get a cleaning service, but you said no," Roommate One said.

"You're all home most of the day. You can take an hour a day to clean yourself."

"Maybe you didn't want to spend the money on a cleaning service."

"Or you couldn't," Roommate Two said, fiddling with the

controller in his hand. Cruelty came so easily to rich kids. "I mean, how does a fifty-year-old wind up renting a room?"

"I'm forty-two."

He patted down his wildly curly hair. "Same difference."

"I told you."

"Right, right. Business venture gone south or something." Roommate Two stood up. I had a few inches on him but felt like the smaller one. "We want to get a cleaning lady to come in. We can afford it. You were the one who said no, and now you're complaining about a messy apartment. Typical boomer."

"I'm not a boomer."

"All those in favor of hiring a cleaning service?"

The guys all raised their hands. I should've let it be. I would benefit from a cleaning service, too, even though I was tight on money. But my pride refused to give in. I wouldn't give them the satisfaction. I'd been working my ass off since I was sixteen; their parents paid their rent. Now I had to pay extra money because they were too lazy to clean? It made my blood rage.

"You know what, I'm exercising that month-to-month flexibility. Nice knowing you guys. I'm sure if I come back in ten years, you'll be in this same spot."

I charged out of the apartment, doing my best to let their snickers roll off my back.

———

So how did a forty-two-year-old (not fifty!) guy wind up having to live in a tiny room in a tiny apartment with three of the grossest, most entitled twenty-something roommates?

I asked myself that question every goddamn day. What were the chutes and ladders of life that brought me here?

Some people, like my friend Leo, knew what they wanted in life and attacked their goals with a single-minded focus. In college, he talked about being a lawyer with his own practice. He made Dean's List, studied like a madman for his LSATs, busted his ass through law school, got recruited by a firm, then broke off on his own. He then wanted to become mayor of his hometown. And by golly, he made it—straight, clear path.

Not all of us were lucky enough to have that kind of internal compass.

I didn't know what I wanted to do with my life, so I went to college to figure it out, but after four years, I remained without an answer. So I went to law school but barely survived my first year before bailing. In the first of many examples of my awful timing, I had this epiphany after I'd taken out boatloads of student debt.

I'd bounced around from job to job, trying to figure out what fit. Pharmaceutical sales was too soul-crushing, running a restaurant was too stressful, working on a cruise ship was too nauseating. Managing rental properties meant getting shit from landlords and tenants. I started a business selling energy drinks, which fizzled quickly, much like the drinks themselves. Each failure added more debt to my life. There were women along the way, but whenever I thought things were going well, they'd bolt.

It wasn't until I reached my mid-thirties that I realized I wanted to work with my hands. My favorite memories were going with my parents' church to build houses for underprivileged people. I got back into carpentry; I'd always done some kind of woodworking or building throughout the years—helping friends repair tables, building cute wooden signs for nurseries. I scraped together all of my remaining money to build spec houses.

Then the market crashed. I had to sell my own house to cover the losses.

I was forty years old, single, and homeless.

And now I was woken up by the sounds of masturbation and *Roman's Choice*.

To make money, I built sets for *Ocean City*. The huge bright side was meeting Audrey, one of the stars of the show. In typical Hollywood fashion, she played a seventeen-year-old but was actually thirty-three. We'd been flirting with each other around the set and finally consummated at the wrap party last spring. We had an amazing summer together but agreed that we'd be professional once the new season started up last month.

I arrived at the soundstage in my loud, rattling car that, after 150,000 miles, wasn't long for this world. I constructed a set for a new pizza parlor hangout where Audrey's character would work after school and eventually have a flirtation with her married boss.

Are you filming today? I text.

I took a quick break and meandered around the set until I found Audrey rehearsing a scene in the school hallway set. I waved, which I knew she saw, but she didn't reciprocate.

After a few hours of working on the pizza place and repeatedly checking my phone, I hopped over to her trailer.

"Yeah," she said when I knocked on the door.

"It's me." I waited a few agonizing seconds before she let me inside.

Her trailer was bigger than my bedroom, a fact I ignored as I kissed her. It was an oddly one-sided kiss. She pulled away.

"What's up, Dusty? I have a big scene I'm trying to prepare for."

"Oh? What is it?"

"Lena is finally losing her virginity to Adam."

"Wow." It was a storyline that'd been building up since last season, but it tightened my chest knowing she'd be in bed with that admittedly hunky actor this week. "Congratulations. For you and Lena."

"It's something they've been driving toward since the start of the show. The fans call us LenAdam, which doesn't have the right ring. Marketing is working on a new name to feed the fan sites." Audrey checked her makeup in the mirror. They had to put it on thick because high-definition TVs made it harder to hide her real age.

"Whatever it is, it's going to be great. What's in a name, anyway?"

"I mean, everything. We need to keep the fans engaged so they keep watching."

I put my hands on her shoulders, and she froze under me. I nearly got ice burn.

"The fans love you, almost as much as I do." She tensed under me, but she was probably nervous about nailing her scene. She was also one of those people with a clear, straight path to their goals. "It's going to be great."

"I know. We've been practicing."

"Practicing?" My stomach dropped into my feet. What the hell did that mean?

"Our lines. Blocking the sex scene. We're working with an intimacy coordinator."

It was still weird dating an actress and having these lines blur. Maybe I didn't need to know everything about her process.

"You know, it's been almost six months since we got together." I kissed her neck, moving her wild hair out of the way. "I've loved every minute of it. Have you given any thought to us taking the next step, moving in together?"

"That seems fast."

"We're both adults here. We know what we want." Audrey was my clear, straight line. I'd known it ever since we flirted at craft services. My twisted, messed-up path had led me to this wonderful point.

"I don't know, Dusty. People might find out."

"And? It's not like I haven't spent the night at your place before. The paparazzi haven't found out."

"I don't want to upset fans who are rooting for Adam and me."

"On the show, though. Not in real life."

Audrey got out from under my massaging hands and went to the far end of her trailer, the distance gaping between us. She had on a new face I hadn't seen before, and after watching all three seasons of *Ocean City*, I thought I'd seen them all.

"What is it?"

"Dusty, this isn't working."

I stumbled back and sunk into her couch. "What? Where's this coming from?"

"You're a great guy."

"Please don't give me the great guy speech. I've heard it too many times."

"This was fun, but you make it feel a lot more serious. And..." She gazed out the window. Was she acting? Did she rehearse this breakup? "There's someone else."

"Who?" And then it hit me like a cliched plot twist. "Adam?"

"It was totally unexpected. Our characters were never meant to get together, but the writers apparently saw us flirting during rehearsals and wrote that into the show. And as we kept filming those scenes..."

"So when you said you and Adam were practicing..."

"We've been having sex. A lot of it. At his house. At my house. Even on the couch where you're sitting." She hung her head, but there was a joyous glint in her eye. Of course, there would be. She was having great sex.

I hopped off like my ass was on fire.

"It's not cheating because at first, we were running lines and then practicing blocking."

I had to sit down, but I was afraid that Adam's bare ass had tainted every hard surface in this trailer.

"It just happened. We're falling in love." Audrey twisted her hands together. I wished she was acting, that she was going method with rehearsing a scene.

"You're falling in love? *We* were falling in love."

"You were," she shot back softly, but it was enough of a bullet to shred through me.

"What happened?" I asked. "I genuinely want to know."

My string of ex-girlfriends was a pattern I couldn't crack.

Audrey sat next to me, trying to be supportive. "I...wasn't feeling it. I think I kept things going because you were trying really hard. I wanted to feel what you felt."

Love wasn't something we were supposed to try at. It was supposed to overwhelm, like this feeling that was unexpected, logical, and all-consuming all at once. Every time I thought I felt that, I was proven brutally wrong. Maybe I was meant to live life alone. Shoved in a crappy apartment with awful roommates.

She patted my back. "I have to get back out there."

Just then, the trailer door swung open. "Hey, babe. You ready to hop into bed? I hope the camera guys don't mind me getting a boner." Adam jaunted inside but stopped when he saw me. "Oh, shit."

On the show, Adam played a brainiac, a stark contrast to

his real life, where he had resting what-just-happened face. It was like he went to the Keanu Reeves school of acting.

"We were talking about a scene in the show..." he stammered out, running a hand over his perfectly coiffed hair.

"It's okay, Adam. I told him."

"That we're having real sex?"

"I know everything," I said, suddenly feeling like a daycare worker to these two.

"Oh. Cool, then?" He gave me a weak thumbs up. "We cool, bro?"

"Yeah. Definitely," I said with a heap of sarcasm.

"It was a shitty thing for us to do," Adam said. His face contorted into a dramatic look. I overheard him once tell castmates that to achieve this forlorn stare, he'd think hard about why we park on a driveway but drive on a parkway. "If it makes you feel better, I always used a condom out of respect to you."

"How is that..." I held up my hand, shaking that line of questioning away. "It's...we're all adults here." I cut my eyes to Adam. "Barely."

"Don't worry, bro! Your soulmate is out there. Do you want some chips?" He offered me his half-eaten bag of Lay's.

I looked at the bag, then at his doofy expression, and something inside of me snapped. I snatched the chips out of his hand and punched him in the stomach.

"Dusty!" Audrey yelled. "What the hell!"

Adam collapsed to the ground. I could've hit him in the face, but that would've set production back, and I wouldn't do that to the crew.

I hoped they appreciated my concern for their jobs since I'd never see them again. An hour later, I was escorted off the set.

4

LEO

My Milkman scandal did not blow over. The first polling numbers came out since the story leaked. My approval rating dropped five points, and in a matchup between Rita and me, Rita had surged into the lead.

Vernita and I ran through potential ideas to turn things around. I could give a press conference, but my comms team had concerns about how much it would help. We thought about having me partake in the latest viral dance craze. Rita and her family had uploaded a lipsync and dance video singing to the latest song from The English Patients, a pop-rock band that was climbing the charts. I informed my team that despite being gay, I did not dance.

I went to my happy place: the balcony of my friend Mitch's bar, Stone's Throw Tavern. It looked out on a tributary of the Hudson River flanked with gorgeous fall foliage. The steady gush of waterfalls brought me calm. I wasn't into the whole concept of zen. That was more Dusty's speed. Who needed to be calm and centered? Life moved too fast for that.

Mitch brought out another round of beer. My other friends, Cal and Russ, joined me out here to brave the chill.

"You're down, but not out," Mitch said, then stopped himself. "Well, technically, you're out."

I tipped my head at him. "I forgot for a moment I was gay. Thank you for reminding me."

"This will blow over."

"I said that last week. And it has not."

"Look at what so many politicians have gotten away with and still won re-election," Russ said.

"And they weren't as attractive as you," Cal said, trying to find a silver lining. "That's got to count for something."

"I took a casual poll of parents on the PTA. There are some who don't like that their mayor is trolling dating apps and having random sex."

Cal put his hand on his boyfriend's chest. "They're just jealous. Most of the women on the PTA wouldn't know good sex if it fucked them up the ass."

"Real classy, Cal." Russ shook his head. "I was trying to make a point."

"You love it." Cal kissed him.

"Not everything has to come back to anal sex."

"Again. You love it."

"Can you guys put a pause on the schmoopiness, maybe? Only until I figure out what the hell I'm going to do." They were still on their new relationship high. Fortunately, they were used to my sarcasm and laughed it off. "I still have the authority to kick you out of the Single Dads Club."

Technically, we were the Single Dads Club. Mitch, Cal, and I had known each other growing up. We didn't know each other was gay in high school, but we all wound up coming out as adults and reconnecting as friends. We were more than friends, though. We were like one big extended family. My parents had passed on, and my siblings were scattered across the country, so these guys were my family. Cal and Russ had started dating a few weeks ago after formerly hating each other. Sometimes I wondered if their bickering was just one long extended foreplay; there was a fourth member of the group, Buzz, but he and his hot manny-turned-boyfriend Shane recently moved to Seattle. They'd be back for the holidays.

"Anyway, what I was saying," Russ winked at his boyfriend for interrupting him, drowning the room in more schmoop. "is that, while the other parents aren't fans of your sex life, the bigger problem is that they love Rita. She and her wife are fun, accessible, warm."

I stood up straight. "And I'm not?"

Silence. Brutal, telling silence. The guys traded looks as if they were mentally flipping a coin to see who had to break the news.

"The videos they post online are..." Cal took a step behind Russ, using him as a shield. "Cute."

"And people know and like Deb. She's a physical therapist in town. She helped me when my carpal tunnel flared up," Russ said of Rita's wife. "People like Deb, so in turn, they like Rita."

"In a vacuum, the scandal isn't that bad. But the scandal up against Rita and her cute family is the problem. You need to fight warm, cuddly fire with warm, cuddly fire," Cal said, echoing a similar statement from Vernita.

I wasn't the warm, cuddly type. I was the take charge, get shit done kind of guy. Why couldn't that be enough? I wasn't trying to be a social media influencer; I wanted to lead a community. I wasn't some pollyanna about politics, but this seemed overboard.

"You need to let people in," Mitch said, never one to mince words.

"What does that even mean?"

"If Rita's going to parade around with her lovely wife, then you need a lovely wife of your own. Er, husband," Russ said. "Er, boyfriend."

"Yes!" Cal jumped up. "People love love!"

"A boyfriend can help show off other sides to you. Humanize you," Russ said.

Humanize was a word I hated more than likable. I was already a human, as evidenced by my body parts and ability to have sentient thoughts.

"You can talk about how you fell in love, and your boyfriend can share fun things about you that annoy him, like how he hogs the covers in bed." Cal's eyes were wild with ideas.

"How about I stick my finger down my throat instead." I looked to Mitch for backup. He was more level-headed than anybody else I knew. But even he seemed intrigued by the idea.

"Single Dads Club, we have a mission here. Our most important mission to date." Cal clapped his hands twice, almost spilling his beer over the balcony in the process. "We need Mayor McCaslin to fall in love."

I wasn't a religious man, but I craned my neck to the sky in the hopes God would save me from this conversation. Cal and Russ had gotten together recently, and I was happy for them. I loved seeing my friend in love, but that wasn't a path I wanted to go down.

"This is the worst idea I've ever heard, and some guy once applied for a permit for a traveling bounce house on wheels."

"Is it?" Mitch asked.

"Mitch, you're saying I should get a fake boyfriend? I thought you were in my corner."

"If it's just for a few weeks." He shrugged. "The right guy could make you seem…"

"Don't say warm. Or cuddly. Or likable."

"Cool. And electable."

It was three against one. I wanted to mutiny this conversation. The thought of being tied to a guy for the next month—hell, even the next day—sounded like torture. I didn't want someone stomping all over my normal, routine life. "I really don't want to do this. I thought I was done with the mushy relationship shit when I got divorced."

Cal and Russ went inside to check in on their kids, who were over at the house of Russ's sister Monica. Their boys were a cute age. Maybe I could rent them and say they were adopted?

"Why are you so against this?" Mitch asked when we were alone, with only the gush of the falls in the background. I knew he wasn't talking about the election. That was the thing about Mitch. He knew how to cut through the bullshit in record time.

"When I was married, I felt like I was constantly making a choice between my relationship and my career. If I wasn't hurting Deirdre and the kids, I was hurting myself. I've finally gotten into a groove as a single dad. I don't want my life to get upended again."

Mitch had an amused grin. "All I know is that a guy who keeps hooking up is maybe looking for something."

I believed Mitch should be hooking up more. Between his quietness, strong work ethic, and lack of sex life, he was turning into a monk.

"Kids are still alive. Phew!" Cal wiped a hand over his

forehead. Russ followed him outside. "Why don't you pull up a dating app and let's find you a boyfriend?"

"I'm not finding a fake boyfriend on an app," I said firmly. "I'm not entrusting my political future to some random guy. I want to go with someone I know and who knows me. Someone I trust who won't fuck up this ridiculous plan."

"So that means you're going to do it?" Cal's eyes bulged as if he were a kid in a candy store. My sex life was now a candy store.

"Who's someone you trust with this?" Russ asked.

I strummed my fingers on the railing. The idea had actually come to me at the beginning of this conversation, simmering until it seemed more logical. "There is one person."

I didn't know if he'd be up for something this crazy.

———

AFTER WE FINISHED HANGING OUT, I got into my car and pulled out my phone. I stared at it, going over multiple cost-benefit analyses in my head.

LEO: Can I call you?
Dusty: Uh-oh.
Leo: Is that a yes?

MY PHONE BUZZED with a call from Dusty.

"Is everything okay?" he asked, his voice heavy with concern.

"Why wouldn't it be? Can't a friend call a friend to see how that friend is doing?"

"You never ask to call. You call," Dusty said, bringing up a good point about our relationship.

It was a shame he quit law school. He had the perceptiveness to be one hell of a trial attorney.

"I'm healthy and safe. So are the kids. But..." I laughed and rubbed my head, messing up my slicked-back hair. "This is going to sound absolutely crazy and ridiculous, and really, it's an indictment on our political system when you get right down to it."

"Go on."

"You're going to laugh."

"I can't laugh until I know what I should be laughing about."

"But you're going to. I'm warning you. It's a real fucking gut buster. I hope you're not drinking milk because it's going to shoot through your nose."

"What am I, six? Leo, spit it out."

I squeezed my eyes shut. My stomach turned. "Do you feel like coming to Sourwood to be my fake boyfriend? I need a boyfriend to help turn around this media coverage, and I thought–"

"Sure."

That was fast. And easy. "It'd be for about a month."

"That's fine."

Very easy. Dusty had no hint of hesitation in his voice, and I was an expert in deciphering his tone.

"We'd have to pretend to be in a relationship."

"Yeah, that's what a fake boyfriend does, right?" he asked.

"And you're okay with that since you're straight?"

"Yeah."

I was at a brief loss of words. Dusty was never one of those straight guys who got all "ew gay stuff." He was supportive from the second I came out to him, and our friendship hadn't shifted. But still, this seemed like quite a leap he was taking for me.

"What about work?"

"It'll be fine."

"Are you sure?" I asked.

"Yeah."

"You don't even know what this entails yet."

"Leo. You're my best friend, and you need my help. Whatever details or caveats you're going to tell me doesn't matter. The answer's yes."

I leaned back in my seat, grateful for this friendship. For the first time, I felt hope surging through my veins. "How soon can you fly out here?"

5

DUSTY

The next day, I settled my affairs in Los Angeles, which consisted of moving all of my meager belongings into storage, and hopped a flight to the east coast. I arrived at the small regional airport that night unprepared for the weather in my shorts and T-shirt.

Fortunately, Leo always thought two steps ahead and had an extra jacket in hand. He waited outside security, and when I saw him, I stopped in my tracks for a good moment.

Whoa. Leo looked good.

I mean, Leo always looked good. He cared about his appearance ever since I'd known him. But maybe it was because it'd been a few years, but seeing his tall swimmer's build in person was like seeing him for the first time. He had flecks of silver filtering through his thick black hair, and his dark gray eyes gleamed with a determined glint. He looked good for a man in his early forties undergoing a major political crisis.

This was my objective opinion.

Leo made me think of all the warm, welcoming feelings most people would associate with home. He was the closest thing to home for me, that constant in my life to which I could always return, and I didn't realize how much I missed him.

"Hey." Leo walked toward me. Right, because I wasn't moving. "Has jet lag hit you already?"

He tossed me his extra jacket, and my body clicked out of its daze long enough to put it on. Leo pulled me into a hug, his sharp, clean scent welcoming me.

"I guess it has. Yeah…it's been a while," I said.

"How long has it been?" His forehead crinkled as he calculated the time gone. "Almost three years."

The number flattened me. I did not understand how time worked, apparently. "Doesn't feel that way."

"We talk all the time." Leo picked up my suitcase. "I'm glad you're here. Thank you again."

"You don't have to carry my suitcase." I reached for it, but he pulled back.

"It's the least I can do. You flew across the country to help me with this dog and pony show. I can carry your suitcase to my car."

I yanked it away. "It's on wheels."

I showed him how it was done, rolling in front of him.

"I can wheel it then."

But it was too late. I was already ahead.

We exited into the cold New York air and dark sky illuminated by parking street lights. Leo pointed straight into the parking lot across from the pickup station. The regional airport was like a strip mall compared to the behemoth of LAX. I was surprised the parking lot wasn't filled with Hot Wheels.

"How was the flight? Were you able to sleep?" Leo wore gray slacks, a fitted black sweater, and shiny shoes. Even picking up a friend late at night, he was dressed to impress.

"Nah. Those seats get more and more uncomfortable."

"What about the neck pillow I got you for Christmas?"

"I forgot it."

"It's made specifically for flights."

"Eh, I don't need it." I didn't have the heart to tell him I lost it or that it might've been crushed in boxes with the rest of my belongings. "I have the guest room waiting for me?"

"The bed's all made up."

My body quaked with excitement. Leo's guest room had a luxurious queen size bed with soft sheets and a mattress that was one giant marshmallow. I never slept better than at casa McCaslin.

Leo clicked his car to unlock, then opened the trunk.

"I can do it," I said, but Leo was too fast.

The suitcase was already in his hands. "I can do it better," he said with a smile.

He bent over to place my suitcase in the trunk, and I... did I check out my best friend's ass?

No comment.

I was really tired. Jet lag. Had to be it. I got into the car without saying a word.

———

THE ROADS WERE DARK, even with the minimal street lighting. Again, not like LA, where there were so many lights and cars and buildings that true darkness was rare. Unless during a regular power outage.

"So, how's the west coast?" Leo asked. "You look tan."

"Benefit of living by the beach."

Leo had a healthy sheen to him that made me wonder if he visited a tanning salon now and again.

"I've been meaning to get out there to visit and crash

with you."

"Yeah." That was literally impossible now that I was literally homeless.

"How's work going? My kids love *Ocean City*. They're excited for the next season. Every time I catch them watching it, I say Uncle Dusty built that set."

My stomach twisted inside me. Leo had enough on his plate to worry about. I wasn't going to add my mess.

"It's good. The show is going really well. I love getting to build all these sets, and the crew is a lot of fun. I'm doing carpentry then coming home to my apartment on the beach. Life is good." I mustered Oscar-worthy levels of enthusiasm.

He looked at me, then back at the road. "Uh-oh."

"What?"

"That sounded terrible."

"Things are great."

"When people say life is good, they're usually about three seconds away from crawling into a hole and crying themselves to sleep."

"That's some real expert analysis. When did you have time to get your psychiatrist's license? I'm doing well! Yes, it's actually possible that I'm thriving in my life. Shocker, I know."

He turned to me briefly again, the concern on his brow cutting through all my bullshit. "What's going on?"

It was no use lying to him. He knew. He could read me like the front headline on a newspaper.

"I don't want to bother you with my typical bullshit. You have a campaign you need to focus on."

"Fuck that. What's going on, Dust?"

I looked out the window. "It was perfect timing that you called because I'm out of a job, homeless, and dumped." I laughed to stave off the patheticness. "Usually, it's one or the other. But you're in luck because this time it's all three."

"A triple crown of shit."

"A royal flush of shit."

"A hat trick of shit. Too bad you weren't able to break an arm or come down with testicular cancer to make it an all-around shitfest."

Damn him. We cracked up with pure, joyous laughter, the kind that cleansed souls.

I regaled him with what happened this week: the lousy roommates, getting dumped, punching a TV star, and being escorted off the back lot. It sounded like it happened to someone else. I was grateful to be three thousand miles away from that shitshow.

"Sounds like quite a week. You okay?" Here was the thing about Leo. He could be a real sarcastic motherfucker. But at the same time, he knew when to shut that off and listen.

"I've been better."

"It's all for the best. Those roommates sounded terrible. Audrey never seemed like a good person. She was stuck up and treated you poorly."

I shook my head, shocked at the Audrey read. "You're giving me your Audrey opinion now?"

"I didn't want to say anything when you were together."

"That never stopped you in the past."

Leo wasn't a fan of my ex-girlfriends. I'd stopped being pissed at him for his honest opinion since he always seemed to be right about them. With Audrey, I didn't ask what he thought, and in turn, he didn't proffer his thoughts.

"I figured it wasn't healthy for me to chime in. I want you to be happy, and if Audrey did it for you, I was going to keep my mouth shut."

"Doesn't matter now." I rubbed my eyes. I was tired on so many levels. "That's it. I am done with girlfriends, dating, all of that. I'm going to be like you. Fun flings. Leave my heart out of it. Focus on my work. I was thinking of getting more into woodworking."

"You'd be great at that."

I tore my gum wrapper into tiny pieces. "Maybe these women know something I don't. They know I'm beneath them."

"Figures you'd prefer doing it on your back."

I flipped him the bird.

"Hey." Leo patted my leg and bore into me at a red light, suddenly getting serious. "You are fucking incredible. The ex-girlfriends refused to see what was right in front of them."

I gulped back a lump in my throat. For a second, I wondered if Leo was talking about me at this moment. Were Leo's features always this chiseled?

"If anything, those women were beneath you. You have a lot going on where it counts. Jobs, apartments. Those are material things. But the things that matter: loyalty, kindness, intelligence. You have that in spades."

He had this way of talking that held you in place and made the world disappear. I couldn't believe people thought he was cold and rigid. They didn't know the Leo I knew. But they would. I'd make sure of it.

"Thanks, buddy," I cracked out.

His eyes stayed on me an extra second longer. I exhaled when the light turned green.

"Put California behind you for the next month, though. First, help me win this damn election."

———

WE DROVE THROUGH DOWNTOWN SOURWOOD, cluttered with mom-and-pop shops. Things seemed peaceful here. I'd only spent brief cameos in Sourwood on my visits, and I was excited to explore what this town had to offer.

We pulled into the driveaway of a familiar white colonial house with black shutters and an American flag sticking out from a pole by the front door. The house was big and picturesque, surrounded by oak and maple trees with colorful leaves. I didn't realize how much I'd missed fall, a nonexistent season in LA.

Leo retrieved my bag from the trunk. He eyed it suspiciously. I noticed a rip in the corner and could feel him judging it.

"Thanks," I said as I took it back.

"I'll get you a new one. And tell me how much I owe you for the plane ticket."

"It's fine." I waved off the offer and carried my suitcase up the front steps.

"I insist. Please."

"Is this part of your campaign budget?"

"No. It's me, thanking you for doing this."

I didn't want pity plane fare. Despite where my life was at, I could afford my own plane ticket, even if "afford" meant "put it on a credit card and deal with it later."

Inside, I could feel the age of the house. Off to the side, the kitchen had been updated, but in the main hallway and living room, the oldness of the house could be heard in creaky floors and seen in classic hardwood.

"Looks the same," I said of the house.

"Do you want anything to eat?"

I was about to say I wasn't hungry, but on cue, my stomach rumbled. It was dinner time in LA. "Actually, yes."

Leo pulled out Tupperware from the fridge. "I made

slow cooker chili for the kids. There's some left. I swear I don't know how I'd feed these kids without the slow cooker."

He glopped chili into a bowl, covered it with plastic, and stuck it in the microwave. I ambled into the living room, which was majestic and cozy and the real selling point of the house—high ceilings, a huge, inviting fireplace, and windows that looked out into the woods.

"How often do you sit on your couch and stare out the window? It's so peaceful."

"Uh, never. I don't have time to sit and stare," Leo said from the kitchen.

True. That was a luxury of the single and unattached.

"While it's heating up, let's take your stuff to the guest room."

"And the bed!" I yelled out. The best sleep of my life awaited me.

Leo came behind me and slipped the luggage out of my hand. He carried it up the stairs like it was a shopping bag. I might have watched his ass as he walked in front of me.

Was this a new thing I was doing? Checking out my friend? Jet leg, man.

I followed Leo to the end of the creaky hall, and he plopped my luggage into the guest room. The bed and dresser were leaps and bounds better than what I was used to—real furniture that came assembled. I was in a comparative lap of luxury. My old mattress was lumpy with springs that jabbed into my back and rang out like a church organ every time I turned.

I sat on the bed, and my body sang in pleasure. Oh, I would sleep well tonight. Did I moan out loud? I might have. I would never take a good bed for granted ever again.

"Is it like you remember?" Leo hung by the door.

"Amazingly, yes." Funny how comfortable everything felt despite it being three years. This house was my home in a way.

Two pairs of footsteps rumbled down the hall, which creaked like a violin.

"Oh, my God! It's the twins from *The Shining*!" I yelled.

Ari and Lucy ran into my arms. I squeezed them in bear hugs.

"Uncle Dusty! This is so cool that you're here," Lucy said. She had the same black hair as Leo, while Ari had inherited his father's slim build and gray eyes.

This was one marker that it'd been three years. The kids were gaining on me. They came up to my chest now, whereas last time, they were belly high.

"Do we call you Uncle Dusty since you're dating Dad now?" Ari asked, head cocked to the side, confused and amused like the rest of us.

I looked to Leo for the official party line. He swooped into the middle of the conversation.

"Uh, yes. Same old, same old for now." Leo put his hands in his pockets and leaned forward, channeling some kind of Mr. Rogers vibe. "As we discussed, your dad and Uncle Dusty have gotten closer, and Uncle Dusty has decided to come stay with us for a little bit."

"I thought Uncle Dusty was into girls?" Lucy asked in that whiplash way that kids spout off questions without regard for social graces.

This was not something we went over. Leo laughed nervously. Our eyes met, and I nodded. I got this.

"Sometimes, people can be into both girls and boys," I said. "Love has no limits. Your dad is one of my closest friends, but we realized that we might like each other as more than friends."

I went over and held Leo's hand. This fake relationship presented quite a conundrum, but we'd figure it out. He squeezed back, sending a zip of pleasure up my arm. We could totally win at this couple thing.

In a desperately needed topic change, I unzipped my suitcase. "I brought you guys stuff from the set of *Ocean City*."

I flashed branded t-shirts and notepads in their eyes to cast off any awkwardness about this arrangement. They gobbled it up like candy.

"This is so cool! My favorite character is Lena. What's she like in real life?" Lucy asked. "Is she just as villainous?"

"Oh, yeah," I answered, realizing how perfect Audrey was for that part.

"We can play *Roman's Choice*?" Ari said. He wore plaid pajama pants and a Sourwood junior high t-shirt. "Have you ever played?"

I had flashbacks to the electronic sound effects and my roommates yelling at each other day in and day out.

"It, uh, sounds familiar." I managed a weak smile.

"Ari, maybe you should focus more on homework and less on video games," Leo said.

"I do my homework," he pouted.

"Your grades say otherwise. You play that thing all the time." Leo very noticeably rolled his eyes. "There are lots of better things you can do with your time. What about playing the piano as we discussed?"

Ari very noticeably eye-rolled back. I stayed far away from this squabble. "I don't like it."

Leo turned to his daughter, but Ari's face burned red, and he left for his bedroom.

"Ari!" Leo called after him.

"That was a little harsh, Dad," Lucy said.

"I know." Leo sighed, the plight of parenthood weighing him down. "I wish he was more into his studies like you. How's my brainiac?" Leo hung an arm around Lucy. "She's going to be our next surgeon," he told me proudly.

Lucy smiled along, the embarrassment coming off her in waves.

"She has some time," I said. "Let her enjoy her adolescence."

She flashed me a grateful smile.

"Fair enough." Leo kissed her on the forehead. "Why don't you get some sleep?"

"It's good seeing you, Uncle Dusty."

"Good night, Lucybug," I said.

She kissed her dad good night, and then it was the two friends. The space between us felt like both a chasm and nothing at all. Leo looked at me, gray eyes warm and sending a bolt of something up my spine. I wondered what he saw in me. I was the fuck up, and he was the success. But our friendship always worked.

The microwave beeped in the distance.

"My dinner's ready." I tried to sidestep him, but he stepped in the same direction, bringing us closer, his heat doing something weird to my head.

"Sorry," we said over each other.

Leo hugged me, the stress of everything coming off him. That was the thing. He refused to let the world see him sweat, but we all had to.

"Hey, buddy. We got this." I was going to do everything in my power to help him win.

"The circus starts tomorrow. We have our first interview. So have some chili and get to sleep. Big day ahead."

I flashed him a confident smile. "No sweat."

6

LEO

Oh, shit. I was in deep trouble.

Asking your best friend to be your pretend boyfriend for a few weeks: smart political decision.

Asking your best friend, who you've harbored a tiny crush on for years, to be your pretend boyfriend for a few weeks: huge mindfuck of a problem.

I never wanted to be one of those clichés, the gay guy secretly in love with his straight best friend. I'd rather be dancing to Kylie Minogue on a Pride float in a rainbow speedo. As our friendship naturally grew, I'd developed what some might call minor romantic feelings for Dusty, but I pushed them down. First and foremost, Dusty was my friend. We had history and practically a shared language at this point; I wasn't going to light that on fire by acting on a one-sided crush.

So as they sang in *The Book of Mormon* musical, I turned it off like a light switch.

Sure, it would bubble up from time to time. A warm spark spreading through my chest when Dusty laughed on the phone. A desire to kiss him goodnight when we met up in person. And perhaps part of the reason I preferred one-night stands was that I hadn't found a guy who was as funny, thoughtful, intelligent, and handsome as Dusty.

Again, I flicked that damn light switch off. And I thought I could keep it turned off while we pretended to be boyfriends. I had an election to win, and Dusty was my best chance of pulling off this ruse. I didn't have time for pining.

But the second I saw Dusty at the airport, and he flashed that megawatt smile on me, I was a goner. Every light inside me turned on. Dusty looked so good. He was as tall as me, looking every bit the California boy: slim yet muscular frame with a broad chest, golden tan, eyes a shade of blue you only saw on Caribbean cruises, blond hair that curlicued over the mature crinkles lining his face. Was it any wonder I didn't want a boyfriend? What guy out there could compete with that?

I used my morning run to clear my head. Dusty is straight, I reminded myself. He was here as a favor to a friend. Pining over him would be a waste of limited cognitive resources that had to be laser-focused on keeping my job and stopping my beloved town from being sold out to the highest bidder.

This was shock. I hadn't seen Dusty in three years. *Okay,* my body was telling me, *he still looks good.* Now that I had that information, I could go on with my life.

"Rough run?" Vernita asked when I arrived back at my house.

I looked down at my sweat-soaked shirt, and I was panting for air more than usual. "Just a lot on my mind. The election."

I had her meet here so we could get an early start. She had wrangled a softball interview with Maria Lopez at *The Sourwood Gazette.* They were fans of my work as mayor and endorsed me for my first two terms. They hadn't endorsed either candidate in this race yet, but hopefully, Dusty and I would put on enough of a show to move that needle.

"Thanks for going along with this," I said. Vernita was shockingly okay with the fake boyfriend idea. Since I wasn't compromising on any campaign positions or breaking any election laws, she didn't protest. In fact, she hoped this was a baby step toward me doing actual dating.

Fat chance on that.

I let Dusty sleep in to help him recover from the jet lag. He eventually stumbled downstairs in a t-shirt and boxers before realizing we had company. Golden blond hairs dusted his defined calves.

Forget turning off a light switch. I needed to cut the power lines.

"Hi." Dusty waved at Vernita with a huge heaping of awkwardness. "I'm Dusty."

"Vernita. Leo's campaign manager."

"I didn't know you were coming over." Dusty glanced down. "I would've put on pants."

I didn't mind the view. Dusty had always kept in shape through the physical demands of his job and his ability to hit up the gym whenever he needed without having to worry about kids. His thick legs jutted out like tree trunks, and his shirt stretched across his chest and arms. I caught very quick glances over my breakfast smoothie.

"I'm here to prep you," Vernita said, hints of an amused smile.

"Like for surgery?" Dusty's eyebrows shot up.

"For the interview."

"Right. That makes more sense." He wiped his hand over his face and wavy hair.

I knew that look. I poured coffee into the largest mug I

owned, poured in a splash of half and half and one sugar, and passed it across the kitchen island.

"Thanks." Dusty gulped it down. "Do you have—"

"Everything bagel is in the toaster."

"Is it from that—"

"Sourwood Bagel Company. I got them first thing this morning, so they're fresh."

"And—"

"Cream cheese in the fridge," I said.

"Is it—"

"Whipped. Not the brick."

Vernita's head whipped back and forth like she was watching a tennis match. The bagel popped up from the toaster. I tossed the hot food on a plate.

"Today's interview is a softball," Vernita said while I schmeared Dusty's bagel. "But it's still an interview. We need to be prepared. This relationship has come out of left field, and the press and voters are likely assuming you've been hiding Dusty away. *The Mayor and the Mystery Man* is what people are calling it online."

"Catchy." I slid the bagel across the island.

"Can you put more schmear on this?"

"You lop on the cream cheese, and half of it winds up in the trash."

Dusty considered it, then nodded in agreement. He bit into his bagel and moaned with delight, sending a very inappropriate buzz to my crotch.

"They don't make bagels like these in LA. I think it's something in the water here," Dusty said between bites.

"Anyway." Vernita handed Dusty a dossier we'd put together.

"What's this?" he asked with a full mouth.

"We compiled a list of potential questions Maria may ask along with preferred answers for each," I said.

"So we're rigging *The Match Game*?" Dusty slid the dossier back to Vernita.

"This isn't *The Match Game*. Your answers need to be aligned to make it believable," she said.

"Aligned," he repeated with a snort. "I don't need a dossier on Leo."

"We need to be on the same page about how we met."

"We were friends, and then we were more than friends."

It sounded surprisingly easy when he put it like that. If only real relationships could be that natural.

"I'm saying that our friendship naturally evolved to a romantic relationship in mid-July," I said. "That way, it comes after the published exposé with Damian."

"And we'll say that you'd flown to Boston for a family event, had come to Sourwood to see Leo, and, well..." Vernita laughed nervously, finding it hard to keep things business. "Sparks flew."

"You'd gone to Boston for your Great Aunt Bernice's funeral," I said, remembering when that news had popped up on our endless text chain. She had lived to 101, making it more of a celebration of life than a tragedy. "You weren't able to stop here since you had to get back to set, but at least the timing will check out."

A part of me felt guilty for roping in his dead great aunt to our scheme, but she'd marched in Boston's first Pride parade fifty years ago. Out of anyone in Dusty's family, she'd be the most game for helping out a fake gay couple.

"Okay, then. Great Aunt Bernice, gay matchmaker." Dusty sipped his coffee.

"Is that cool?"

"Yep. That's settled. We don't need to do any other prep."

Vernita flashed a cautious squint at me, probably regretting this Hail Mary idea. "We need to make sure you know Leo, so there aren't any questions—"

"I know Leo better than anyone. Test me." Dusty flashed me a wink.

"I get that you two are close friends, but there may be questions that come up. We need this interview to go as smoothly as possible."

"Test me," Dusty said.

"Dust." I nudged the dossier his way.

"Ask me a question in your dossier." Dusty wiped schmear off his lips, perfectly calm, while Vernita seemed primed to blow a coronary.

Vernita looked at me, and I gave her the green light.

"I know this seems weird," I said to Dusty. "But we—"

"If I get a question wrong, then we can prep until the cows come home." Dusty added a splash of half and half to his coffee. "But that's only if I lose."

He knew how I couldn't turn down a competition. My pilot light had been lit.

"Ask him," I told Vernita.

She turned to the first page. "What do you like most about Leo?"

"His eyes. They're technically brown, but they look more like a charcoal gray, like a finely tailored suit."

I checked myself in the toaster reflection and only now realized that my eyes did have some gray in them.

"Why did Leo decide to run for mayor?"

"Because the old mayor of Sourwood was caught taking bribes. It angered Leo so much, he decided to do something about it." Dusty tipped his head to me. We were playing the oddest game of chicken.

"What's his most annoying habit?"

"That when he's bored, he tugs at his right ear lobe."

I felt my ear lobe self-consciously. I did that?

"Where's Leo's favorite restaurant in Sourwood?"

"There are two answers." Dusty quirked an eyebrow. "What he tells the public is that his favorite restaurant is Caroline's. He loves their chicken noodle soup and meatloaf. Food from locally-owned restaurants just tastes better." Dusty hopped off his stool and took an assured step my way. "But the real answer to the question, the restaurant that Mr. Fancy Shoes Mayor loves with all his heart..." He got right in my face, shit-eating grin and all. "It's Applebee's," he whispered.

Vernita's mouth dropped. "Is that true?"

Dusty tipped his head, giving me the floor. A huge spotlight blasted on my face while my stomach rumbled in shame at the thought of their nachos.

"No comment," I said.

"Any other questions?" Dusty asked Vernita in his most victorious gloaty voice.

She slapped the dossier closed. "I guess we're good here."

———

After breakfast, I went upstairs to get showered and dressed. I wore a baby blue button-down shirt that Vernita said would "soften" me, whatever that meant. I kissed the kids goodbye and sent them off to the school bus.

All that was left was Dusty.

Vernita and I waited in the living room. I took the spare moment to do as Dusty suggested last night and stare out my living room's expansive windows. The view outside was gorgeous. An artist's palette of fall colors dotted the trees.

"Dusty, do you need help?" Vernita called upstairs.

"Nope," he said after an extended pause. "Not used to getting so dressed up."

She gave me a screwy look.

"Dusty wears a t-shirt and jeans to work," I said in his defense.

The guest room door creaked open, followed by footsteps coming down the staircase. Vernita and I made our way into the foyer. And that was when I lost my breath and my mind.

Dusty walked down the stairs in a crisp, plaid button-down shirt, dark blue khakis, and a sharp gray blazer. His scruff had been shaved away to reveal fresh-faced cheeks. His shaggy hair was combed into refined waves. He was a preppy, clean-cut dream, and I was in so much fucking trouble.

Dusty descended the stairs with grace as if modeling for a catalog spread.

I opened my mouth to comment, but that whole losing my breath stuff kept the words at bay.

"Thoughts?" He took off his blazer and threw it over his shoulder. The shirt pulled at his toned chest and had the fitted cut that showed his lean torso.

"You clean up nice." I played it cool, even though a jumble of mixed feelings ballooned inside me.

"I told Vernita I don't need the blazer. It's too stiff. What if I rolled up my sleeves? That's what politicians do when they want to show they care, right?"

"Rolled-up sleeves works for me." I glanced at Vernita, who gave a nod of approval.

She draped the blazer over the banister.

"I made sure to keep the tags on." Dusty pointed to the

paper squares outlined on his upper back and just over his, *gulp*, round butt. "You can return them next month."

"They're yours to keep."

"Leo. No." Dusty didn't have a political spouse wardrobe at the ready, so I'd made an emergency shopping trip before swinging by the airport.

"It's the least I could do."

The smile that sprung to his face was priceless and sent a warm feeling through my body.

Vernita checked her watch.

"Is it that time?" I checked my watch, too, then went back to checking out Dusty.

What the hell was I doing? I scrambled out the door.

Dusty followed behind me. "Let's cross our fingers and hope this doesn't blow up in our face."

Oh, I was crossing every finger and every toe.

And reminding myself not to check out my straight best friend.

7

DUSTY

Leo had arranged for the interview to take place at his friend Mitch's bar. It was safe, neutral ground that he said would help him stay at ease. Stone's Throw Tavern was off the main strip of Sourwood, and much nicer inside than its outside suggested. It was surprisingly expansive with windows that overlooked the river.

I jumped when Leo's hand pressed on my lower back.

"What are you—"

"She's here," he said through his smile.

Leo guided us to a corner booth where Maria Lopez from *The Sourwood Gazette* waited with a glass of orange juice.

His warm hand pressed firmly into the small of my back. I sunk into his touch.

"Maria. Always a pleasure." Leo stuck out his free hand for a shake.

"Mr. Mayor. Good to see you again." Her long hair fell over one shoulder. She had the kind of amiable smile that belied a curiosity lighting up her eyes. I'd seen this smile on journalists interviewing Audrey when they wanted her to let her guard down so they could get a juicy quote.

"This is Dusty Michaelson."

"Great to meet you," I said with my own amiable smile. I wasn't going to let her score any gotcha moments.

"Likewise," Maria said and jotted something down on her notepad. "I'd thought Dusty was short for Dustin, but it's not. It's just Dusty."

"My dad was a preacher, so I am a literal son of a preacher man."

"Dusty Springfield." She nodded and jotted.

"How did you know my name wasn't Dustin?"

"I did a little background research."

"Oh." My stomach dropped. Was background research necessary in a light, fun interview? Seeming to sense my nerves, Leo rubbed my lower back, and damn if his hand didn't feel good down there.

"I wanted to find out about the mayor's new mystery man! Don't worry. I don't know your social security number. Yet." She laughed as she pointed to the booth. "Here, have a seat."

I slid in, then Leo. Our knees touched under the table, and I flinched for a second before remembering that this was part of the plan.

He wrapped his arm around me and pulled me close, sending jolts of something into my veins. Maybe I should've looked at the dossier to see what the protocol was about touching.

Is this okay? his eyes asked me.

I replied with a terse nod, nerves from the touching and the background research flooding me. I placed my hand on his knee, which was new after twenty-four years of friendship, but to my pleasant surprise, felt natural.

"How are you feeling?" he whispered in my ear while Maria set up her tape recorder.

"If I go off course, give me a sign," I whispered back.

"I'll tap on your foot."

"And I'll squeeze your thigh."

He leaned in close and pressed his nose to my head, obviously for Maria's sake, but his warmth and fresh scent sent a fuzzy spark through me.

"You're not using a shampoo that was in the bathroom." He growled into my ear. He was clean-shaven with that million-dollar smile, and not a piece of him was out of place.

"I brought my own. It's an organic coconut shampoo from this shop on Venice Beach."

I listened to Leo inhale the scent into his lungs, watched his chest puff up with air.

"You smell like the beach." His whispered growl was doing something funny to my stomach.

"Is that a good thing?"

"Oh, yeah."

I placed my hand back on his heavenly thigh. We were ready to roll. How could anyone think we weren't a real couple? Even I was getting a little confused.

Maria tapped the recording app on her phone. The red record light glowed on screen. Every word I said was going to be recorded or written in her notepad. No pressure.

"Dusty, how does it feel to be thrust into a campaign?"

The word thrust made me think of Leo (don't ask me why!), and I lost my answer. "Uh, I'm game. Yeah, I want to support Leo. He's an incredible mayor. He cares so deeply about every aspect of Stillwater, from the people to the parks."

"Stillwater?" Maria quirked an eyebrow.

"What?"

Leo tapped my foot. His grin tightened.

"Babe, you mean Sourwood."

"I do!" Two seconds into the interview, and I was one of those rockets that imploded on the launching pad. "I was thinking that I still need to water my plants, and my brain got…confused."

Maria jotted a note in her pad. What commentary did she need to write down that her phone wasn't capturing? The blood rushed from my face. Leo was probably at Defcon Five.

"What have you planted?" she asked.

I smiled weakly. "Y'know…plants."

"I'm surprised your plants are thriving since it's October." Maria leaned forward.

Her phone stared me down. My brain was spiraling.

"We planted a little basil," Leo said, completely at ease. "A little pot of it in the kitchen. We use it to season our foods. Dusty's from California, and you know how crazed they are about natural foods." Leo threw his head back and laughed, but I recognized that laugh. It was fake and filled with terror. "I picked up seeds from the free seed library at the Sourwood Library."

"The library has seeds?" Maria asked, taking the words out of my mouth.

"They do. The library has lots of great resources for Sourwood residents." Leo slipped into his infomercial, campaign trail voice. I squeezed his leg, hoping to steer him away from talking points. All that did was make him jump and hit the table.

"Are you okay?" Maria asked.

"Fine," he squeezed out. "I remember when Lucy tried to

grow cantaloupe in our backyard. Sadly, the animals got to it before we did."

The three of us enjoyed a laugh, though my laugh was more of my throat forcing out air in a ha sound as if I was an alien mimicking human behavior.

"Well, this is quite a development." Maria motioned between us. "Mr. Mayor, we had no idea you had a boyfriend."

"We were keeping things lowkey as they developed. It was as much of a surprise to us as it was to you." Leo had an ease and charm to him. He could tell me the sky was lime green, and I'd believe him.

"And now you're official?"

"I feel like teenagers labeling our relationship official. It was all very natural. They say the best relationships grow out of friendship..." Leo gazed at me and flashed his confident grin, and damn, I really believed that.

Pull it together, Dusty.

"You two have known each other for a while. Over twenty years."

"I hope you're not calling us old." Leo chuckled. "But yes. Dusty is my best friend. We met in college."

"So, you just decided to turn this into something romantic?" There was a slight tone to Maria's voice that put me on guard. Was she leading us into a trap?

"It wasn't a decision per se, but something that developed naturally." Leo's voice had an edge to it, a pleasant pushback.

"Did the article from Mr. Damian Van Drew have any influence on your relationship?"

"I don't see why it would." Leo tightened his arm around me. "That was an experience from earlier this year. Dusty and I have been romantically involved since the summer."

Maria whipped her head to me. "Dusty, what do you think about the scandal?"

By the panicking look Vernita shot me, I had a feeling this answer was in the dossier that I ignored.

"I don't think about it at all," I said coolly. "I'm not sure what it has to do with Leo's ability to lead. In fact, I'm surprised it's even a story, frankly. Slow news day?" I cocked my head to the side and shot her a smile that informed her two could play at this game.

She jotted away in her notebook, remaining unnervingly objective.

"So, how did we get here?" Maria asked. "You two were friends, and then you suddenly became boyfriends."

"Dusty was in Boston for a family event."

"A funeral. Great Aunt Bernice," I added, wanting extra credit for remembering the cover story.

Leo tapped my foot.

"We met up for dinner at this little French restaurant on the Charles. Little candles on the tables." Leo pulled me closer to him, perhaps to keep me in line.

We had gone over this story on the car ride over, Leo and Vernita drilling down every last detail. My vote for the fake story was Italian because a French bistro was too cliché, and the food was never as good as the ambiance, but I was shot down. Italian food was too heavy and could stir mafioso connections, according to Vernita.

The funny thing was, our date was something we would never do in reality. During the times when we'd hang out in person, Leo and I didn't meet up at fancy restaurants. We grabbed a booth in the back of a sports bar, sharing apps while catching up for hours. Or we went to Applebee's, but I knew the A-word was verboten.

"We both got the coq au vin without asking what the

other was getting. It was a fun coincidence that happens a lot with us. And something started to click." Leo chuckled at the non-existent memory. I wanted to fake order the veal, but that would've offended animal rights people too much.

"We talked about families and life and what we've been up to, nearly shut the restaurant down. Then we walked to an ice cream shop around the corner, and I'm usually not a dessert person. But Dusty insisted. He said no meal can end without dessert."

I never said that. Only grandparents said shit like that. I suggested we fake go for gelato, but that was shot down because French food plus gelato would've been European overkill and made us come off as snobby. Vernita decided that if it came up, Leo ordered rum raisin, a flavor she decided was mature and sophisticated.

"We walked along the river on this perfect summer night. I didn't want this night to end. It was something in the air."

Leo stuck to the script perfectly, hitting every beat of the story. Great, right? But as he went on, I found myself getting annoyed. Things were too fake. Candlelit French restaurants and long walks along the river? It was like something out of a dating ad.

Maria nodded accordingly, but I could see the boredom coalescing in her eyes. It was the equivalent of listening to an economics lecture. Even she could tell Leo's answers were too rehearsed, too safe.

"That's a lovely story," she said. "Our readers will get a kick out of it." She flipped her notepad shut and turned off the recording.

"Did you have any other questions?" Leo asked. "We still have a half-hour booked for the interview."

"I think I have what I need. And I know you have a lot to

do. I don't want to keep you." She stood up and put on her coat. Leo and Vernita traded looks while he desperately clung to the cool, casual persona he'd been cosplaying for this interview.

"Did you know Leo was in a band?"

All eyes turned to me. Panic washed over Leo's face, but at least I had Maria's attention.

"In college. He played guitar in a band with other guys on his debate team. They called themselves The Master Debaters." Leo and his bandmates were ridiculously proud of that name. Even back then, they were dorks for using it.

"Dusty, we don't have to get into that," Leo said.

"Mr. Mayor, you were in a band?"

"Oh, he was," I said. "He was a total rock star—in his head. They played at speech and debate events, sometimes at frat parties. Not any of the cool frats. The nerdy, academic-based ones." Leo shined in my head, playing on tiny stages for crowds of twenty people max, but he played it like it was Madison Square Garden. "He'd wear a sweatband around his head and ones on his wrists and flick them off at the end of a show. Once in a while, a girl would catch them."

"She doesn't need to—I played music in college. A long time ago." Leo's reddening face motivated me to keep speaking. As did Maria sitting down and taking out her phone, reopening the recording app.

"What kind of songs did they play?"

"Covers of what was big back then. 'Nookie' by Limp Bizkit was a cornerstone of their shows. Leo got so into it, especially the part about taking a cookie and sticking it up your—"

"That's not—" Leo squeezed my side extra hard, making me emit a sharp tickle-induced laugh. "That was a popular song when we were in college. Every band sang it. Back then, we as a society didn't recognize how those lyrics could potentially come off as problematic."

"Didn't you give yourself laryngitis from that song?"

"I don't remember."

"The Master Debaters performed more than 'Nookie,'" I assured Maria and Leo. His shows came back to me crystal clear. By default, I was their number one fan. "Leo crushed 'My Own Worst Enemy' by Lit and 'The Middle' by Jimmy Eat World. And anything Foo Fighters. He worships at the altar of Dave Grohl. He tried to grow his hair out like Dave. It did not go well."

"I looked good!" Leo chimed in.

"Your hair doesn't grow long. It grows out." I fumbled fingers through his black locks. "Like a Q-tip."

Memories flooded my mind of Leo, young and vibrant, the guy who would rip off his tie the second his debate was over and chug a beer in the parking lot. Maturity had stuck a yardstick up his ass.

"You'll have to dig up pictures from that time. I'm sure they're out there," I said. "And Leo would do this dance on stage." I got up and imitated his moves. "He'd try and do the moonwalk while playing. Or this shimmy thing like he was slow dancing with his guitar." I rocked in a circle while air-guitaring pitifully. "I'm not doing those moves justice. Get up, Leo."

He pursed his lips, but it was performative. I caught the sparkle in his eye. Nostalgia had taken hold.

"It was actually more like this." Leo jumped up and showed off the moves he still had, swaying his hips and bobbing his head, and absolutely rocking out on air guitar. We were hurtled twenty years into the past. "Doing speed debates had made me good at talking fast, which made me really good at the Barenaked Ladies song 'One Week.' I would go into the crowd and dance with them while singing."

Leo had this incredulous look, amazed that he actually did that. Maria was just as surprised but hung on every word.

"Mr. Mayor, do you still play?"

"No." He shook his head to underline his point. "That was a long time ago. I put my focus on my family and my work."

"I'm going to change that. That's my campaign promise," I said. I squeezed his leg when he sat back down. Just because.

"Any other Leo McCaslin intel?" Maria leaned forward, chin in hands.

"Did you know that Leo tried to be a professional surfer?"

"Wait. What?"

"Uh-huh. The summer after he graduated from law school, he had this idea that fuck it—am I allowed to say 'fuck it?'"

"Don't include that," Leo said.

Maria nodded.

"He had the idea that he was going to make a living from being a surfer. He'd give it a year, and if it didn't pan out, he'd take the bar and become a lawyer." I fell back into the booth howling with laughter.

"Did he?"

"He lasted two weeks."

"I lasted three months, sweetheart," he said in the most lovingly acidic way possible. He ran a hand up and down my arm, sending welcome goosebumps across my flesh.

"Two of those months were practicing." I cocked my head at him, daring him to say otherwise. "What even made you want to be a surfer? You hate the beach because of the sand."

He stared at me for a hot second, his lips curling into a blazing hot, satisfied smile. He turned to Maria. "Did you know that Dusty has a lifelong fear of clowns?"

"Wow. We're going there, are we?"

"They terrify him." I tried to clamp a hand over his mouth, but he escaped my clutches. My fingers unexpectedly buzzed with the feel of his lips. "He came to my kids' fifth birthday party and ran inside the house when the clown got there. All the kids were cool with it. Not Dusty."

"I see. That's how this is going down, huh? Looks like somebody woke up and chose violence today."

In my defense, clowns were terrifying. They were demonic straight drag queens with funhouse mirror faces. How did we, as a society, decide they were suitable for children's entertainment?

"Hey Maria, do you know what Leo's absolute, number one favorite restaurant is?"

Leo clamped a hand over my mouth, but we could barely keep up. He collapsed into my shoulder, tears of laughter at his eyes. We were hysterical for a good, long minute.

"Remind me why I'm dating you?" Leo asked, inches from my face.

We locked eyes, and everything around us seemed to stop. Was he going to kiss me? Was that something we should do? I began to tilt my head and go in for the kiss. A flash of something—panic, shock?—flashed on his face.

Leo turned to Maria. "Any other questions?"

She looked at Leo, studying him, it seemed. I worried how much of this she saw through.

"What?" he asked.

"I've never seen you laugh like this, Mr. Mayor. You're a lot of fun!"

He shrugged modestly.

"You two are a cute couple."

Leo smoothed one of my dangling pieces of hair into place, his thumb sliding down the side of my face. "I like to think so."

"The best relationships grow out of friendship," she said. "That's how it happened with my husband and me."

"Dusty knows me better than anyone. I think I reached this point where I realized I was searching so hard for love when it was right in front of my face the whole time. Everything just..."

"Clicked." I met Leo's hand with mine.

My entire body craved Leo McCaslin in a weird rush of need that had to have been the high of laughter and nostalgia. I would've given my left nut to kiss him at that moment.

But Leo scooted away from me the second Maria left. The space between us turned cold and expansive.

Too bad we were just a pair of really good actors.

8

———

LEO

"You were in a band and never told us?"

I reached for the pizza slice Cal offered, but he snapped it back.

"It was a long time ago." I made another attempt and was thwarted again.

"The fact that you sang 'Nookie.' Nay, the fact that you even knew the lyrics to a Limp Bizkit song...I feel like I'm meeting you for the first time."

"Surprised I have such good taste in music?" I swiped the plate from his hand. It had Batman logos around the perimeter, fitting since we were celebrating his son Josh's birthday.

Dusty and I were surrounded by screaming, sugared-up nine-year-olds. Cal and Russ hosted the birthday party at LeapWorld, an indoor amusement park with obstacle cour-ses, go-karts, jungle gyms, and the pièce de résistance: epic gladiatorial platforms where kids (and adults) tried to bump each other off pedestals using oversized foam poles. Leap-World was pretty much a rite of passage for Sourwood kids. Ari and Lucy had their birthday here years ago.

I sat at a kids' picnic table with the Single Dads Club, minus Russ, who was monitoring all the kids like an umpire, especially his son Quentin. Quentin was on the scrawny side, and according to Cal, Russ had a habit of being a bit overprotective with him. Cal gave us a sneak peek at Josh's birthday cake, shaped like the Batman logo.

"Josh is going to love that," Mitch said, his burly body comically hunched over a tiny table. We all looked ridiculous, like Gulliver crashing a Lilliputian party.

"I'd wait until the very end of the party to feed the kids cake. Otherwise, this place is going to be covered in puke," I said from experience. It was a good call having every inch of this place covered in plastic. LeapWorld could be hosed down each night.

"Don't change the subject." Cal shut the cake box. "Why didn't you tell us you were in a band? I don't remember you playing in high school."

"I didn't. I picked it up in college."

"Let me guess: to pick up girls?" Cal asked.

"No," I said at the same time Dusty said an emphatic, "Yes!"

I cocked an eyebrow at him. Traitor.

"You should keep playing. I can host an open mic night at Stone's Throw," Mitch said.

"I don't think I can still play. It's been a long time." I waved off the music talk. Lots of people did stuff in college that they stopped once they entered the real world. Playing in a band was fun when I was twenty, though it was quite a rush to relive those memories. "Thank you for bringing that up in the interview, Dust."

"That was a great article," Cal said, pouring himself a cup of Coke into a matching Batman cup.

"You have no idea." I squeezed Dusty's arm, my hand

lingering for a second. My appreciation knew no bounds—and neither did my impulse to touch him, apparently. "I've gotten so many great messages from people saying how cute we are, asking if I can perform at the next town meeting. Most importantly, the first round of polling came in this morning, and I'm slowly closing the gap with Rita."

"Mission accomplished." Dusty clinked Batman cups with mine.

"I could not have done it without you. Have I mentioned how glad I am you're here?"

Dusty looked away, his cheeks blushing. Shit, I should've rephrased. Light switch, light switch, light switch.

But the thing was, I meant every damn word. I was so happy Dusty was here. Not just for the article, but having his support and spending more time with him has made campaigning enjoyable. Dusty came with me to other campaign events this week, and we had a blast. All politicians should campaign with their best friends.

"My pleasure. I have lots more embarrassing stories to share," he said with a playful threat.

"Please give us all the embarrassing stories," Cal said.

"Oh, I will. I have to dole them out thoughtfully, like morsels."

Cal hi-fived Dusty. "We finally have someone to take you down a peg, Leo. The world makes sense again."

Dusty had met Cal and Mitch over the years when he swung by town. They all got along, which was something I was nervous about when different friends met. Mitch even offered Dusty a bartending gig in case he was staying in town.

He politely declined. He still planned to return to the West Coast, which made my heart sink. And not because he'd given my public image a shot in the arm.

"I'm gonna hit the can." Dusty stood up and rubbed a hand through my hair.

"Why do you keep insisting on messing up my hair?"

"Maybe I'm making it better. You ever think about that?" He smirked and left.

"He's awesome," Cal said. He then shot up from the picnic table and pointed at a pair of twin boys. "Mason! Aiden! Stop wiping your boogers on the blocks!" He turned back to us. "Excuse me. I have to thwart a viral contagion."

He pulled a box of wipes from the floor, something he seemed to have on hand perpetually, and dashed into the obstacle course.

"So..." Mitch said, looking toward the bathroom, then me, then back at the bathroom.

"Mitch, do you need some fiber supplements?"

"Can I ask you a question?" He crossed his arms over his flannel-covered chest, really acing that lumberjack look.

"Does this have to do with small business licenses?" I joked, trying to delay the inevitable question I knew was about to pop out of his mouth.

"Why were you and Dusty never a thing?"

"We're friends," I said, almost offended. I didn't know why the question bothered me so much. "If I were straight, you wouldn't be asking me this."

"Well, you're not."

"He is," I said firmly.

Mitch cocked a skeptical eyebrow. The man said so little and so much at the same time; it was infuriating.

"Oh, stop. Why don't you go back to the Bounty paper towel logo where you came from?"

"You two are good together. In the article. In person."

"Because we're best friends. That's what twenty million years of friendship gets you. And as I previously stated, he is straight. If you're going to keep asking me the same question repeatedly and expecting a different answer, then we're going to be here a long time, and I'm going to need to sit in an adult-sized chair." I got extra verbose and extra lawyer-y when I was annoyed.

"Maybe it's not as black-and-white as straight or not."

Mitch, champion of the full spectrum of sexuality? I had to excuse myself to go die of shock.

"We're faking it. Women aren't the only ones who can fake it."

"That joke hasn't been funny since the '90s," Mitch said. Apparently, my sarcasm had been rubbing off on him. "If you are faking it, you're doing a really good job."

My frustration expanded in my chest like a cough that wouldn't go away. I glanced over at Dusty, who was now chatting with Russ, his smile brighter than the oppressive fluorescent lights of LeapWorld. My damn heart did this loopy-swoop shit as if I was in an elevator that decided to plummet ninety stories.

"Dusty is my closest friend. We tell each other everything. *Everything*. If he were the slightest bit gay or bi or whatever, he would've told me. Also, when did you become a hopeless romantic? I don't think it goes with your aesthetic."

Fine, so I was a little bitchy. I didn't want to be fielding questions about my relationship status with Dusty from my friends on top of all the relationship questions I was getting from voters and the media. My friends knew what was up. This was a fake relationship. Dusty was on board with the little touches and petting during the interview because he was a good sport. It was on me not to read more into it. There was no "there" there.

"Hey!" Dusty returned and massaged my shoulders. I

refused to look at Mitch. Lord knew what kind of self-satisfied grin he had poking out from his bushy beard.

"Hey, yourself," I said.

"Did you know that the gladiator setup isn't just for kids? Do you want to give it a go?"

"I don't know if I'm dressed for it." I had come from work, which meant slacks, a button-down shirt tucked in, and dress shoes.

"If you're not up for it because you're afraid of losing, just tell me." Dusty ground his fist into the knots of my shoulder. His fingers danced up to the hairs on my neck. He'd really run with the public affection part of our ruse.

"I'm not dressed in official gladiatorial footwear. Any results from our matchup would have an asterisk."

"But what if you win? Remember when we played soccer in that piazza in Spain, and you were in sandals?"

"You're new here, Dusty. I don't want to embarrass you in front of these kids by whooping your ass."

"Mitch, what do you think?" Dusty asked.

I looked up at Mitch, who was enjoying the hell out of this show. I didn't think I'd ever seen him smile this much.

Mitch stared me in the eye. "Leo, I think you should go for it."

———

AFTER STEALTHILY FLIPPING Mitch the bird, Dusty and I got strapped into our protective helmets and pads. We were given oversized foam poles with paddles at the ends, like an enormous oar, and hopped onto our respective pedestals. I felt like a doofus, but Dusty looked like one, too, so I wasn't alone.

"Let's go. You and me, amigo." Dusty climbed onto the pedestal.

I climbed onto mine. The pedestal was smaller than it looked. Made for kids. Not adults. It took me a second to get my bearings, what with all the gear I had on and balancing the large pole, which was a neon-colored, comically over-sized Q-tip.

"You okay there?" Dusty asked from his pedestal. He looked as ridiculous as me, his blond curls shoved under a helmet.

"Never better."

"Okay, let's do this." Dusty hunched forward, ready to attack. "You're going down, McCaslin."

"In your dreams, Michaelson."

"No junk shots," Dusty said.

"That's a given." We were guys. We knew the pain a shot to the groin caused.

Russ did a double-take when he saw us up here. "If either of you pulls a muscle or breaks a hip, don't blame me."

"Can you count us off, Russ?" I asked.

He rolled his eyes but was ultimately game. "Three, two, one."

Dusty lunged his pole at me and almost fell off from the momentum.

"Watch yourself, old man." I gripped my pugil stick tight.

"Who are you calling old man, geezer?"

I swung my pugil stick and made a direct hit to his hip. He stumbled but caught himself. His stick smacked into my arm. We might've been decades too old for this, but we were a force to be messed with. Our swordplay took on a rhythm. We swung, we hit, trading blows, but neither of us giving in.

"Thanks for being so cool about the interview," I said. "With all the touching. I know we didn't discuss beforehand, but you rolled with it like a champ, especially considering..."

"Considering what?" Dusty took a swing to knock out my legs. I jumped up to evade. I didn't know my body could jump like that. Adrenaline seemed to do the work.

"Considering you've...never done that stuff with men." I had a pained expression as I got the words out. What was I so afraid of? Dusty pounced on my moment of weakness and smacked me off my pedestal. I fell onto the bright red gym mats, which was like falling onto a hard mattress.

Above me, Dusty had jumped off his pedestal and held out his hand like a knight. His blue eyes were clear and warm, and I suddenly got an image of Dusty on top of me. I had to cool off before another pugil stick came out to play.

"That's one. Best of three?" I smacked away his hand and got up all on my own.

His smile took over his face with childish glee. "All right. You're on."

I hopped onto the pedestal. From my perch, I caught Cal and Mitch on the sidelines, watching with perverse enjoyment. Who knew what the hell they were thinking. Mitch probably assumed this was me flirting or some shit like that.

We got into position, and both counted to three. Each time I swung my pugil stick, Dusty sensed my move and blocked.

"That's not one hundred percent true," Dusty said in between trying to knock me off.

"What?"

"That I haven't fooled around with guys."

I went stock-still. Dusty tried to use that moment to hit me, but I punched away his pole with my fist in a flagrant regulatory violation. "What are you talking about?"

"One of my ex-girlfriends liked to bring in another guy sometimes." Dusty looked around to ensure no kids were in earshot. "For some two-on-one stuff. And lines blurred."

"Lines blurred?"

"Lines blurred. Only once or twice."

What the hell did that mean? Was he on top or bottom, or did it go that far?

Dusty tried to use my confusion to smack me, but as he pulled back for the kill shot, I jammed my pole into his stomach (a legal move!), sending him flying.

I was a good sport and helped him back on his feet, but my mind was swirling with questions.

"We're tied," Dusty said, squirming with a flash of pain as he stood. We might've been too old for this shit.

"One more," I uttered with grisled determination and an edge that took Dusty by surprise.

We got into position. On the count of three, I lunged for him with my pole.

"Whoa, Leo. Easy there."

"So you've been with men, and you never told me?"

"I mean, I didn't set out to be with them. It happened. Randomly." Dusty fought back with equal force. "Are you angry?"

That was a good question, something I was trying to figure out, too.

"You never told me this. We tell each other everything. And this was a big thing you could've told me." I heaved my pole back and forth, Dusty escaping my hits.

"I guess I was embarrassed." He made a direct hit on my side, but I turned to stone, not budging from the impact.

"Of what?"

"I don't know."

"Because of anyone, I would've understood."

"It wasn't something I wanted to talk about."

"Why?" I slammed my pole into his arm, anger still rising in me despite having no reason to. I was usually much better about holding in my emotions, but the thought of another man putting his hands on Dusty made me as bright red as the gym mats.

"I don't know, man. Who cares? It's in the past. Why do you care so much?" Sweat beaded at Dusty's forehead.

Why? That was the million-dollar question. The frustration boiled over within me—that he'd been with a guy and didn't tell me, that I was finding out years later at a children's birthday party, and worst of all, that it hadn't been me.

I launched my pole at him as if it were a javelin, clearly breaking the rules of the game. It barreled Dusty in the chest and sent him flying.

"Dusty!" I climbed off the pedestal and ran to him. He was on his back on the mats, the full wear of his age coming to him.

There was something in his eyes, like begging to make this water under the bridge. He was confused, and I was, too.

"Want to go three out of five?" I asked.

"No, I'm done for the day. You win." He sat up and rubbed his back.

"I think you win. My move wasn't a regulation move." I took over back rubbing duties, massaging the muscle corded across his broad frame. By the sharp winces he let out, I could tell it was quite a fall.

"I'm really sorry. I don't know what got into me."

"I do. You're too damn competitive. It's going to get me killed." He snorted a laugh, and the twinkle in his eye said all was forgiven.

I was glad we were fine. He managed to stand up by

himself, and we joined the party to sing Josh a Happy Batman Birthday.

Even if Dusty wasn't one hundred percent straight, he was still one hundred percent not into me in that way, no matter how it played for reporters. This was a fake relationship, and if I didn't cool myself down, I was going to destroy a real friendship.

9

DUSTY

In my bed, phone half under my covers, I did something I'd surprisingly never done before: I googled my best friend.

It was some ungodly hour of the early morning, and I hadn't gotten a wink of sleep. It wasn't because of my back. The pain from the gladiatorial fight had gone away by early evening. The jet lag had worn off a few days ago. There was some inkling in me that wasn't ready to call it a day.

I went from checking Facebook to reading random articles online about everything from the history of lip balm to "7 Signs You Have Early Onset Alzheimer's." Googling my best friend was a better use of cell phone battery.

I came upon images of him on the campaign trail, Leo at ribbon cuttings and town events. He was a man in his element. I read about all he had achieved in Sourwood—making it an affordable, wonderful place to live. He had mentioned those things before, but it was something else to read an objective article about his accomplishments.

There was one piece of content I'd tried to avoid, but curiosity got the best of me. My thumb tapped on the

Milkman expose article. I had already read the poorly-written piece, but this time, I looked at the pictures posted from his profile.

Leo looked good. Really good. Hairy, muscular chest, thick arms usually covered in pressed suits, confident smile.

I went to the section with his naughty texts, telling Damian what he wanted to do with him. My dick responded by getting hard.

It was words. Anyone reading salacious texts would've been turned on. I made a mental note to look up an article that backed up this idea.

The article warned the following image was NSFW. I was nowhere near work, so I clicked.

Whoa, daddy.

Leo was sprawled out on a bed in nothing but white boxer briefs, grabbing his dick. His thick shaft and bulging head were outlined in the white fabric. Everything was in clear view.

I told myself to look away, to keep scrolling. This was a picture I shouldn't be looking at.

I kept looking.

My eyes devoured the image. Morbid curiosity. That's all this was.

I'd wondered here and there over the years about Leo, if he was packing heat. I got my answer.

The kicker was his look into the camera, his smoldering eyes and pouty lips. He was acting tough and confident, taking full control of my screen. The gray flecks in his eyes popped out like crystals.

Before I knew it, my hand was palming my dick. First over the covers, then over my underwear. Just a little touching to see what was going on down there. Maybe I was comparing us. Lengthwise, Leo had me beat, but I edged him in thickness.

I'd never spent this much time thinking about Leo's dick. But to be fair, it was now part of the political conversation.

I *had* to.

To stay on top of current events.

I kept going, my throat going dry as I slowly stroked myself over my underwear.

Fuck, I'd never been into dicks, but Leo's mesmerized me. All this time we'd known each other, and he'd been working with *that*. I licked my fucking lips, suddenly and inexplicably hungry for cock, specifically that which belonged to my best friend.

My eyes traveled to the bulge underneath his shaft, his balls heavy. I caressed mine, heat roiling in my core.

This was research. If we were to be fake boyfriends, I had to know his body.

Another picture was of Leo shirtless at a pool or beach. Water trickled down his chest and abs. He had a little dad bod action, but overall he kept it tight.

I pulled my dick from my underwear and full-on jerked off, my dick swelling with desire. Desire for, uh, research.

I tugged at my balls, felt their weight in my hand. I rubbed my thumb over my head, biting back a groan. Leo's sizzling smirk stared back at me.

I wanted...I didn't want to say. Because there was no way it was happening.

But fuck, he was good-looking.

I was like a fucking teenager again, quietly sneaking a wank and praying to God nobody heard me. I hoped I was quieter than my former roommate.

My balls drew up, and I rubbed my hand back and forth harder against my package until I soaked my stomach with come. It trickled in between my thighs and sack, coating me in sticky warmth. My heart rate came down to regular levels.

I could've sworn the smile in Leo's picture changed to one of shit-eating victory.

———

THE NEXT MORNING, the sounds of footsteps on the creaky floorboards woke me up early, before the sun had even come up. I tried to ignore them, but they were persistent like woodpeckers. I left the bed to go to the bathroom, giving my suitcase, which contained my come-crusted underwear, the evil eye.

"Good morning." Leo passed me in the hallway decked out in a black running shirt and running shorts, accentuating his muscles and figure. He had a spring to his step as he jaunted down the stairs.

Did Leo even realize how attractive he was? Besides being in good shape, it was the little moments when he showed new cute sides to him.

"Don't mind me. I'm gonna try and go back to sleep."

"Really?" Leo said, almost as a challenge.

"It's five-thirty in the morning," I whisper-yelled since there were other people in this house smartly asleep. I followed him into the kitchen.

"One of these days, I'm going to break you from being a late sleeper."

"Five-thirty is sleeping in?"

"By nine—"

"—the day is over." I shook my head and laughed at this common Leoism, one he'd been saying since trying to convince me to wake up for early study sessions. Were it not for a mandatory class or kegs n' eggs, no college student wakes up before ten of their own free will.

"Nobody says that except morning show hosts," I said. "In fact, most sane people agree that nine is when the day usually begins."

"Slackers." Leo stretched an arm across his chest to limber up.

I rolled my eyes. "Sleep is the most important part of the day."

"First thing in the morning is the perfect time to run." Leo pulled his leg into a quad stretch, holding onto the wall for balance. "It's beautiful out there. Sun coming up. Quiet. Peace."

"You know what else is quiet and peaceful? Sleep."

"You had plenty of sleep. You turned in early last night."

Instantly, heat crept up my neck. I might've been in my room, but I was not sleeping. I prayed he never checked my browsing history.

"Join me," Leo said.

"For a run?"

"It'll be fun."

"Exercise is not fun." Fortunately, carpentry was an active profession. I was on my feet and working, so I didn't have to worry about doing soul-crushing, numbing exercises to keep my body from atrophying.

"Didn't you use to run on the beach?"

"When I was like twenty-six." Back then, I could get drunk the night before, wake up and run six miles, then eat a mountain of pancakes for breakfast. The young folks truly didn't know how good they had it.

The sounds and smell of coffee brewing in the kitchen filled the space. Leo walked past me. "I'm making a fresh pot."

"I'm not a runner."

The coffee smelled too good to pass up. I turned my head to Jesus and cursed. Looked like I was running this morning.

———

ONCE I HAD my medically necessary morning cup of coffee, Leo lent me shorts and a moisture-wicking T-shirt. Outside the house, Leo showed me stretches for my calves, quads, and something called an IT band that ran up my leg. A crisp autumn chill swept through the air. Leo watched me with a perverse entertainment, amused by my hatred of running.

"It's cold and dark out." The first flecks of sunlight streaked across the sky.

"It'll get lighter and warmer at the perfect point in the trail. The view will blow you away. I run this path every morning, same time. Trust me."

"I always trust you." He was lifting my expectations of this view, but I wouldn't give him the satisfaction.

"What kind of exercise do you do, Dust? You're in good shape."

"Carpentry is exercise enough."

"Seems to be working well for you." He looked away for a moment. A residual surge of blushing hit my face. "You should do some stretching first."

Leo bent down to touch his toes. I followed his lead but could only reach my shins. I would've done better had I not been thinking about what he looked like from the back in this position. His ass was the only part of him I didn't see in the pictures last night, but he had a nice curve from what I'd gathered from my trip so far.

Why the fuck was I gathering data on Leo's ass? If I were more flexible, I'd smack my head against the ground.

"Don't pull up yet," he said. "Let your top half hang there and lower itself inch by inch."

"You sound like a yoga instructor." My spine unraveled as I inched closer to the ground, heat stretching through my legs.

"You took yoga?" he asked.

"No. But I once dated a yoga instructor. She could fold like a pretzel."

"Thanks for that visual."

I smiled to myself. Fun times.

Next, he had me do a quad stretch, where I pulled a leg to my butt to match Leo. I held onto the side of the house for balance. I had flashbacks to gym class and holding onto my ear lobe for balance.

"Tuck your tailbone so you get a deeper stretch." Leo tried to demonstrate, but I couldn't tell the difference.

"How do I tuck my tailbone? Like how drag queens do it?"

Leo snorted. "Wrong tuck."

He moved behind me and pushed into my lower back, applying gentle but firm pressure. "Feel your tailbone? Now tuck it so that your spine straightens and you really feel the stretch in your thigh."

I was putty in his hands. In fact, the only part of me straighter than my spine was my dick, which didn't have the leeway for a random erection in these shorts. I pushed my foot into my hand harder, feeling the pull of my quad muscles to stop thinking about Leo's warm hands dangerously close to my, uh, danger zones.

"How does that feel? Do you feel it?"

Oh, I felt something.

I stepped out of his clutches for the sake of our friend-ship. I then stretched the other quad, watching him do the same, his body long and lean like a flamingo on one leg. Hopefully, exercise would help me, uh, exercise all this pent-up–confusion? Horniness? Weird form of jet lag?

"Ready?" Leo clapped his hands together.

"No."

———

I WAS RIGHT. Running sucked.

Pain edged up my legs and knees like bags of cement wedged under my quads. Muscles that I thought I used on a daily basis came to life, yelling at me for not stretching enough.

But Leo was also right. The view was glorious. The pre-sunrise light shaded our surroundings in a dark blue glow. We jogged down Maple Street, the town's main drag, which was empty and quiet, a sharp contrast to the hustle and bustle that would come in a few hours. In Venice Beach, there was always something going on. I didn't get to experi-ence this kind of peace, and the quiet stirred thoughts in my mind, some of which I didn't want to think about. As we kept running, the thick cluster of businesses and buildings disappeared into spread-out houses, then nothing at all. We took a sharp turn into the woods, running through a vibrant palette of fall foliage that came more into view as the sun rose.

Somewhere in the middle of our run, my body began to acclimate and find niblets of pleasure. Oxygen filled my lungs, and the soreness in my legs morphed into power. Our path got steeper as we charged up a hill, but I kept up.

Leo slowed down as the trees cleared to a bench and railing. He faced me, practically giddy.

"Are we taking a break?" I asked sarcastically, though I was grateful for the rest.

"Here's that view I was talking about." Leo nodded for me to follow him to the railing.

And there it was.

"Oh, shit." My mouth hung open. It was the only appropriate response to the tableau in front of me.

We were high enough to overlook Sourwood with the Hudson River and mountains in the distance. Sourwood was a pocket of civilization against the mighty water, dotted by shimmering golds and maroons of foliage. All those people down there...did they know they were living in paradise? I was looking at a painting, right? Or a heavily doctored photo that had been posted to someone's Instagram page. I had to be.

"What do you think?" Leo asked. "Worth all the fucking exercise?"

"Yeah," I breathed out, still catching my breath.

Leo leaned against the railing, gazing out mesmerized. He looked at this every morning and continued to be blown away.

"This is gorgeous," I said.

"It's beautiful now with all the leaves. And in the winter, it's blanketed with snow and reflecting people's Christmas lights."

"Amazing."

"It doesn't get old. I can't believe I get to live here and I get to lead this town. I'm the luckiest schmuck on earth."

"Now I see why you've lived here your whole life."

He nodded. I had an unexpected surge of jealousy hit me. I wish I were one of those people who could find a home like this and spend my life there. I hated my home-town. Central California was arid, boring, and a good ten years behind the rest of the state. As an adult, I bopped around different cities as a direct reaction to my hatred of where I grew up. That's what most of us did. We ran to big cities or new countries or into the country. Running, escaping, making a new life to forget the old one. But Leo stayed. He didn't run from anything.

"Come over here." He nudged his head for me to get closer. Out of his pocket, he handed over a small pair of binoculars.

"What are you doing with these?"

He rolled his eyes at any insinuation. "Giving you a special bird's eye view tour."

I looked through the binoculars, Sourwood up close. Leo stood behind and positioned me just so, like an astronomer lining up his telescope. I became very aware of his hands on my hips and found myself catching my breath in a whole new way.

"Do you see that small house at the corner with the pale blue shutters?"

"I do." It was on the older and smaller side and could use some upkeep.

"That's the house where I grew up. I painted those shutters when I was fourteen. My mom had wanted to go with yellow, but I convinced her to do blue."

"Good choice." I imagined Leo on a ladder in the hot summer sun, getting the shutters the perfect shade of blue to prove himself right.

"I offered to repaint them for the couple who moved in. I think they're planning some major renovations." There was a resignation in his voice, an acknowledgment that life moves on.

"Don't you have the authority to stop them?"

"I'll have to check the bylaws." I could feel the smile just behind my ear. "Moving on."

He turned me a few degrees to the right, my body heeding his touch. "Do you see a hair salon?"

"I do. Is that where you go?"

"I worked there in high school; only it wasn't a hair salon. It was a video rental store. I'll never forget how two sets of parents almost got into a brawl over renting the last copy of *Babe* for their kids. I got one of them to agree to rent *Monkey Trouble.* I consider that my first successful negotiation."

"The kid's movie compromise."

"One of the other customers watched me handle that situation and said I'd make a good lawyer. He was a lawyer and offered me a summer job working in his office right over..." Another twist of my body. "There."

The office was now a vet clinic, but I pictured Leo with a familiar spring in his step rushing to his internship, gleefully handling volumes of paperwork. He had ambition, only unlike me, his panned out.

"Am I boring you?" he asked.

"No." I might've leaned back into him. I was being taken on the Leo tour, and I loved every second. We'd been friends forever, but there was so much I still wanted to know about my friend.

With his hands on my hips, he guided me to view Caroline's in the heart of downtown, where he first sketched out his plan to run for mayor. He told me he still had that piece of paper, and it still had grease stains from his burger.

"And now for the final piece, one of my proudest achievements," he said into my ear as he shifted me to gaze upon a grassy knoll along the river surrounded by construction cones and tape. In the center was rusted over machinery from an old plant.

"This is Renegade Park. There was a bottle factory in town that'd been closed ever since I could remember. The land had been abandoned for decades, used as a place for teenagers to come hook up. I had Sourwood buy it, and we're turning it into the area's largest public park, similar to Gasworks Park in Seattle. We're commissioning artists to create sculptures out of the unused equipment and scrap metal. We're designing jungle gyms for kids based on the old assembly lines. We're putting in an outdoor theater. And the remaining part of the factory building is going to be converted into a public greenhouse."

As he spoke, my mind filled in the details he sketched out. I could see it all. This patch of desiccated land turned into a vibrant ecosystem. Children playing. Artists creating. Families picnicking.

"You are a man with a plan."

"It's definitely my most ambitious project to date. Some people aren't thrilled about it."

"Who wouldn't love a public park?"

"Housing developers who want to build on primo real estate." Leo huffed out a breath. "Don't get me wrong. I'm all about building houses and bringing more people."

"If you build one of the best places to live, they will come."

"I know that, but the riverfront should be for everyone, not a select few who can pay for multi-million dollar mansions. I don't want Sourwood to turn into yet another overcrowded suburb that's all strip malls and housing developments. I've seen that happen with other towns in the area. It sucks all the personality out of them."

I nodded my head in emphatic agreement. Los Angeles

was filled with expensive suburbs with the same chain stores and cookie-cutter houses.

"Renegade Park can be something that lasts in Sourwood, that builds community. It will keep this little enclave a special place."

I turned and looked at him. I didn't need binoculars to get a good view of Leo. His eyes were wide and alive, brimming with ideas, concern creasing his forehead.

He cared. Truly cared about this town. It was inspiring to be around someone like that. I wished I'd brought the same to our friendship, but too often, it felt one-sided—that I was taking more than giving.

"You care," I said.

"Is that a bad thing?" He didn't step back. Our bodies were close, magnets trying to resist.

"It's a wonderful thing." A pain hit my chest. I was the one who stepped back, breaking whatever moment was happening between us. "We should get back to it." I jogged in place, forcing a smile on my face.

"What's wrong?" Leo didn't budge.

"What? Nothing."

He saw right through that.

I bowed my head and sat on the bench with a dedication plaque from 1936. "I wish I had what you had. You have something you care about. You have something that literally gets you up in the morning." I flung my head back and covered my eyes with my arm. I felt so ridiculously inadequate. "I have a trail of failures. Forty-two years on earth, and all I have are dead-end careers, belly-up businesses, and crushing debt. My apartment on Venice Beach was actually a tiny room I rent from three obnoxious twenty-somethings who spend every day playing video games and jerking off."

I wanted to crawl into a hole. My life sounded even worse said aloud.

"I don't think of you as a failure. I've always been a little envious." Leo sat next to me, rubbed my shoulder.

"Bullshit."

"Not bullshit. You're a renaissance man. You've tried lots of different things. You know more than me about wood-working, sales, owning a business. You've taken risks, and that counts for something."

I hated that Leo wasn't being sarcastic and roasting me. The fact he was being genuine made me feel like an even bigger joke.

"I feel like a fucking disaster. Sometimes, I wonder why you're even friends with me." A chill ran up my back. I hated hearing these words, putting them out there. I looked down. I couldn't let myself see his reaction.

"That's why I didn't tell you about those threesomes. It would make me seem even more like a mess of a person. Did you know that my ex-girlfriend left me for the other guy in the threesome? I was literally the odd man out. I didn't want to lose any more of your respect."

I couldn't be here. Whatever Leo said to make me feel better, whatever non-sarcastic rebuttal he had, I couldn't hear it. It'd hurt too much. So I got up and ran.

I ran faster than I had that morning. But my body wasn't ready. A new kind of pain tore through my calves, the bad kind that sent alarms to my brain. I tried to keep running, but the agony ripped through my leg. I stumbled against a tree.

Leo jogged up to me and examined the scene of his friend slumped against a sapling with two pulled calf muscles. So much for making a grand escape.

"Well, for a supposedly straight man, you sure know

how to make a dramatic exit." He held in his laughter, barely. There wasn't a hint of pity anywhere to be found on his face. "I probably should've told you that it's best to start with a jog before breaking into a full sprint."

"Fuck off."

"Are you sure you want me to fuck off? You're going to need someone to help you down."

"See? I can't even run away properly!" I broke out laughing, and then he followed. Our laughter echoed in the quiet forest.

"Are you done?" Leo came over and massaged my calf, getting the blood flowing. I hissed at the pain.

"If you want to leave me to die here, I'd understand."

"When I'm finally gaining in the polls? Nah." His strong hands breathed life into my leg. And other places. "Dust, I don't call you my best friend just because it sounds cool. Yeah, so you aren't some multi-millionaire CEO with a house on the beach. But you always pick up the phone when I call. And you flew across the country at the drop of a hat when I needed help. I'm lucky to have you in my life."

Leo looked up at me, and behind his sarcastic grin were eyes blazing with intensity. We stayed locked in that moment; my heart pounded in my ears, and all my sexual fantasies about Leo came roaring back.

I pushed them away.

Leo needed me to win this election and save his career. For the first time, I could be the one to help him. I wasn't going to fuck this up like everything else in my life.

He kneaded his fist into my calf.

"You're good at this," I said.

"I have practice." He cleared his throat. "Over the summer, I pulled a glute during a run."

"You pulled your ass running? Then how were you able to keep using Milkman?"

"I hooked up with very limber men."

A bolt of jealousy lashed through me like I'd torn another muscle. Why did I suddenly care about Leo hooking up with other guys?

He gave my leg a final all-good slap. Wordlessly, Leo threw my arm around his shoulder, and we started the trek down the hill back to his house together.

10

LEO

Vernita was my professional ride or die. We came together as a fluke. When I decided to officially run for office, I needed an experienced campaign manager who'd help me unseat the corrupt current mayor. Over coffee at Caroline's, I interviewed an experienced, Ivy League educated consultant who came highly recommended. He turned out to be a pompous ass who repeatedly informed me that mayoral races were beneath his usual work, but he'd make an exception.

Having lunch in the booth behind us happened to be a woman who'd been a speechwriter years ago but left the industry to raise her two kids. She was considering getting back into the game and took our chance meeting as a sign. People told me I was crazy to hire a speechwriter who hadn't worked in a decade to lead my campaign. My gut told me otherwise, and my gut was never wrong.

After a decade of working together, Vernita and I knew each other inside and out. We could predict how the other would react to new ideas and situations. I knew the volumes of opinion behind the slightest facial expression. So when

Vernita came into my office on this Tuesday afternoon wearing an expression others would call poker-faced, but I recognized as concerned, my stomach dropped.

"What is it?" I stood up from my desk.

"Have you not seen Rita's latest video?" She entered my office and shut the door.

"I have a budget meeting in a few."

"Do Ari and Lucy not show you anything from social media? It's been making the rounds." She pulled out her phone and queued up a video.

"Lucy is busy with her studies. She's not into social media stuff."

"She's thirteen and has a phone. I guarantee she's into social media."

"And Ari is busy with...video games." I rolled my eyes. Deirdre and I had multiple arguments about letting him have a gaming system, which she ultimately won.

Vernita leaned her phone against my penholder. On screen was a cute video of Rita and her wife reminding everyone to get their flu shots. The two women lovingly play-fought about Rita being nervous about getting the shot, their young kids nestled in their laps.

"Okay, I can tell people to get their flu shots. I'll have the surgeon general of New York make a cameo in my video." She and I had met at a conference and then later at a secret poker game where she beat me to the tune of five hundred bucks.

"It's not over. Keep watching." Vernita gritted her teeth and watched me watch the video.

I didn't know how much cute lesbian banter I could take until I finally got what Vernita wanted me to see.

The video cut to Rita walking by the closed-off entrance of Renegade Park, construction and orange tape behind her.

"Getting a flu shot is about preparation so we can grow strong!" She cooed into her daughter's face, who smiled wide back at her.

"But mommy, how can Sourwood grow if we're not allowing people to come here?" She gave her mom an exaggerated frown.

"I know, sweetie. Our current mayor is making it very difficult for new families like ours to join our wonderful community."

"He wants us to be all alone? I don't want to be the only girl in my class." Her lower lip trembled exactly on cue. Damn, this kid was good.

"I don't either." Rita turned to the camera. "Because of Leo McCaslin's Runaway Park—"

"Renegade Park," I muttered at the screen.

"—we are threatening to stagnate Sourwood's growth. Our children could grow up in empty classrooms, teachers losing their jobs, store owners going out of business."

"What?" I jumped out of my seat and looked at Vernita as if she should be calling balls and strikes on this bullshit. "That is ludicrous! People move into and out of Sourwood all the time."

"We could fall behind in diversity and innovation. If our population dwindles, we could be annexed by a bigger town, wiped off the map." Rita's lips curved downward into an exaggerated frown. I had to be watching a parody commercial for *Saturday Night Live*. "It's time to fight for our future. I'm Rita Buchanan, and I want to see Sourwood flourish."

I tossed the phone back to Vernita. I needed to take a bath after watching that. I paced in my office. "Nobody takes that seriously, right? They think we're going to turn into a ghost town because we build one or two fewer housing developments?"

Sweat trickled at the back of my neck. Vernita and I shared a look. She didn't need to answer me. We'd been around politics long enough to know the golden rule. Never overestimate the intelligence of your constituents.

"Her family put her up to this," I said.

"I know." Vernita watched me from her seat, staying calm. The wheels were always turning in her head.

I gripped the back of my chair, leaning into it, hoping it could absorb my stress. "I've played nice with Buchanan real estate for years, but they're spoiled children. All they want is more. They'll build, overpopulate, and be out of here while we clean up the mess."

"I agree with everything you're saying, Leo. But it doesn't sound captivating. It's not viral or a sound bite."

"Maybe I should hire a five-year-old to say it with a pout. Can we do that? Go through a casting agency?"

"No," she said firmly, shutting down what would've been a horrible idea anyway. "But we can fight back."

"I thought we were. That's what the whole fake boyfriend thing is supposed to be doing." A twinge of pain lanced my chest at calling Dusty a fake anything. "Dusty's been doing a great job. People like him. We got a huge response at the latest campaign rally."

"We did," she said with hesitation.

"The tone in your voice is terrifying me right now."

"I've been monitoring social media reaction, and there is some chatter about people wondering if you're still just friends."

"Fucking internet." My job was reduced to pleasing anonymous commenters online. I was a step above YouTube influencer.

"They're not completely wrong." Vernita tapped on her phone, bringing up another video. "This is from the campaign rally."

On screen, I was giving a rousing speech at Renegade Park, the plant in the background, talking about the plans for the space. People were cheering. I didn't have sweat half-moons under my arms. What was the problem here?

And then I saw it.

When I left the stage, Dusty and I hugged. He clapped me on the shoulder. It was as if we were two distant cousins forced to see each other at a family function and were pleasantly saying goodbye. It was downright clinical.

"I don't see anything wrong," I said, lying through my teeth.

Lying was useless to Vernita.

"What do you want? Me to get off stage and start dry humping him?"

"You two seem platonic. Not as flirty as you were during your interview with Maria Lopez. We don't want to arouse any suspicion."

Arousal was not my problem. I was doing that just fine. Being around Dusty was giving me a constant erection. There were a few close calls when I almost crossed the line between us—namely our first run together—and maybe my clinicalness was merely insurance against dry humping my best friend.

"I'll make sure to do more light petting and handholding. Sound good?"

"Actually..."

Another familiar Vernita face. Her lips pressed together into a forced smile that meant she was going to ask me to do something I really didn't want to do.

"What?" I asked.

11

DUSTY

I had the day off from fake boyfriend responsibilities. Ari was home sick, so I agreed to be home with him. After going for another run with Leo, I came home, showered, and had a relaxing breakfast while he left for City Hall. I stared at the sagging bookcases in the living room. They were so warped it was like the shelves were smiling at me.

Ari stumbled downstairs in his pajamas.

"Hey, champ. How you feeling?"

He sniffled and coughed. "Fine," he said in that flat, nasal tone that belonged to everyone suffering from a cold.

"I'll toast up a bagel for you with a side of orange," I said. Ari gave me a grateful thumbs up. "Show me your tongue."

"What?"

"Just do it."

Ari stuck out his tongue. A white film coated the surface. "Yep. You're still sick. Healthy tongues are red."

"Gross." He flopped onto the couch. I went into the kitchen and prepared breakfast. My phone buzzed with a text.

Leo: Is Ari up yet?

Dusty: Affirmative.

Leo: How is he feeling? I'll pick up more DayQuil and Airborne on my way home.

I smiled at my phone, feeling a special tug at Leo getting into total dad mode.

Leo: Thank you for watching him.

Dusty: If he gets to be too much, I'll lock him back up in the basement.

Leo: Perfect.

Leo: It's fine if he watches TV and plays video games a little bit, but I don't want him to spend the entire day playing. I worry his brain is turning to mush.

Dusty: He's recuperating.

Leo: He doesn't have the plague.

Dusty: Let the kid chill. But yes, I will monitor.

I pulled the bagel from the toaster and confirmed with Ari that he wanted butter. I peeled his orange and put it in a separate bowl.

Leo: How are you feeling? Sore from this morning?

Dusty: Only a little bit. I think my legs are getting used to this torture.

Leo: It's good for you.

Dusty: Exercise is a Ponzi scheme.

Leo: Uh.

Leo: How?

Dusty: I don't know. I just always wanted to say something like that.

Dusty: I really enjoy our runs together.

They were quickly becoming a highlight of my day. We talked about anything and everything—careers, kids, families, fun memories, movies. Well, everything except how I sometimes think about us rolling around naked together.

My heart raced as I waited for a response. The three dots bubbled up, then vanished, then bubbled up again.

Leo: Me, too.

I breathed a sigh of relief.

Familiar blinky, electronica sounds from the living room brought back memories of my old roommates.

Ari was playing *Roman's Choice*. The creatures hopped and jumped on screen as he clicked at his controller ferociously. I watched from the doorway, silent until there was a break in the action.

"Nice job." I placed his breakfast on the coffee table.

Ari whipped his head around. He had the same no-nonsense stare as his dad, those hawkish eyebrows raising. "Thanks," he mumbled.

"You're good at this." I watched his avatar go through a scary forest that I'd seen many a time. At least Ari had the decency not to perpetually scratch his nuts while playing. "There's a dagger-wielding dragon down that way. I'd do the center path."

"Yeah, I know. You can get around him by going through this shortcut." He pressed away on his controller, sliding his avatar down a hole in the ground to a new level. My eyes jolted open, like seeing the Matrix for the very first time. My roommates never found this secret passageway, nor did they navigate the world with such dexterity.

"Go left," I said, backseat driving.

But it was too late. Ari's avatar bit the dust.

"I told you so," I said into my coffee.

He spun his head around and shot me a glare. "You play?"

"I could." I'd watched my roommates play endlessly.

Ari nudged the second controller in my direction and set up a two-player game. "I have no mercy when I play."

Like father, like son.

The game started, and we tore through the course. Ari played with definite skill, but I was no slouch. I was not one of those adults who let kids win to bolster their self-confidence. Our two avatars engaged in combat, scrambling through the course. Ultimately, it was no contest. Ari left me in the dust; his skill on the controller was undeniable.

"I'm a little rusty," I said. "Wanna go again?"

We went again. He kicked my butt again. And again. We kept playing until my fingers cramped, but I pushed through the pain, my competitiveness overcoming discomfort. The only sounds in the house were the clicking and clacking of controllers.

"That move you did to leap over the drawbridge was awesome," I said. "My roommates played this game every day, and they could never master that jump."

"They're probably tapping one second too late. Try doing this move." Ari demonstrated, though there was no way I could mimic correctly.

His face was bright with excitement. "Thanks for not..."

"Not what?"

He struggled to get out the words, looking at the screen. "My dad always has this look on his face when he sees me playing like he's watching my brain rot in real-time."

"He sees a lot of potential in you. He doesn't want it to go to waste."

"He sees a lot of potential in Lucy. The brainiac." Ari rolled his eyes, but I saw how much it dinged him. It must've been difficult to have a twin who was so smart. It lent itself to a lot of comparisons.

"Your dad loves you. He wants you to have a great life when you get older. And frankly, nobody makes a living off playing video games."

"Yeah, they do."

I whipped my head to look at him. "Say what now?"

He proceeded to pull up an app called Twitch on his phone, which had livestreams where people watched other people play video games. Ari explained that those video game players got paid, sometimes six figures or more, based on the number of people watching. It seemed that the warning to us when we were kids that video games led nowhere belonged in the graveyard next to doctors doing cigarette commercials.

I officially felt like an old man.

"Oh."

"Really good players can go on tour, win money in tournaments, create branded merchandise," he said.

"Man. Let's go in the backyard and burn all of your textbooks in a bonfire." I was maybe half-joking.

Ari inched closer, a secret on his lips. "Can I show you something?"

"Of course, bud." I laughed to myself. I pounded his fist. "No limits here."

When I'd visit in the past, Ari and I would talk about all random things. Kids loved to blabber on, I'd learned, and it was our job as adults to listen. We didn't need to chime in with our thoughts or make this into a conversation. They wanted to be heard.

I followed Ari up to his room, cluttered with lots of boy things and clothes on the floor. He opened a program on his laptop. It was a computer game called *Forest Quest*.

"Never heard of it. Where'd you get it?" I asked.

"I made it."

I did a double-take at the screen, appreciating all the details of the animation and intricacy of the world. "Ari. You made that?"

"I took some free online classes in video game design and have been working on it since the summer." He demonstrated which keystrokes to use to move in the game. "Did you want to play?"

"Yes. And I'm not saying that to be a nice quasi-uncle."

Quickly, I was sucked in. The forest was a maze, intricately designed with endless paths and holes. I calculated in my mind how long this must've taken, how painstaking the detail.

My avatar died a few minutes later, but in the real world, I was all smiles. Ari watched me, waiting for an official response. I gave him two of my hardiest thumbs up.

"Really?" he asked.

"Oh, yeah. I know I shouldn't curse around children, but holy shit, bud. That game rocks! When did you have time to work on this?"

"Usually when I'm at my mom's. She doesn't judge me for being on the computer all the time."

"Your dad would love Forest Quest. The ingenuity—"

"I'm not showing him this," he said with absolute certainty.

Honestly, I didn't blame him. Leo did not hide his disdain for Ari's hobby. Leo would be proud of his hard work, but I was concerned he wouldn't take it seriously because it was video games.

"Your dad and I, we're of a different generation where video games were fun, but not much more than that. There was the whole 'Guy who lives in his parents' basement' stigma. But this is more like computer programming."

"He won't care. He'd be impressed if I was getting straight-A's."

I sat on his bed, trying to figure out how to broach this delicate subject. Major feelings were on the line. "Your dad has opinions on things. That's just the price of getting older. You see a lot, so you think you know. But above all, he appreciates hard work. He works very hard, and when he sees how hard you worked on this game, he will know."

We heard the front door open, and Ari immediately shut his laptop.

"Why don't you lie down and get some rest. I'll work on your dad." I winked at him to let him know I had his back. I'd known Ari since he was a baby, googoo and gagaing across the floor. Now he was a full-fledged person with thoughts and ideas. Time was a funny thing.

Downstairs, Vernita poured herself a glass of water while Leo stood at the kitchen island, staring at the discarded orange rind.

"I was going to clean that up," I said.

He looked at me, and orange skin seemed to be the furthest thing from his mind. "We need to have a little talk. We got some interesting data back on the campaign."

Leo sat me down. He looked at Vernita, who shared his weighted look.

I crossed my arms, waiting for someone to break. "Jesus, what is it? If someone has cancer, then spit it out."

Leo looked at me with dead seriousness. "We need to kiss."

12

LEO

"What?" Dusty asked, just as flabbergasted as I was.

I couldn't believe it either when Vernita mentioned it at the office. I thought this election should be about the issues. Oh, how naive I was.

Vernita whipped out a report and slid it onto the kitchen island. "The good news is that according to polling, the numbers are continuing to trend up." She pointed to a graph that showed this exact fact. Up and to the left. What any organization or political campaign wanted to see. "Leo's favorability and," she cleared her throat, "likeability are up. We're seeing great progress."

"I'm confused. This all sounds like good news." Dusty leaned against the island, looking only at Vernita. He had trouble meeting my eyes. "Yet you sound like you came back from a funeral."

"They're headed in the right direction, but we're not in the clear yet," she said. "We need to keep up the momentum. Remember, Leo's still coming back from the brink of scandal. Dusty, you're helping to get people to forget that, but then that only brings us to zero essentially."

"So us making out is the answer?" Dusty asked.

He hated this idea. And I hated that I didn't hate it.

Fortunately, Vernita stepped in here as I was frozen with awkwardness.

"There is some social media chatter about you two. Some people wonder if you're just friends."

Dusty let out a nervous laugh. "I mean, they're not wrong."

I shut my eyes. One day, far in the future, this would be funny. But not today. "We reviewed some of our public footage. And it does seem that way. We need to get better at acting like a real couple, and that includes a kiss."

"Applefest is coming up, and this will be huge," Vernita said.

"What's Applefest?"

"Applefest is Sourwood's fall festival downtown. Vendors and local artisans line the streets, and a popular local cover band plays the concert Saturday night. It's the biggest event of the season and attracts huge crowds."

"Read: voters," I chimed in.

"The mayor always has a booth there. And it'll be your best opportunity to meet with a large swath of Sourwood residents."

"Voters, right?" Dusty asked sarcastically.

I made a face at him.

"You two can be more intimate there," Vernita said with all the swoon of a cardboard box. "Light petting, holding hands, a kiss here and there. We're thinking that when Leo introduces the band performing that night—when crowds are at maximum levels—you two can passionately kiss. It'll be a real moment, like when Al kissed Tipper Gore at the 2000 DNC."

"Didn't he still lose?" Dusty asked.

I held up a hand. "Let's not relitigate that election, please." I still had nightmares about the 2000 election and hanging chads.

"So all we need to do is kiss?" Dusty asked with a touch of nerves in his voice.

I cleared my throat. "Yes. I know. This is—this whole thing is nuts."

He shrugged. "If you don't win, then all of this will be for nothing."

Not for nothing, I thought. I'd enjoyed having Dusty here, not just in texts and phone conversations. A part of me had worried what our friendship would be like if we were around each other all the time. It only got stronger.

"Do you have a problem with this? Are you on board?" Vernita asked me when I walked her to her car. "Just remember—this dog and pony show is only to get elected, then you can continue to be the great leader you have been. This is the spoonful of sugar to help the medicine go down for voters."

She'd been at this game for a long time. As had I. We knew how it went. But this felt different, more personal.

"It'll be okay," I said. I had to kiss my best friend, something I'd wanted to do for years.

No problem. I was a professional.

———

THAT NIGHT, I couldn't sleep. No surprise there. I had something new to keep me up. I lay down on the couch after drinking a glass of red wine. A fire crackled in the fireplace, and for a moment, things felt peaceful enough for me to find a window for sleep. As I closed my eyes, I heard footsteps by the fridge.

"Don't mind me. I needed a snack." Dusty came into the living room a minute later with cream cheese on a pumpernickel bagel and an empty wine glass. "I can't get enough of these bagels."

"Don't make a mess," I said, a force of habit.

"How can I make a mess with a bagel?"

"Life finds a way," I said, lying back on the couch.

"Do you want half?"

"No."

Dusty nudged his wine glass my way. "Fill 'er up."

I poured him a glass.

"I knew you'd be drinking wine out here. Oof, and it's red."

"What does that mean?"

"You only drink red when you're really stressed. White wine is for a general unwinding of the day. Something light and airy, you once told me. Red is when you need to be calmed down."

I both hated and loved how much Dusty knew about me. I topped him off and pushed the glass over. Dusty took a seat on the opposite end of the couch.

Flames crackled behind us. The fire framed Dusty's face in silhouette, showing off his hard jawline, which had only gotten stronger and more refined with age. I could see the soft pout of his thin lips.

"I'm not much of a sleeper." Dusty sunk into his end of the couch. "That's why I can handle all of our late-night calls."

"I don't think I've slept the whole night through since I was in elementary school." The smell of toasted bagel became too tempting, and I found a new pocket of hunger. "Can I have a bite?"

Dusty handed his plate over. I took exactly one bite, then

handed it back. I didn't want to overstep. Why did I suddenly worry about overstepping with Dusty? I used to think we didn't have any limits, but maybe I was pushing up against them.

"What's keeping you up?" Dusty asked. "Mmm, this is good wine."

"What doesn't? Keeping a town on track, the constant looming elections, making sure my kids are okay."

"The kids are all right. I promise you that. Everything you want to teach them, you are. It's getting through. I promise you that."

I smiled into my wine. The crackling fire made Dusty's skin glow shades of amber. My heart beat in my ears. Fire made everything sexier, didn't it?

Shit. So did wine.

"So about today…"

"I'm sorry. Vernita was out of line."

"She wasn't." Dusty tapped his fingers against the arm of the couch. "Should we practice kissing?"

My eyebrows went up. Maybe another part of me did, too. "What? Are you serious?"

"Yeah." Dusty had a mix of playfulness and fear flickering in his eyes. "If we need to pull off being a couple, then kissing is part of that."

"Is a kiss something we need to practice?" I tried to maintain my reserve and professionalism, even though my insides were shaking and begging to suck face with Dusty. "We've been around the block."

Dusty put a faux-outraged hand over his heart. "Are you calling me a slut?"

"Of course not," I said with my best sarcastic tone. "But we've kissed people before."

"We want it to be believable."

"People will believe it because they'll see it. You can't fake a kiss."

Dusty brushed his hand through his hair, making it all shaggy and cute. "Do you want to be on that stage at Applefest bumping our noses or making faces when our lips and tongue touch?"

"Making faces?" But more importantly: "Tongue? Applefest has kiddie hayrides and artisan craftsmen selling candles. It's not the tongue type of place."

"Well, see, these are things I need to know."

"You were going to kiss me with tongue?" I gulped a heavy lump in my throat, which relocated to my balls. Dusty's tongue, sweeping over mine...I drowned that urge in wine before it had a chance to come up for air.

"Go easy, there," Dusty said as I refilled my wine glass. "Or else you're going to give yourself a nasty hangover."

He didn't realize that this was top-quality wine from Italy, which didn't include sulfites, i.e. hangover-free. And I needed this sulfite-free wine to calm my growing nerves.

"You're nuts."

"I think we should kiss with tongue." Dusty edged closer to me on the couch. "Not like slobbering teens. But a classy amount of tongue. How many couples barely touch lips when they kiss like they're blotting lipstick?"

Deirdre and I kissed like that. We went through the motions years before I finally admitted the truth to myself that I was gay.

"We aren't necking at Applefest."

"Necking? Where are we, Lover's Lane?"

"A nice peck on the lips," I said.

"We should practice. It has to be believable."

The more I pushed back, the more logical he sounded. If our kiss looked bad or fake, it would cause more headlines than any of the good. It would be a salacious detail that elections get hung up on.

"Why do we have to practice?" I felt like we were going in circles, but that was me filibustering on kissing my best friend.

Because what if I liked it? A lot?

"Think of it as rehearsal. On TV shows, the actors block the scenes so that they don't stray off-camera. Again, we don't want to make asses of ourselves at the Pumpkin Party."

"Applefest."

"I'll need to know which way you tip your head, for one."

He maybe had a good point. We couldn't look like a first kiss up there.

"We'll try one kiss. No tongue." I put my authoritarian voice to good use, laying down a law I was dying to break. Dusty licked his plump lips. My dick jumped in my pants.

"Deal."

He inched closer to me on the couch. My heart rate shot up. Thoughts of us over the years, thoughts of those early times in college when I freaking mooned over him in my own very private way, they all came crashing into my head. I shoved them away. I had to.

This was a professional kiss.

Dusty had a relaxed smile on his face. This was business for him. Not the culmination of a years-long crush I thought I had properly extinguished.

"Awkward, I know," he said with a dimpled grin, breaking some of the tension. But not enough.

"I don't really kiss guys," I blurted out.

"Why not?"

"Huh?" I asked, caught off guard.

"Don't you hook up with guys via your handy-dandy apps?"

"Not all the time. When I do, we just...I don't really like kissing them. I've never been that into kissing. Kissing has been about getting to an endpoint."

I scanned through my past relationships and hookups, and the truth smacked me in the face. I liked to get down to fucking. Kissing brought an intimacy that scared the shit out of me.

"That's how most people are. Kissing gets engines revved up. I like kissing. I like luxuriating in the soft feel of someone. There's a special kind of energy when two people kiss."

"Every day, I learn something new about you."

"I'm an enigma."

An enigma wrapped in a nice body. I couldn't stop looking at his lips, thinking about what kind of energy we could create.

"So how about it, bud?" he asked. "It's go-time."

Dusty leaned forward. He tilted his head to the right, probably because he was a lefty. He would show off his lefty hand smudge after a night in the library working on notes. A small smile flitted on my lips as I tilted my head to the left.

Our lips met for the briefest of seconds.

He pulled back. "Your eyes were open."

"They were?"

"Keep them closed."

"Even for Applefest?"

"Yes! You kiss with your eyes open?"

"I wanted to make sure we didn't bump noses."

Dusty shook his head, his lips just a bit wet from our contact. "Dude, never kiss with your eyes open. That's like watching a movie with all the lights on."

"Why are you being such a stickler?"

"Because kisses matter. That's one of my quirks of being a romantic."

"Even if this isn't supposed to be romantic?"

Or was it? I was getting confused, tangling myself in excuses, anything to push away the abject thirst I had for my best friend.

"How did it feel for you?" My breath hitched in my throat, waiting for an answer.

"Good," Dusty offered. "Let's do it again." He pointed at me. "Eyes closed."

I steeled myself for round two. Awkwardness faded when I looked at Dusty, and I thought about how eagerly I wanted to be close to him. Before I could regret this fake relationship idea altogether, Dusty closed the space between us.

Our lips pressed together with no intention of coming loose. His warm breath coated my mouth. As if we were playing on instinct, things clicked together. I opened my mouth for his tongue to enter. It slid against mine, swept around my opening, sending sizzling chills throughout my body. The heat of his chest right up against mine made me melt into him. I slid my tongue between his soft lips hungrily, our breaths getting shorter and more urgent.

Dusty rested a hand against my cheek, and I wanted it to drift lower. My dam of need had exploded like a shoddily built levy.

And then it was over. Dusty pulled back again, this time taking all my oxygen with him. I couldn't describe how I felt, but the look on Dusty's face seemed to say it for me.

"Better?" I asked.

"Uh, yeah. I'm, uh, surprised you don't like kissing. You're good at it." His cheeks clouded with red. "What did you think of my hand?" He mimicked the movement of it on my cheek, and I nearly swooned all over again.

"Good. Yeah, it was good."

"Because I just went with it. That's something I do."

"No, yeah, I get it." I hopped off the couch at lightning speed. If I spent any more time with Dusty, my resistance would evaporate, and I'd ruin this entire operation. Falling apart over an engineered kiss? That wasn't me. I didn't let emotions get the better of me. The only thing that kiss was supposed to do was bring me closer to re-election.

"The wine is kicking in, so I'm going to get to sleep. Night, Dusty." I made an awkward gesture that was part-hug, part-hi five, part leg pat. I brought awkward back better than Justin Timberlake brought sexy back.

DUSTY

I woke up the next morning the same way I went to bed the night before—thinking about that kiss.

That amazing

Spellbinding

Heart-thomping

Boner-inducing

Meeting of the mouths

I was still catching my breath. Hell, I needed four oxygen tanks and a year of Lamaze classes to catch my goddamn breath.

Oh, this was bad. Heavenly, amazingly bad. I was here to help my friend in need, one of the scant opportunities when I had the chance to restore the friend balance. But instead, I chose to blatantly mack on my best friend.

And to use the word mack, which should've been retired in 1997. Ugh.

I was jerking off to intimate pictures of him. I was using polling as an excuse to kiss him and then shoving my tongue inside his mouth. I had to play it cool because if Leo knew how much I was enjoying this, he'd freak out, and our friendship wouldn't recover.

I mean, we'd been friends for years, and Leo had been gay that whole time, and he never showed any interest in me. He saw me strictly as a friend.

I thought I did, too.

Leo knocked on my door. "You ready to run?"

It was a cold morning. I was still in bed. Maybe he could join me?

Oh, for fucks sake, no, he will not!

"Yeah. Give me a minute," I yelled from the comfort and safety of my bed. After a night of tossing and turning, sometime in the earliest parts of the morning, I came up with an idea to help me with this odd little crush I'd developed.

I pulled on a pair of running shorts and a fresh T-shirt. I laced up my sneakers and checked myself in the mirror. Shockingly, I looked like an athlete.

"Finally," Leo said once I joined him downstairs for coffee. "I was about to leave without—"

I shut him up with a kiss. A quick kiss, more in-depth than a peck, but without tongue. I topped it off with a caress of his chin with my thumb.

"Morning." I poured myself a cup of coffee then hopped onto the island. "Could you put a dash of half and half in?"

Leo, stunned into a zombified silence, went to the fridge for the half-and-half. He touched his lips when he thought I wasn't looking.

"Uh, here." He handed over the carton.

"Thank you, sir."

We drank our coffees in silence. I smiled into my cup, hoping like hell I knew what I was doing. When I finished, I placed my cup in the sink, then kissed Leo again, sending him into another state of stupefied silence.

"I'll be outside stretching."

————

AT FIRST, we ran in silence, which was fine since the beauty of Sourwood was enough to admire. Each time we ran through town, I found more things to love about this hamlet. The old storefronts that belied decades of history. The bright yellows of the turning maple leaves. The glorious view at the top of the hill, where the grays and brown of town were encompassed by autumn leaves and then the bright blue of the river. I thought living by the Pacific Ocean was beautiful, but the Hudson River took the cake.

Eventually, Leo struck up a conversation about our day ahead. Keeping it business. We were set to visit a senior citizen's home for a Q and A session. Seniors were the most reliable voting block, he explained. He then went on to regale me with tales from past Applefest celebrations, all the weird questions he'd get from residents, some of whom had imbibed too much hard cider from local breweries. Apparently, the reference librarian had flashed him at the mayor booth in one particularly rowdy year.

"Thanks for watching Ari yesterday. When I kissed him goodnight, he seemed to be doing much better. I'm shocked you were able to pull him away from his controller," Leo said with a light-hearted laugh that immediately sparked something within me.

He started up his jog again, but I didn't follow.

"What is it?" he asked.

"You gotta stop that," I said.

He turned back to me, utterly confused. "Stop what?"

"Shitting all over your son."

"Excuse me." He went into protective dad mode, which I found endearing, yet also a touch scary since it was turned on me. "I love Ari."

"I know you love him, but you have a weird way of showing it. You put down his interest in video games all the time."

A pained look crossed Leo's brow. "I want him to find a more enriching, challenging hobby."

"Belittling his interests and always comparing him to his sister isn't pushing him in that direction."

"Are we really doing this? Let's just continue our run."

For a man who loved to give speeches and debate, Leo was a king of not talking about things.

"Ari designs video games," I said defiantly. "Really good ones. I played one of them."

A pinch of regret stung my chest. Technically, Ari hadn't sworn me to secrecy. I felt bad for sharing, but I wanted Leo to see how incredibly talented his son was.

"Ari?"

"Yeah. He designs them on his computer. The graphics, the schematics of the levels, all of it."

"I thought he only played." Leo put his hands on his hips like he was catching his breath at the new information.

"He does a lot more. And I'm sure he'd share that with you if you were more open and accepting of his hobbies. He might not be a brainiac like Lucy, but that doesn't mean he isn't smart."

"I never said he wasn't smart," he said curtly, every muscle tense. "That's what was frustrating. Ari has great potential. I didn't want to see him wasting it."

"He's not. I promise you that. But maybe Lucy is."

"What's wrong with Lucy?" Leo plopped down on a rock.

"Maybe calling her a brainiac is putting all this pressure

on her. As the son of a preacher man, I know the stress of trying to live up to a certain image." It was stress I learned to alleviate in high school with bong hits and cheap beer.

Leo rubbed his hands through his hair. I could feel the weight pressing down on him. "It gets harder as they get older. When they're young, they tell you everything. They won't stop talking. All their hopes, all their fears, all their strange thoughts. It all comes pouring out nonstop." He laughed to himself. I had a pinch of jealousy that I never went down the path of fatherhood. I remembered how chatty the twins were. "But then there's a turning point. They hold back. I have to pry information out of them. They become mysteries, and I go from knowing everything to being constantly in the dark."

I squatted beside him and placed a supportive hand on his knee. "You're a great dad, Leo. Really."

"Am I? Has all this mayor shit ruined everything? I've tried so hard to keep balance, to be there as much as I can for my kids. It's so hard. As a single dad, I feel like I'm constantly playing catch up, and one day, it's going to be too late."

His dark eyes clouded over to the gray side, whole and vulnerable. This was a Leo most people never saw. Hell, I barely saw it. He made juggling balls in the air seem effortless, but there was always effort involved.

"Hey, it's never too late. And thinking back to when I was their age, I wanted to feel heard more than anything. My parents didn't listen to anything I wanted or cared about. It was their way or the highway. I'm not saying you have to agree with everything they do, just listen."

Leo patted my hand. "For a lifelong bachelor, you seem to know a lot about kids."

"I guess I never grew up." I stood back up and shook out

my legs. Squatting was painful. My quads were very mad with me.

"The twins love you. Uncle Dusty."

"I'm crazy about them. It's been cool watching them develop personalities and become mini-adults."

"It's terrifying."

"Let's finish the fun." I held out my hand to get Leo back on his feet.

He joined me in standing up. I planted another kiss on his lips, leaving him yet again shocked.

"All right. Let's do this!" I jogged in place to get my body moving. As soon as I pushed off to start my run, Leo grabbed my shirt and pulled me back.

"What the hell are you doing?"

"What?"

"What's with all the kissing this morning?" He looked at me like I was crazy, but there was a glimmer of something in his eyes I couldn't decipher.

"Whatever do you mean?"

He cocked his head. "The kissing over coffee, and now. I didn't dream all that out of thin air."

Like the way I dreamed about kissing you last night?

"I had this epiphany this morning. It's kind of brilliant when you think about it. To get better at kissing—I mean, to make it more believable. Because you're already good—" I shook my head, forcing myself to get words straight and not dig myself into an even more awkward hole. "The more we do it, the more comfortable we'll feel, the more natural it will look at Applefest and anywhere else we have to swap spit."

"Who says swap spit?"

"Who says Lover's Lane?" I crossed my arms.

He laughed like he was staring down a crazy person.

That might have been forty percent true. But the majority of me made sense. My plan sounded better when I said it aloud, even if it was actually a cover. Because for some odd reason, I really wanted to kiss Leo more.

I wasn't ready to unpack that. Hell, I hadn't unpacked my actual luggage yet.

"So you're going to what? Keep kissing me randomly throughout the day?" he asked.

"If that's what it takes." My dick jumped in my shorts. "It'll help to wipe the shocked look off your face when we kiss."

"I'm shocked because you're kissing me at random!"

"That's what couples do!" I yelled back, my voice going to Seinfeld-octave levels. "Has it really been that long since your last relationship?"

He grumbled in frustration, which I found incredibly adorable.

"Soon, we'll be kissing like it's old hat. Old tongue."

Leo pulled his leg into a quad stretch, which made his shirt stretch across his chest...and made me stare blatantly.

"What are you looking at?" Leo peered down at this chest.

"I'm gazing at you lovingly for practice. Man, you belong in a nunnery." And not because he looked damn fine in black and my mind was scrambling with what he could do to me in a tight confession booth with a pair of rosary beads.

Oh, heavenly father, I am sinning, and I can't stop. I really hoped this plan would help me mellow out. The more I kissed Leo, the faster I'd get these weird feelings out of my system.

"This is ridiculous. We can't kiss all the time." Leo laughed it out, but his voice was still strained in frustration.

But then I remembered who I was dealing with.

"If you insist." I leaned down for a stretch. "I had a feeling you couldn't handle this."

Leo quirked an eyebrow. "What's that mean?"

"I'm obviously the better fake boyfriend here."

He stepped toward me, eyes boring into me. "Says who? I'm a damned good fake boyfriend."

"No, I'm better. I'm more willing to kiss you and play this up for the public. But not like it's a competition or anything." I jogged in place. "Though if it were, I'd be winning."

Off I went, running down the path as fast as my feet would take me, bobbing and weaving around roots and bramble. I charged ahead, determined to beat him down the hill. My blood circulated through my body, a nice change from engorging in my dick. Behind me was the determined gait of Leo, crunching over leaves and gravel.

I let out a laugh deep from within my chest. I was having pure fun and had to let it out. Wind rushed through my hair, making it vertical. My heart beat crazily like I was being chased.

I was being chased.

The bottom of the hill was in sight, but before I could claim victory, Leo hulked past me, giving me a tiny shove in the process. He stuck out his tongue as he passed.

Real mature.

I stuck my tongue out at his back.

He waited at the bottom, jogging in place, smarmy grin lighting the hazy forest. I took my sweet time going down the rest of the way. Let the fucker wait.

"Don't wait on my account," I said when I reached the bottom.

Leo grabbed me by the shirt and pulled me into a passionate, forceful kiss with all the tongue. It out-amazed, out-spellbound, out-heart-thumped our kiss from last night. And boner-inducing? My dick was so hard it'd set off the metal detectors at the airport.

"You're right," he said, close to me, face flush. "It is starting to feel like old hat."

"Wait, what?" I was still coming back down to earth.

He managed a victorious smile through catching his breath. "Who's the better fake boyfriend now?"

Leo jogged away, leaving me stunned and hard.

Shit.

14

———

LEO

Dusty was dangerous. Each day—hell, each hour—we spent together was another land mine I came close to stepping on.

Kissing for sport was easy for him. He was in this for the ruse. He wasn't the one swooning like a fucking teenager every time our lips met. He wasn't the one instantly transported back to being the closeted college student pining over his friend.

And damn, of course, he had to be a good kisser.

So we kissed.

A lot.

Saying hello. Saying goodbye. Over morning coffee. Over dinner. Vernita gave us curious side-eye at the office, but she grinned with acceptance. My staff and everyone in the city council building watched and found it adorable. True love. They were buying it hook, line, and sinker. Some kids had even posted us kissing on social media, and people called us "Couple goals."

That part of the strategy was working. The part where the more we kissed, the more old hat it would be? Big old flop. The more I kissed Dusty, the more I wanted to kiss Dusty. I struggled to stay glued together. God, his lips and his stubble and his breath...it was all better than I ever imagined. You could spend years being close to someone—talking, knowing everything about him, hugging. And sure, that was close. That was its own form of intimacy. But kissing? Feeling him in your arms. That was a whole other level.

Even if it was all for fucking pretend.

Three days before Applefest, I tried my absolute best to concentrate on the city council meeting I was leading, even though the prospect of kissing Dusty when it was adjourned heated me up like a tea kettle.

"The next item on the agenda is authorizing funding to break ground on Renegade Park," I called out.

"Actually, I think this should be tabled until next month," Rita said into her microphone. She shot me a smile that was less clueless than usual.

Next month. After the election.

"We want to be sure we can secure the contracts to begin building early in the new year so that it's ready for spring. We had agreed to this timetable and the funding over the summer. This vote is mostly a formality, Rita."

"Yes, but in light of recent events, this should be tabled until next month," Rita said, all sharp politeness.

"Well, as an elected official now, we need to continue to conduct business. We can't hold everything until next month. I was elected to do my job now, not wait a few weeks."

"With all due respect, Mayor, polling is showing that a majority of Sourwood residents are not aligned to your objectives. And considering the population increase over the past four years, we don't want to discount the opinions of new residents who will be voting. I think we should at least put it to a vote with the city council."

Was she really taking over my meeting? We faced each other down, all polite small-town smiles. I could barely keep mine on.

"I think she has a good point, Leo," Herb said, another city council member who'd been there since the turn of the millennium. He had petitioned (and was denied) for a bomb shelter in the center of town to safeguard against the world ending with Y2K.

The other city council members seemed to nod or at least be on board with a vote.

"Fine. All those in favor of tabling this discussion for one month, say aye."

The ayes had it. Five out of eight city council members voted yes.

After the meeting, I caught up to Rita at her office.

"Nice move," I said.

"It wasn't a move."

"Tell me, do you have any ideas of your own, or are you being fed everything by your family?"

She busied herself with shoving papers and folders into her attaché case. "We have plenty of parks in Sourwood. What's one less?"

"You want to cut off the riverfront to the public and turn it into mansions and high rises for a select few. It will permanently alter the fabric of this town."

"Well, that's not up to you to decide. That's why we have elections. And I'm still ahead."

"Barely." The last Vernita checked, Rita was up four points. Dusty had helped me cut her lead substantially. "I'm gaining on you."

"Not for long, MisterWood." And there it was again.

That smile. That not-so-clueless, knowing smile that made chills slink up my spine.

"What've you got up your sleeve, Rita? More cute videos with your family?"

She stopped filling up her bag and stared right in my eye. "Dusty's great. Really nice guy. It's very serendipitous that you two fell in love. Convenient."

My insides seized up inside me, but outside, I played it cool. "Don't sink to that level. You're better than that. Barely."

"You asked what I've got up my sleeve, Leo?" She tossed her bag over her shoulder. "You'll find out very soon. I'll see you at Applefest." She flicked a piece of lint off my shoulder and left.

I trudged back to my office, where Vernita waited patiently.

"What's up? Shouldn't you go back home to your wonderful husband and kids?" I asked in the doorway. Vernita's husband was an incredible cook. I was lucky enough to eat at their house a few times, and I always wished I had left with a doggy bag.

"Wanted to make sure you were okay."

"Rita is planning something for Applefest."

"Probably."

"She seemed very confident. Oddly confident. Have you heard anything?"

"Only that she is planning something. I asked the Applefest organizers, and they said she's hosting a booth. She was probably trying to psych you out."

"It wasn't working." It was a little.

Vernita shrugged and scrolled through the emails on her phone.

"You and Dusty are working out well. My hairdresser

gushed to me about how cute you two seemed. All the PDA, as my kids call it, is getting noticed."

"Right. Yeah, good." It felt weird hearing her talk neutrally about my relationship, even if it was fake. There was something real there, and I didn't like that it was for public scrutiny.

"He's a good guy," she said, and there was a weight to her words I didn't expect.

"He's my best friend."

The tips of her lips curved into a smile.

"What?" I asked.

"Nothing. But..." She strummed her fingers on her dossier. "What's the plan if you win?"

"*When* I win."

"When you win." She waited for an answer. "We should start planning an exit strategy for Dusty in November. I assume Dusty is going back to Los Angeles when this is all done."

A new terror clenched me in its fist. I dipped my head, stared at the single scuff mark on my right shoe, which I'd buff out tonight.

"Yeah, uh, that's the plan for now."

"Do you think he'd be open to staying through the holidays so we can break you two up with a smooth landing?"

"Can we talk about this later?" I snapped at her. She lurched back slightly from the contact of my words. "Sorry. I'm just tired. We'll talk about it later."

"You got it, Mr. Mayor." She stood up and patted me on the shoulder in a way that felt maternal. Her warmth beamed through her. "In my opinion, I hope he stays."

Me too, Vernita. Me fucking too.

15

DUSTY

Applefest was officially cute, and I said this as someone who was overall ambivalent on apples. I was more of an oranges guy, especially when they were muddled in a glass of vodka.

A huge Applefest sign with apples for the Ps stretched across the street. The main drag was shut down to traffic. We entered through one of the entrances where a stage was set up for tonight's concert. Throngs of people shuffled around from booth to booth. The buzz in the air crackled in my veins. There was the distinct feeling Sourwood was going all out today. No autumnal stone would be left unturned.

Along the street, booths were set up with vendors and local businesses. A few stray clouds sifted through the brilliant blue sky. Food stations and food trucks were set up at corners advertising apple cider (kiddie and adult kinds), apple cider doughnuts, and caramel apples. One place had the audacity to advertise deep-fried Oreos as if they were staging a protest against the fruit of the hour.

Well, the real fruit of the hour was Leo. He was downright presi-fucking-dential. Leo was so damn good at commanding a room—or a festival in this case. He remembered everyone's name, shook hands with all the local business owners, and sampled their wares. People waved and greeted us as we walked through the crowd to the mayor's booth. He wore a button-down shirt with rolled-up sleeves, jeans, and a maroon quilted vest. Leo held my hand and kept smiling at me. Was it for show? Was it for real? I didn't know anymore. All this kissing had made me crush-drunk.

I was a minor celebrity, too. Residents asked me questions about how I was enjoying Sourwood, what my favorite stores were, what I was excited for with Applefest. Anytime I felt nervous about the crowds, I squeezed Leo's hand, and he squeezed back, and I knew I could take on anything. Sometimes, he'd look over and give me this stealth smile and wink that made the festival disappear.

We strolled down the row of vendors, caramel apples in our hands that we'd watched the owner of Lazy Sundae make in front of us. I was never a fan of them—it was sugar on sugar—but this one was delicious. I breathed a huge sigh of relief when we came to Mitch's booth, where he served burgers and hard apple cider. The line stretched into the street, and I dutifully waited for my drink.

"Enjoying your first Applefest?" He came to our table, where we knocked back a beer.

"I didn't know people cared about apples this much. It's like a town of schoolteachers."

"Yeah, it's a lot to take in. You get used to it." Mitch wiped down the empty table next to ours.

"I love this, though. There are so many things I want to buy. Candles made out of craft beer bottles? Yes, please. Your booth is busy."

"It always is."

"That's because he serves alcohol," Cal said, decked

out in full scouting uniform. He was taking a lunch break from manning the Falcons scouting booth, where he, Russ, and their troop were doing rope-tying demonstrations.

"I'm only serving hard apple cider," Mitch corrected.

"Which is alcohol. Festive alcohol, but still alcohol."

Mitch shrugged his shoulders. He was busy and proud of it. Across the way, Leo was chatting with people at his booth, which had a sign that read, "AMA: Ask Mayor Anything."

"He's like the Energizer bunny. He can keep going and going," I said, watching Leo.

"Every vote counts," Cal said.

"He loves it." Mitch watched with a twinkle in his eye.

"I never want to get into politics, but some people are born for it." Cal wiped off excess ketchup from his mouth. "Leo's found his calling."

I felt a pang in my chest. I didn't want to fuck this up for him. The mayorship meant too much to him. Whatever feelings I felt for him had to stay tucked inside.

"How are you doing with all the campaigning?" Cal asked in between large bites of a hamburger.

"Campaigning is just a stuffy synonym for talking with people. Everyone I've met in Sourwood has been really nice and down to earth."

"I'll bet you'll miss them when you go back to the airheads on the West Coast." Cal chuckled to himself, then stopped. "No offense."

"None taken. I'm an East Coaster at heart."

"I'm an actor, so I'm part airhead anyway."

Jokes aside, a cold burst of reality hit me. Sourwood wasn't my home but seemed more like it each day.

"The election will be over soon. Keep your head in the

game," Mitch said before he had to jump on the register to serve more walkups.

My head I could do. My heart was another story.

I had Mitch make a chicken caesar wrap and ferried it over to Leo's booth, catching him in a rare moment without a visitor.

"Thank you. It's hard to be charming and hangry at the same time." He looked in the bag. "Chicken caesar wrap! It wasn't on the menu."

"I asked Mitch for a special exception."

"How'd you know—"

"Remember that time you came to visit me? You made us go on a Harold and Kumar-like quest for a chicken caesar wrap across Santa Monica."

"That was a great wrap. Where was that place—"

"Finley O'Connor."

Leo let out a chuckle, his eyes creasing at the corners, making me swoon. "An Irish pub with the best chicken caesar wrap."

"America is a melting pot. Eat. Before you get bombarded with more visitors."

Leo gestured for me to get closer. He planted a glorious kiss on my lips—soft but with intention, a guiding hand on my cheek. I loved how his body felt on me, how protective he was.

A guy could get used to this. Though he very much should not.

"What do you think of Applefest?" he asked.

"You are the eight billionth person to ask me that. I love it. Yay apples! Yay fall! This is an Instagram post come to life."

"Have you been on their Instagram page? There's a cute picture of us."

He pulled up the page, and my heart and belly flipped. A candid shot of Leo and I walking through the crowds, his arm around me whispering something funny into my ear. I was smiling like my lips were made of rubber bands. It was an interesting sight to see an objective picture of myself being unabashedly happy. I wanted to be that guy in the picture all the time.

"We look good," I said, a bunch of nerves twisting their way through me.

"You look good. I'm lucky to be standing next to you." Leo gave my hip a light pinch. He scrolled to the top of Applefest's feed. "Holy shit."

"What?"

"They announced who's playing the concert tonight. The English Patients."

"I thought you said it was local cover bands. The English Patients are like a real band. They played *Saturday Night Live* last week. *Ocean City* used their music in three episodes."

"That's quite a get. Someone in the Applefest organizing committee must've had a connection. Surprised they didn't mention anything to me."

"I guess they wanted to keep it under wraps?" I nudged the bag of food closer to him. "Here. Eat."

"I will."

"You say that, but then you won't. Something will come up. You'll think of another email to write. You run on ninety percent caffeine and ten percent Microsoft Office. I'm surprised you haven't wasted away." I took the wrap out of the bag and plunked it in front of him. "I'll take over while you have lunch."

Leo quickly figured out he wasn't going to win. He bit into the wrap, and I watched as hunger faded away.

"You need your energy to conquer Applefest. I'll cover for you."

Two people came up to the booth while he ate, and while I could've filled in, Leo spoke with them. They gushed with excitement about The English Patients playing. When he finished lunch, things were still quiet. There was a lull on our side of the fest, and Leo was a jittery mess with nobody to talk to and nothing to do. He was a man of action. It was killing him not to be mingling with the crowd, especially since he shared his concern that Rita had something up her sleeve.

"Let's go for a walk," I said. "If the people won't come here, we will have you go to the people."

"I'm supposed to stay at the booth."

"Switch things up!"

I wrote out a Be Back in Thirty sign with a black marker and stuck it on the table under a rock. The afternoon was turning late. Soon it would be night, and everyone would gravitate to the concert. We had to take advantage of the sunlight.

Leo and I walked into a more crowded area where there were games. Kids enjoyed hay bales and slides, while carnival games were for the adults.

"So, what's your plan?" he asked.

"Win me one of those stuffed animals." I pointed to the booths where they were giving away prizes. The baseball throwing booth had large panda bears hanging up top, tempting me.

"You want a stuffed animal prize?" Leo asked. "Aren't you a bit old?"

"I've gone to fairs my whole life, and I've never won one of those things." I leaned into Leo's ear. "If I'm going to have a fake boyfriend, I might as well make the most of him."

Leo smiled to himself, and I could feel his stubble get close to my lips. So I kissed him. Vernita said that every time I kissed him, his numbers went up. Something of mine went up, too.

"You really want that panda?"

"People will like seeing a mayor who knows how to win, and they'll find it cute that you're winning me a stuffed animal."

"I have to win. I don't want to crap out in front of my constituents."

"You thrive under pressure." I rubbed Leo's shoulder. He was so easy to touch. "I guess I could always ask Rita to play for me. She probably plays softball and could get it no problem."

Determination stamped across his brow. "Let's win you that panda."

———

LEO LED ME, hand on my ass, to the baseball booth. This time, he didn't apologize. I didn't object. My mind came up with multiple scenarios for where else he could put his hand.

Leo shook hands with the man Sedrick running the booth. He operated the sporting goods store Balls and Strikes, which was situated behind us. "How are Lorraine and the girls?"

"Hayley lost her first tooth last night!"

"Congratulations." Leo passed him money to play the game. "You can put this under her pillow."

Sedrick handed over the three packed softballs to Leo.

"My guy wants one of those pandas."

My guy. I was drowning in swoon. Fake swoon, but still tasty. Like Diet Coke.

Leo pushed up his sleeves, exposing his thick, furry forearms. The panda wasn't the only bear I wanted.

"You got this." I slapped his butt.

He arched an eyebrow at me. I arched one back. *Yes, I slapped your cute butt.*

Leo wound up for the pitch and hurled the ball into the pins. He cleared the platform.

"Yes!" I threw my hands in the air, unafraid to cause a scene.

Since Leo was the celebrity of Sourwood, people inevitably crowded around to watch. Leo didn't bristle at the attention. He was always on. He knew how to hold a crowd in his palm but make each person feel special. I was under his spell.

"Let's see what you got, Leo!" yelled an onlooker.

"Prepared to be amazed," I yelled back.

Sedrick handed him the softball and set up the pins again. "If you can do that two more times, you got yourself a bear."

I clapped and turned to the crowd. "Let's give the mayor some encouragement."

The crowd joined me in clapping and cheering him on. I slapped Leo on the butt again.

"It worked last time," I said to him. And it was a nice butt to slap.

Leo stared at me for an extra second. "It must be very fun inside your head."

Usually, yes. But currently, my head was surging with hormones like I was a teenager who had just discovered porn.

"I played little league. Shortstop for the Sourwood

Badgers about thirty years ago." Leo wound up his pitch and launched the ball into the pins. He cleared the platform again.

The crowd cheered him on without my prompting. Was there nothing he couldn't do?

"You think you can make it three in a row?" Sedrick passed over the softball. According to the rules, Leo had three more chances to clear the pins in order to win me the panda. Sedrick did not make this easy.

"You ready?" Leo tossed the ball in the air.

The crowd cheered him on.

"You guys can do better than that!" I yelled back to him and raised my hands to approximate the levels of noise we were expecting. They got louder, filling Applefest with noise.

Leo wound up his pitch but stopped. "Wait, this isn't right."

"What?"

"I need my lucky butt slap."

"Oh? You want me to spank you?"

Leo turned red at the collar. My mind was apparently hard-wired for dirty talk.

I got into position, wound my hand back, and made contact with his right cheek. My hands lingered for a second and squeezed.

Oops.

Leo laughed along. His whole body seemed to levitate with enjoyment. He threw the ball and knocked down the pins.

I jumped up and down. I ran through the crowd of onlookers and hi-fived them. I was a ball of energy. And when I came back to Leo, he held up the panda for me.

When I grabbed for it, he took my hand and pulled me into a kiss.

And just like that, I finally admitted what I'd been too scared to think: I was totally sprung for my best friend.

Our moment was cut short by a woman with a Vote for Rita T-shirt tucked into a pair of mom jeans. Another woman wearing a different-colored Rita T-shirt and culottes was right behind her.

"Hello, Mr. Mayor." Rita and her wife were wearing matching smug smiles, but if I were wearing that outfit, I wouldn't be smiling.

"Rita. Deb." Leo gave them terse nods. "Good day for Applefest."

"It's gorgeous. Bill was saying attendance was likely going to break records." Rita had the judgy eyes that I knew very well from years of being around church moms. My balls jumped into my stomach when she and Deb looked my way. "And you must be Dusty."

"That I am."

"We've been hearing so much about you. You formed out of thin air," Rita said with a high-pitched laugh that sounded like hyenas being drowned, in my humble opinion.

I threw my arm around Leo. "Isn't that how love goes, though? You're going along, going along, and then suddenly bam! This guy who's been in front of me this whole time is the love of my life!"

"You've been getting a lot of visitors to your booth?" Rita asked Leo.

"Yeah. This is the first break I've had all day. People love talking to the mayor."

"I had a thought. Next year, I'm going to repaint the AMA booth. It could use a new color, maybe mauve."

"Does it now?" Leo's smile was so rigid it could cut glass.

His grin read one hundred percent fuck off. Was it weird that I found it a turn-on. "That's sweet that you have dreams."

"You're funny. Occasionally." She and Leo smiled and waved at residents passing by. Their facades were A-plus.

"Have you seen the latest polls? Your lead is receding."

"Oh, Leo. The only thing receding is your hairline." Rita breathed in a gust of fresh, fall air, venom glinting off her white teeth. "You and the rest of Sourwood are in for a treat tonight."

"How so?" Leo had an edge of curiosity to his voice, which he tried to play down.

"Did you hear that The English Patients are playing later?"

"Yeah. It's quite a get for Applefest."

"Who do you think pulled the strings to book them?" She revealed a Cheshire cat grin.

Oh, shit.

"The city council doesn't get involved with Applefest. I didn't see any change in the line-item budget for the event." Leo went full business mode while squeezing my hand. Tight.

"There was no extra charge. Something Buchanan Real Estate wanted to do for the town it loves. I worked with the committee to keep it a secret since we were working down to the wire to clear it with their schedule. The drummer's mother is a close family friend."

I regretted living in Los Angeles for decades and not having any cool music connections—unless you counted my roommates who sang songs from *The Little Mermaid* when they got high.

"Sourwood is so excited to get a special concert from a huge band, not the usual local cover bands. And can you imagine their reaction when they find out it was because of me? Who do you think is going to be up there when they go on, receiving a ringing endorsement from the lead singer?"

Leo tried his best to keep his poker face up. I was less convincing. It was an unfortunate part of our political system that people listened to celebrities, even when we told them to shut up and sing. The festival was abuzz with The English Patients performing. Now they would find out why.

"No campaigning is allowed at Applefest," Leo said.

"It's frowned upon, but not a violation. I'm sure people won't mind once they start playing. I'll be sure to look out for you from the stage." She waved good-bye with a giddy lift of her shoulders.

"It was good seeing you, Mr. Mayor. How's the rotator cuff doing?" Deb said quickly before being ushered away by her wife.

Leo beelined back to his mayor's booth. I was our eyes to ensure he didn't bump into anyone, as he was texting Vernita the whole time.

"It's no big deal," I said to Leo once we got back.

"It's a very big deal."

Vernita joined us point-two seconds later with a large stick of cotton candy. Leo filled her in on the music situation. She tossed her snack into the trash.

"The town is going to eat this up. This is the biggest thing to happen since..."

"It's going to wipe away our article, all of my good press." Leo paced in the booth.

I searched my brain for something to help.

"People will have fun tonight, but they won't remember anything by morning," I said.

"Unless they're using that neuralizer from *Men in Black*, that ain't happening." Leo rubbed his forehead. "It's all anyone's been talking about since they were announced last week. Once the band says 'Vote for Rita,' it'll be lodged into their minds."

"I can put out feelers to my network to see if I know any celebrities we could ask for an endorsement," Vernita said.

"Like we can get Ariana Grande to drop what she's doing and drive up to Sourwood last minute?"

"Keep talking with people," Vernita said. "Keep being yourself. You're great at events."

"He's doing so great, Vernita," I said. "He's being super social. Everyone loves Leo." Since I couldn't help here, the least I could do was shower him with compliments. "And he won me a panda."

"A panda?"

"Should I leave before the concert starts? I don't want to look like some idiot out there while Rita is getting all the glory." Leo gripped the panda, nearly popping off its head.

The wheels turned in my head, an idea coming to light. "Guys."

"Leaving will look even worse," Vernita said.

I held up my finger. "Guys."

"But staying and enjoying a concert by a group of young assholes who endorse my competition is better? We have two weeks left until the election. We need to think of something big to pull focus."

I clapped hard, making my hands go raw. "Guys!"

I got their attention. "I think I have a plan."

Leo and Vernita went silent. Their eyes were spotlights on me. I gulped down hard.

Right, saying I had a plan meant I had to keep talking.

"So, what's this plan?" Vernita asked.

A smile snaked onto my lips. "For one night only, we're going to turn Leo back into a rock star."

16

LEO

Remember that Eminem song where he talked about his knees being weak, his arms being heavy, and barfing spaghetti on himself when he went up to perform? That was my current state.

Minus the vomit. For now.

Dusty led the way, carving a path through the throngs of people gathered at the stage. I held his hand tight; he didn't say a word about my palm being drenched in sweat. I had visions of bombing and getting tomatoes thrown at me, but Dusty had such a fervent look in his eye it had to be worth a shot. I'd never seen him so focused.

Nerves filled my stomach. I pulled back.

"I don't know if I can do this. It's been a long time," I said. "I haven't picked up a guitar in what? Fifteen years?"

"It's like riding a bike. You got this."

Not everything was like riding a bike.

"Are you sure you can do this, Leo?" Vernita asked, tailing us. "Because if you can't, it's going to backfire spectacularly."

That was a good question. A very good question.

I wanted to be truthful and say I had no idea, but Dusty piped up first.

"He can do it. He's going to blow them away."

We reached the front of the stage. The sun had set, and Applefest was illuminated by street lights, festive lanterns, and the glow of cellphones. The set for The English Patients was empty, minus a roadie checking equipment. The nerves in my stomach expanded like water spilling over a surface. Vernita was right. If I choked up there, my campaign was over.

But if I crushed it...a teeny tiny part of me kept that dream alive.

Dusty hopped on stage and chatted with the roadie. While I knew how to gladhandle residents of Sourwood, Dusty had a great ability to connect with others. He spoke animatedly, rubbed his hands together, and kept looking at me, shooting me that easy smile. Even though I was a bundle of nerves, I was able to swoon over him. I could multitask. The roadie seemed into it and brought Dusty backstage with him.

"Is this crazy?" I asked Vernita.

She arched an eyebrow at me. "You tell me."

I didn't want her to worry. She'd invested years of her life into my political career, as did the rest of my staff. Dusty was sticking his neck out, too, to make this happen. People counted on me, and I had to deliver.

Dusty poked out from backstage and crammed his way back into the crowd.

"All right. It's done."

Awesome and crap. He actually fucking did it. And now I had to fucking do it.

Vernita had a confused look, as she was as doubtful about this as me. "How'd you get them to say yes?"

"I said that the mayor wanted to say a few words. And I also told a white lie."

A lump formed in my stomach.

"What lie was that?" I asked.

"I said Sourwood abided by the Fairness Doctrine."

Of all the things I expected to come out of Dusty's mouth, the fucking Fairness Doctrine, an old US law that stipulated that both sides of political issues were required to have equal television air time, was not on the list. I'd be less shocked if he started speaking Mandarin.

"How do you know what the Fairness Doctrine is?" Vernita asked.

"I actually paid attention in high school here and there." Dusty made a funny face at her. His spirit was infectious.

"Not enough attention. The Fairness Doctrine was eliminated in 1987," I said.

Dusty took the historical update in stride. "Luckily, these guys didn't know that. I told them they have to let you on that stage after Rita, or else it's a violation of campaign ethics." Dusty glanced Vernita's way. "Is any of that true?"

It *sounded* truthful. I turned to Vernita as well. "Do you think? Applefest is resolutely apolitical, and the band endorsing her could be seen as a violation."

"She could say that the mayor's booth is a form of campaigning." She shrugged her shoulders as she scrambled through her political knowledge as quickly as possible. "Frankly, it's uncharted waters. Sourwood's mayoral election has never been this scrutinized."

"We'll score on truthiness then." Dusty clapped my shoulder. His eyes sparkled blue. I could stare at them all day. I'd forgotten how entrancing they were after all those years of texting and calling. I'd look for them in the crowd.

"You can do this, Leo."

"I don't know if I can. Literally. Fifteen years since I picked up a guitar."

"I'm telling you. Like riding a bike." Dusty threw both arms over my shoulders.

"Probably five years since I rode a bike, too."

Dusty kissed away my hesitation. His kisses were feeling less like a campaign tactic, and I savored their warmth.

"Thanks for believing in me."

The crowd roared as The English Patients took the stage. The guitar player saddled up his instrument; the drummer adjusted his seat. All that was missing was a meddlesome mayor clinging to his last chance to salvage his campaign.

"Sourwood, are you ready to rock?" the lead singer, Jimmy Bart, yelled into the microphone. He was clean-shaven with a neat head of hair and a white button-down shirt. He wouldn't look out of place selling bibles door-to-door.

The crowd roared again. Dusty yelled back.

"We are so flippin' excited to be at Applefest. I'm a fan of McIntosh. Dave on Bass is a freak because he likes Delicious, which is probably the biggest misnomer for a piece of fruit in history."

People held their phones in the air. Kids sat on their parents' shoulders. I spotted photographers snapping pictures, which would be all over social media and local press tomorrow.

If I flopped, I would go viral. I'd have to change my name and live in the woods. Without Wi-Fi or my favorite coffee pot.

"But before we start the show, we wanted to bring out the woman who made tonight happen. Rita Buchanan lobbied to bring us to Sourwood since we usually don't play at festivals. She wanted to do something special for the town because she loves you guys so much. Rita, come on out."

Rita stepped onto the stage with Deborah and their small kids. They were the picture of a cute family. She waved confidently to the crowd, a far cry from the woman who was quiet as a mouse at city council meetings, except when it came to land issues. She was a puppet, and once she wormed her way to the mayor's office, the Buchanans would take over.

"Rita is running to be mayor of this here town, and that's because she cares, because she wants a better life for every resident. She wants to see Sourwood grow, not be held back. But most of all, she wants you guys to have fun tonight!"

The lead singer spoke with surprising poise and sincerity, which generated more applause from the crowd. He should consider a run for office. It couldn't have gone better for Rita.

She beamed to the crowd, who began chanting her name. Each *Rita* was another hammer of dread slamming into me. Dusty rolled his eyes like this was a minor inconvenience.

She took the mic from Jimmy. "Sourwood, I don't want to keep you waiting. This is but one small example of how I will work hard for you. Sourwood is a town on the verge. We've got one of the biggest music acts here today! Let's keep growing! Without further ado, The English Patients!" She handed back the mic, and the chants got louder, mixed with general applause about the show starting.

She and her family were leaving the stage when the roadie from before darted out to Jimmy and whispered in his ear.

"In fairness," Jimmy began with diminished enthusiasm.

"We have the current mayor of Sourwood here tonight. Leo McConklin."

"McCaslin," I hissed under my breath.

"I wanted to thank him for letting us play, and if he wants to hop on up here and give the crowd a wave…"

"That's your cue." Dusty gave my butt a lucky slap. "I believe in you."

I kissed him for good luck and walked onto the stage where I received a supportive round of applause—though nowhere near the decibels Rita garnered. Not like we had an official sound meter to judge. The crowd stretched all the way down the street.

"Mr. Mayor, make it quick," Jimmy said off-mic. He stepped back.

It was at that moment I shunted aside my trepidation and found my gumption. I was Leo McCaslin. I wasn't going to be pushed around. I took a breath, ready to rock.

"Thanks, Jimmy." The roadie handed me a new mic. I walked to the center of the stage. "We're all here to see The English Patients, not listen to speeches. Am I right?"

The crowd wasn't sure whether or not to applaud.

"Well, my wonderful boyfriend Dusty challenged me to a bet." Dusty's name got some cheers, and I pointed him out in the crowd. "He said 'Leo, even though it's been a long while since you fronted your own band, you can still rock with the best of them.'"

A low rumble of curious cheers emanated from the crowd. That was enough wind to keep me sailing.

"Rather than say something boring like 'Have a great show' or 'Thank you to our Chamber of Commerce,' Dusty said I should pick up a guitar and play."

The cheers got louder. Even though everyone was here

for The English Patients, at this moment, the stage was mine; the crowd was mine.

The crowd went silent again, hanging on my every word. I found Dusty in the crowd and winked at him. "For those who didn't read about it in *The Sourwood Gazette*, I was in a rock band in college. Yep, before I thought about the law and government, I was thinking about trying to be the next English Patient." I spun around to Jimmy. "Or pre-English Patient, since it was before your time." Back to the crowd. "I thought I was the next Dave Grohl. We weren't half bad. We played all over campus."

"What was your band's name?" Jimmy asked, his interest piqued.

"Because the band was made up of members of the Speech and Debate team—yes, we were that cool—we called ourselves..." I paused for embarrassed emphasis. "The Master Debaters."

The crowd came alive with laughter. Barrels of it. Jimmy tried to resist, but he couldn't help but crack a smile.

"Are you serious, man?" Jimmy asked, failing at holding in his laughter.

"In our defense, this was the era of the Butthole Surfers. Anyway," I spun on my heel. "Jimmy, could I play a song with you guys?"

"Play a song? With us?" Jimmy seemed caught off-guard, which was the point, but he seemed into it.

"I know you're a big Foo Fighters fan. I already said I pretty much idolized Dave Grohl. Do you know 'Everlong'?"

Jimmy threw his head back and laughed. "Seriously? That's one of my favorite songs to cover."

I tipped my imaginary hat to Vernita for quickly coming upon that tidbit in her frantic, last-minute research.

"Yeah, what the hell." Jimmy checked with the other bandmates, who nodded in agreement. "Let's do it!"

The roadie ran out with an extra guitar and plugged it into the amp. My hands were slick with nervous sweat, but adrenaline was going to carry me through. He handed the guitar and earplugs to me.

And once I put the guitar strap on, the crowd truly went wild. They could've heard us up in Canada.

"You ready, man?" Jimmy asked.

Rita grimaced from the wings. It was a glorious sight. Dusty mooned at me from the crowd like I was fucking Superman. Now *that* was a glorious sight.

I leaned into his microphone. "Let's rock."

Jimmy smashed his lips to the microphone. "One. Two. One two three four!"

It turned out Dusty was right. Playing guitar was like riding a bike. I was the kid in *E.T.* riding his bike over the moon.

Muscle memory took over my fingers as they plucked the immortal first chords of "Everlong." The music hurtled me twenty years back in time. There I was on stage at college shows, small crowds jamming out. Barely a cell phone in sight. The only space I knew was that stage, that bar. Each note I played unlocked more skills and made me more confident. My fingers zipped up and down the guitar, keeping up note for note with The English Patients. After circling the stage, Jimmy ran to his microphone to start singing.

I barely made out the lyrics over the music and the cheering. The crowd was aglow with cell phones raised in the air, even a few lighters for us older folks. Electricity crackled in the air. Sourwood was alive.

And I was immortal. I transcended space and time,

playing in tune with my younger self, playing with The English Patients, singing until my throat went raw. Sweat soaked through my crisp button-down shirt.

I smooshed next to Jimmy's microphone to join him for the chorus, something I used to do at old shows. To say the crowd went wild was an understatement. Sourwood was losing its collective mind. I looked down at my fingers, amazed at what they could remember, calluses reforming on the skin, sweat trickling down my face.

Jimmy glanced back at me and gave a nod. He was asking if I was ready for the ending. I jammed out on the guitar, rocking the final chords of the song until my fingers wanted to bleed.

If one looked up "going out in a blaze of glory" online, they'd find the video of this moment.

The volume of the crowd was deafening. The only thing louder was my heart racing in my ears.

"Mr. Mayor." Jimmy looked back at me and extended his hand, which I took in one of those arm-wrestling-esque handshakes. "That was awesome!"

I took a bow and pointed at the band, trying to be modest but also loving the fanfare. Let's just say you didn't go into politics if you hated attention.

I scanned the mass of people and found the face in the crowd I cared about most, the one I wanted with every cell of my body.

I waved for him to join me on stage. Dusty didn't hesitate. It wasn't for PR or appearances. I wanted him by my side.

Dusty pointed at me and looked at the audience like *Can you believe this guy?*

But I didn't care about the audience. I wanted Dusty so bad I was going catch fire.

I pulled him to my chest. He wrapped his arms around me, and our kiss elicited a more ravenous response from the crowd. His lips tasted amazing, salty and warm. I couldn't get enough of them. I couldn't stop looking into those eyes, couldn't stop thinking about the way he looked up at me.

I rested my forehead on his and the world faded away for a moment.

A brief moment.

"Sourwood, you guys know how to party!" Jimmy yelled into the mic. "All right, let's start this show!"

The roadie ran out, unhooked my guitar, and motioned for us to get offstage. I didn't acknowledge my scowling opponent when we got into the wings. I pulled Dusty into a curtain for another kiss, my hands cupping his waist.

"That was incredible." His breath danced on my lips. He spoke and kissed me at the same time. We couldn't keep our hands off each other.

"You are fucking incredible," I said, fully in the middle of an out-of-body experience. I pulled him closer to me so he could feel my erection. He let out a tiny moan. "You know, they say sex is the fastest way to ruin a friendship."

He stared back at me with a dark storm of lust in his eyes. "Promise?"

17

DUSTY

I once read a study that said willpower was like a battery that got drained throughout the day. If that was the case, my willpower was running on fumes because when Leo kissed me, I lost all resistance. Every warning in my mind that told me not to cross this line melted away. I was left with a primal hunger to jump my best friend's bones.

When he left that stage, Leo had transformed into a full-blown rock star. People mauled us as we left Applefest. They wanted selfies and to tell him how awesome he was. A not-insignificant amount of men and women propositioned him for sex, with a few saying I could join in. Small town Sourwood had a kinky side, but I wanted none of it.

I only wanted Leo.

"Did you want to stick around?" I asked him, scared of his answer.

He looked at me with a force I felt in my core. "No."

Through sheer force of will, we made it to the car, where I lunged for Leo again. Our tongues twisted and swirled in each other's mouths. We were well past the nice kisses. This was hardcore making out with an end goal. I wanted Leo inside me. I wanted him on top of me. Nobody tell Scarlet O'Hara, but I had a feeling my heterosexuality was gone with the wind.

"If we keep going like this, we're not going to make it back to the house," Leo growled into my mouth. His warm, calloused hands caressed my cheek and down my chest. I never realized how strong he was. But I'd seen the pictures. I knew the body that hid under those suits and button-downs.

I was so revved up I would gladly lose my butt virginity in the backseat, to hell with the logistics and lack of lube. Ever since I arrived in Sourwood, every minute with Leo had been foreplay in disguise.

"Baby." Leo pulled back, his pupils wide as saucers. "Let's go home."

"You called me baby," I said while still catching my breath.

"Is it weird?"

"Yeah."

"Should I stop?"

"Not on your fucking life." I pulled him against me for more kissing. He stroked me through my jeans. "Actually, say my name."

"Dust?" he asked, a new gruff edge to his voice.

I licked my lips. "You say it differently now. Like you want me."

"Because I do. I want you in ways you can't even fathom. Baby," he dragged his teeth along my jaw, sending heat racing through me.

Tonight. All bets were off tonight. Leo was my best friend. In twenty-four years of friendship, he'd never talked to me like this. He'd never looked at me like this. Hungry.

Possessed by lust. But in his eyes was the same Leo who cared about me.

I trusted him completely.

"Let's go home," I said.

———

I THANKED all religious deities for having Ari and Lucy stay with their mom this weekend. As soon as we got in the house, I was on my knees, undoing Leo's belt.

"Baby, let me close the front door first."

He clicked it shut. And I unclicked his belt.

"Where are you going?" I asked as Leo shuffled backward, right before I got to the good stuff. "Should I stop?"

"I needed to rest my back against a wall. I should've stretched before playing guitar."

"Will you not be able to perform like a US Olympic gymnast tonight?"

"I'll take some Advil before I fuck your brains out." Leo pushed his pants to the floor. "As you were."

There it was. As big and thick as I'd been dreaming about. No screens or scrim of boxer-brief separating us.

And that was when it hit me: I'd never done this before. I had a dick myself, but how well did I know my way around one? The last thing I needed was to ruin this moment with my ineptitude.

"That's not good," said Leo above me.

"What?"

"You seem deep in thought." He pulled his pants up. "Thinking and blow jobs usually don't go well together."

Just as I was about to make an excuse, I remembered that this was still Leo. He was still my best friend. Our friendship didn't have to pause.

"This is going to sound like such a line, but this is truly the first time I've ever done this with a guy."

"What about those other guys from the threesomes?"

"I didn't go down on them. I don't want to screw this up. I know that's a difficult thing to do, but don't underestimate me." I felt my neck go red. It was difficult being over forty and admitting I was still a total novice at certain things.

A trustful, caring grin beamed down at me. He brushed a thoughtful hand through my hair. "So we'll do this together."

This was Leo. We'd been through so much shit together over our lives. I was flooded with a wave of gratitude that I was going to get to experience another first with him.

I pushed down his pants and boxers. His thick cock jutted before me. Heat pressed through my body.

"Take it in your hand and lick up to the head," he said with a gentle but firm command.

His dick tasted hot, a bit like soap and his own natural scent. He groaned above me. I licked a stripe on the under-side of his cock before taking his head in my mouth. I was today years old when I took a dick in my mouth.

Heat and bitter pre-come hit my tongue in a thrilling elixir. My fingers fluttered through the hair on his upper thighs and bush. I was a more eager student than I realized, daring myself to take him completely in my mouth.

"Damn." Leo moaned. "Not bad for a straight guy."

"How many straight guys have you been with?"

"No comment." He pulled his cock from my mouth and moved it along my bottom lip before sliding it back inside. Like he was on that stage, Leo had me in the palm of his hand. "But you're one of the best."

"*One* of the best?" I stroked and dragged my tongue down his length. "I think we can change that."

"Man, you're as competitive as me, you know that?"

"You're just figuring that out?" I took a ball into my mouth. I tried to do all the things I enjoyed during fellatio, this time as a giver. My body was on fire with these new sensations. "By the end of tonight, I will be the best straight guy you've been with."

Though I didn't know if the straight moniker would make it to the morning. I had to at least be bisexual at this point. The labels could be sorted out tomorrow.

I took him down to his base, his thick rod stretching my lips. Leo groaned out my name and pulled me by the hair to keep me in place for a few seconds until I gagged. I loved this rough side to him.

A slight chuckle brushed past his lips.

"What?" I asked, slightly offended.

His chuckle turned into a full-fledged laugh. "I can't believe I'm doing this with you."

"That makes two of us," I said between stroking and sucking.

"I've wanted this..." He seemed to stop himself just when I wanted to hear more. "I've only done the one-night stand thing with guys. I didn't know what it could feel like to be with someone who knows me and who I feel so comfortable around."

"Word of advice: maybe don't talk about other guys while this one has your dick in his mouth."

"Good point." Leo gently pushed me back and stepped out of his pants. "Stand up."

He pressed me against the front door and planted wild kisses on me, our tongues sword fighting in the hot caverns of our mouths.

Leo lifted my hands, and I held onto the top of the doorframe as he greedily canvassed my body, scanning the surface, thinking of what to take. His hard cock brushed against my jeans.

"You are so hot," he said. His fingers found my fly. He unzipped and reached inside to stroke my achingly hard cock.

A guttural moan ripped out of me. His hand didn't mess around. It stroked with a laser-focused determination, testing the limits of my boxers.

I was not one built for patience. I unbuttoned my jeans and dropped trou, exposing my rock-hard dick for him to have.

"I wanted to make things easier for you," I said.

"For me?" He let out a sexily sinister laugh. "Sure."

Leo jerked me in torturously steady strokes, his thumb rubbing the pre-come around my head.

"Suck me," I gasped out.

"Is that your pick-up line for women?"

My body was too busy being set on fire for me to be eloquent. Leo got the hint and lowered to the floor, his hot mouth taking my cock. I groaned with need, instantly ranking this the best blow job of my life. My dick disappeared into his mouth, and it was an extra turn-on to watch Mr. Always-in-Charge be the one taking it. I pushed back the orgasm swelling within me.

My legs wobbled, unable to keep functioning under all this intensity. Leo stood up slowly, bringing up my underwear and pants with him.

"Baby, I want to take you upstairs." His lips traveled down my neck, leaving a fiery trail in their wake.

"Then what the fuck are we doing down here?"

He took a step back and studied me. It was as if I were standing there naked, his stare ripping off my clothes.

"Dusty." He shook his head and smiled. My name had never sounded sexier.

"Leo, I want you to play me like you did that guitar." I saw what his fingers were capable of on stage. I wanted them all over my body.

Traveling upstairs while making out and groping each other was a challenge that we managed without falling down.

His room had a king-size bed with thick comforter and expensive-looking cream sheets. I hadn't spent any time in here. Maybe that was a subconscious move to keep me from dreaming about sleeping with him. There was a small fireplace in the corner.

"Can we light a fire?"

He nodded yes as he stripped off his shirt. While he set up the wood, giving me sexy naked caveman vibes, I got my own wood ready, stroking myself until my cock was a metal rod. I ripped off my clothes and lay on the bed. I watched him build the fire, leg muscles tight while squatting, his thick hands handling the logs.

"I didn't know you were also a lumberjack."

"I didn't chop down the wood. Bought it at the grocery store." He turned around and raked his eyes over my naked body. "Dusty, I could stare at you all fucking night."

My name sounded extra special on his tongue.

"Oh, we're going to be doing a lot more than staring."

Leo approached the bed, his muscular, hairy chest silhouetted by the fire crackling behind him. I could've come just looking at him. His brown eyes glimmered in the darkness, keeping me in place.

I didn't know I could find a man sexy in this way. This wasn't "oh, yeah, this guy's good-looking" like when I saw a

Marvel movie. This was a deep-seated lust that possessed every cell of my body.

I was slightly jealous he had such a manly body. My chest and stomach were hairless, and I could get by shaving once a week. At times, I felt forever boyish, especially now when I was with a man.

"Come here," I said.

He joined me on the bed, his strong body stretching over mine. More kissing, more touching, more grabbing.

I slapped his firm ass cheek. His chest hair bristled against my smooth chest, making me feel warm, like one of those weighted blankets that everyone kept telling me to buy.

I could trail my fingers along his hot skin all day and night and never get bored. I was like Columbus discovering this great man, minus the slaughtering and raping and pillaging that Columbus did. Scratch that; I shouldn't bring a known genocidal maniac into sex.

I was on the USS *Enterprise*, discovering new worlds!

"To Infinity and Beyond!" I said as I slid a finger down his crack.

He pulled up, his dazed dark eyes coming into focus. "What?"

"Sorry, just thinking of *Star Trek*."

"You quoted *Toy Story*."

"I did?"

"Yeah." He kissed the spot where my neck and shoulder met, sending waves of pleasure shooting through me.

"Are you sure?"

"I have two kids. I know my Disney shit." He stuck his tongue in my ear, and that was that.

I moaned into his broad shoulder. My cock dug into his

furry belly, and his rod poked into my thigh. We were like two lightsabers.

"Are lightsabers from *Star Trek*?" I asked.

"*Star Wars*." Leo threw my legs over my head, exposing my ass to him and the world. And that was that.

"You okay?" he asked, probably seeing the surprise written on my face.

"Yeah. It's all interesting."

"Curious choice of adjective." He stroked a hand down my thigh, bristling through my light leg hairs. "Have you ever been rimmed?"

Leo's question sent my mind spiraling forth with lust-filled scenarios. My tongue went thick and heavy in my mouth as I pictured everything Leo could do with his.

"No."

"Is that something you'd let me do tonight?" His hand slid down the back of my thigh, getting teasingly close to my ass before zooming back up. Hunger built within me.

"I've never bottomed before. Or really, any of this."

"You're doing great so far." His grin spread across his face. "Dust, I plan to have my way with you tonight, but only if you want that, too. We're still friends. We still talk to each other."

Guy or gal, I'd never felt more comfortable during sex than I did with Leo. There was none of that needing to hide or pretend.

"Is that all you want to do?" I asked.

He shook his head no. "Don't tease me, Dust."

"I want to try having sex." It was crazy when I heard it, but it sounded right, too. Start before you're ready was a common refrain of business owners. Why did that mantra have to stop at the bedroom?

"Okay, then." He cracked a lazy smile.

I could stare at him all day, towering over me. His chest had definition and tone, his arms were thick and ropey, but there was some dadbod going on in his midsection. Despite how much he worked out, age caught up to him, lending him maturity and experience and extra sexiness.

The best part, though? "Your hair's messed up."

He looked at himself through the mirror over the fireplace. His hair product couldn't resist my hands and the roughhousing of two men in lust. Leo smoothed it back into place.

I shook my head no. I wasn't here for business in the front. I was ready for Mr. Party in the Back. I put my ab muscles to use and sat up, tousled his hair, and bit his nipple for good measure. He hissed in pleasure.

"Didn't your mother tell you that the more you play with it, the less you'll have?" I said.

"I have good genes. I'll go gray before I go bald."

I pictured Leo with more salt and pepper dusting his hair, and another wave of heat hit me. I needed this man.

The sounds of the lube bottle snapping open and the thick liquid coating his fingers filled the room. They were the mechanical logistics of gay sex, but they somehow managed to turn me on. They added to the anticipation. As did the way that Leo's eyes never left me.

"Mr. Mayor? As you were." I threw my legs closer to my chest, showing off more of my ass.

A wicked glint hit his eye. He slapped the back of my thigh.

A loud gasp escaped my lips when his tongue made contact with my hole. It flicked on the exposed skin, circling my opening.

"Holy shit. That feels so good." I was alive with ecstasy.

"I wanted to taste you before I fucked you."

"And how do I—" I stopped myself. That question could've been real graphic.

Chills ran up my body as I felt his puffs of laughter.

"Good, Dusty. Real good."

I groaned with want, my head spinning and hands grasping for fistfuls of blankets. I was on fire in the best possible way, his mouth lighting me ablaze.

"Fuck me, Leo. Please fuck me." I cried out in pleasure as his finger entered me. I know it was a finger and not his dick. I'd had his dick in my mouth. I knew how thick it was, how it would stretch me.

"Baby, what do you want?"

"In laymen's terms: I want you to rail me." The only poll I cared about was the one he was going to impale me with.

He laughed again—more hot breath on my sensitive skin. I breathed out a yes when I heard the condom wrapper crinkle open. His fingers didn't leave my ass as he prepared himself. My pre-come slid down my stomach and chest, pooling at my nipple. Leo sucked on my balls, then dragged his tongue up my length and hoovered up the pre-come from my engorged head as I lost control, my body splitting apart with pins and needles. My balls ached with the drive to shoot my load.

"You're not coming yet," he growled at me, moonlighting as a psychic amid all his sex-goddery. "I want to feel your ass clench around me as you come. That's going to be so damn hot." His voice had a thick rasp to it, heavy with lust.

"Want that, too." I could barely speak, and his dick hadn't even been inside me yet. I was going to see stars and blackout the second he entered me, wasn't I?

His tongue followed the trail of my pre-come down my torso, licking it clean and swirling around my nipples.

"If you don't want me to come, then you need to fuck me

right now. Like, don't even give me some smoking hot retort. We don't have time for that." I was a minefield. One step and I would explode.

Leo shoved inside me, stretching me like I'd dreamed, filling my ass with his hardness. I winced in pain—well, more shock than pain.

"Are you okay, Baby?"

Before I could object, the pain began to subside. It was overtaken by my aching desire to have him inside me.

His fingers dug into the backs of my legs as he slid into me slowly, locking eyes to ensure I was all right. Soon, pleasure took over.

"You're a natural."

He gazed down at me, and I laughed. I realized that I was having fun. Sex had always been awkward or boring or tense with past lovers. But on top of the blinding lust that possessed my core, I was enjoying myself, enjoying being with him. I realized I never laughed during sex with other people. But with Leo, we could go from dirty talk to banter like it was easy, another extension of our friendship.

"Oh, fuck. Baby you are so tight. You feel so good." He grunted as he humped me, pushing me closer and closer to an already dangerously close climax. He leaned down, our bodies hovering, our eyes locked, his hairy, sweaty chest slick against me.

"Give it to me, Leo. Put your lightsaber in my infinity and beyond."

Leo cracked up, full-on guffawing while still fucking me senseless. The next time a concerned voter claimed he couldn't multitask, I would point to this as a prime example.

"You've ruined my kids' childhoods."

"I do what I can." I moaned into his shoulder. The orgasm gushed through me.

Leo thrust into me in short, jagged moves. He strained to prolong this as much as he could. We were both on the edge. Neither of us could speak. I grabbed a fistful of his hair and pulled him close. He jammed my legs closer against my chest and nailed my opening with greater force, forcing the come to shoot out of me and coat our chests in the most spectacular seconds of my life.

Leo shivered and shook above me, his face contorting in pleasure as he emptied himself into the condom.

"If this was what sex could be like, then I'll never wear pants again." I heaved out a breath as he rolled off me and used his boxers to wipe us off.

"Damn, Dusty. If you keep talking like that, then we're going to have round two sooner than we think."

"There's going to be a round two?" I asked.

"You bet your fucking ass."

18

DUSTY

I woke up the next morning to a strange sight: sunlight. It was the first time in two weeks when I wasn't up before the sun. The light was blinding, and it made me wonder if Leo and I had sex with open curtains. I supposed that wouldn't completely surprise me if Leo was an exhibitionist. It seemed there were still things we didn't know about each other. Like I preferred to be the little spoon.

My body ached with an exquisite soreness. My legs were tight from regular running and needed a stretch. But now I could add another body part—a sore butt. And it felt great.

A sore butt given to me by Leo, my best friend, the guy who'd been by my side for most of forever.

Twenty-four hours ago, I was mostly straight. But after two vigorous rounds of lovemaking, I was a big ole question mark—and a fan of anal sex.

Charred logs sat in the fireplace, remains of last night. I sat up in bed and watched birds buzzing around a nest in the tree outside the window. The house was quiet, peaceful. And I was alone.

Where *was* Leo?

I pushed my way through the comforter until I put both feet on the cool hardwood floor. My shirt hung off a chair in the corner. My underwear bunched in a ball between the bed and nightstand. Scenes from last night flashed in my head and put a smile on my face.

But then I remembered I was alone, and my bedmate was nowhere to be found.

"Leo?" I said to the empty room. I checked the en suite bathroom. No sign of him.

After relieving myself and splashing cold water on my face, I pulled open his dresser and put on a pair of charcoal gray boxers, so I didn't have to walk through the house naked.

When I opened the door, I heard the faint buzz of breakfast downstairs. The warm smell of toasted bagels and freshly-brewed coffee traveled up my nose. My stomach rumbled with hunger. I hadn't eaten since Mitch's booth at Applefest. Last night qualified as a workout, and daddy needed to replenish his calories.

I went to my bedroom and slipped on a sweatshirt and shorts. I tiptoed down the stairs, my heart racing as I got closer to seeing Leo.

"Morning." Leo smiled at me from above his iPad. He was decked out in full running gear. His black T-shirt was soaked with sweat, and he had that post-run glow glimmering on his cheeks. I was a little taken aback he ran alone.

"Good morning."

"Bagels are in." He pointed to the toaster, all levers down. "Did you want cream cheese or butter on it?"

"Since when do you know me to put anything but whipped cream cheese on my bagel?"

"After last night, all bets are off." He pulled open the fridge door and removed the familiar tub of cream cheese.

"You went running this morning," I said.

The bagel halves popped violently out of the toaster as if they were on pogo sticks. Leo went to work schmearing them up.

"I didn't want to wake you."

"You wake me every other morning whether I want to or not."

"This morning felt...different." He opened his mouth as if he were about to say more. Instead, he put his attention on the bagel. "I figured you'd want to sleep."

He had a point. I'd been getting up early naturally over the past few days, but I was out like a light until the sun came up this morning. Still, it would've been nice to go running with him. Did sex have to change everything?

"I wasn't sure if you'd be up for running. I didn't want to wake you. You looked so peaceful, fast asleep. I was tempted to stay in bed with you." A warm smile stretched across his lips.

"Lie."

"Truth." He tossed the bagel on a plate and slid it across the island my way.

"Did I hog all the blanket? My exes said I hog the blanket."

"Oh, yeah. There was a point in the middle of the night when you turned over and took everything with you."

I smacked a hand to my forehead. "You should've pulled them back."

"I tried, but you got tangled in them in a way I've literally never seen before." He drank his smoothie from the blender.

"You could've woken me."

"I didn't know where you were. You were sucked into your blanket cocoon." Leo waved it off. "It reminded me of that time we shared that motel room at the Grand Canyon."

"Oh, God. That place." The Canyon Inn. Home of the used damp towels, perpetually dripping sink, and the allegedly king-size bed that could barely fit two grown adults.

"I almost got an elbow to the face that night. How did we wind up there?"

"I might've forgotten to check what room I booked for us." The innkeeper gave us the weirdest look when we checked in, and I took it upon myself to thoroughly explain that we were just friends on a post-graduation road trip. This conversation felt a little bit like that, but at least we hadn't lost any of our bantering skills post-sex.

He poured me a cup of coffee into a #1 Dad mug. His hand rested easily on my back as he handed it over.

"Anyway, sorry about last night," I said. "The blanket tug-of-war."

"All good."

Pins and needles prickled on my skin. I should've laced up my shoes before coming down because we were dancing this morning. Dancing around the thing that happened. Dancing wasn't what we did in our friendship.

Leo nodded, trying to come up with the next dance move. "The run was good. How are those sneakers working for you?"

"Good."

Who cared about sneakers? We had sex last night! We said things to each other that couldn't be written off to the heat of the moment. I had my best friend's dick in my mouth, and he licked my ass like it was Tootsie Pop.

I put down my coffee cup and toast. "Leo." I found myself getting breathless again. "Last night..."

Before I could finish that sentence—or more accurately, figure out how to finish that sentence—someone knocked at the front door. Leo was all too happy to bolt to the foyer, but admittedly, I felt a wave of relief, too.

Vernita clacked into the kitchen, looking so happy you'd think she was the one who had mindblowing sex last night. Maybe she did. Her husband was quite handsome.

She pointed at both of us. "You two. A-plus. Amazing. Gold stars. Academy Awards. All of it. Dusty, I was nervous about your plan yesterday. It had the potential to backfire greatly. But it didn't. It didn't at all." She grabbed a mug from the cabinet and poured herself a cup of coffee, which she did not need at all, judging by her enthusiasm. "And Leo, you...you blew me away."

She pulled him into a hug, ignoring his sweaty attire.

"If I'd known you could play the guitar like that, I would've had you do more fun things like that. That was...that was Clinton playing the sax on *Arsenio Hall*. That was huge."

"Haven't I always been fun?" Leo asked.

"No," Vernita and I said at the same time.

Leo sipped his coffee and shut up.

"My emails have been out of control. I've gotten inquiries from media outlets across the state about you. You've gone somewhat viral."

Leo shrugged modestly while I beamed like a proud boyfriend—err, fake boyfriend.

Vernita pulled up a video on her phone from YouTube of the performance. The clip ended with me kissing Leo. Even from this distance, it was obvious that this was no fake kiss and that kissing had not become old hat as my plan had presumed. My heart jumped as I remembered that moment when everything went quiet, and our mouths met.

"Unfortunately, there are rumors being spread that you weren't actually playing," Vernita said, rolling her eyes. "Somebody is saying your guitar wasn't plugged in, and you'd hired a professional guitar player to play for you backstage."

"That's one thousand percent fake news," I shouted out.

"Reddit loves a conspiracy theory," Vernita said.

"Rita." Leo laughed to himself. "Anyone who was there knows it's bullshit. They can look at my calloused fingers."

Leo stuck out his hands, showing off rough fingers that caressed my skin last night, that plunged inside me, that held me as I slept. My dick got hard all over again.

"I'm not worried, but I am continuing to monitor." She took back her phone and resumed checking her email. "And Dusty..."

I held my arms out, showing that I was da man. Anything to get the blood pumping elsewhere. "I was amazing."

"That was the best fake kiss I've ever seen. You two really sold your relationship. That'll shut up all the doubters."

Except for the two doubters in this kitchen. Leo studied the consistency of his coffee while I examined the crumbs on my plate.

Vernita turned to Leo with more intense energy than anyone at this hour. "Harlen Carruthers reached out to me, too."

Leo almost dropped his coffee cup. "Harlen Carruthers?"

"He wants to endorse you."

"Shit." Leo took stunted steps around the kitchen, hands cupped over his mouth.

"Who's Harlen Carruthers?" I asked like the political noob I was.

"Harlen was a beloved state senator in the '90s," Leo said.

"Now he's like the godfather of Hudson Valley politics," Vernita continued. "People love him. He fundraises like a champ. His endorsement carries a lot of weight around here."

"Nice! Now he's riding the Leo train."

Like I did.

"It's not a done deal. He might attend your debate against Rita this week. But so long as there are no more surprises, my hope is we can ride this momentum to the election." Vernita tried to stay business, but the excitement broke across her eyes. "Mr. Mayor, get dressed because we have debate prep to do."

Leo looked at me, and for a split second, it almost seemed like he wanted me to say something. "Duty calls." He grabbed my arm and leaned into my ear as he passed. "We'll talk later."

He kissed my cheek and retreated upstairs. We would talk later. Maybe by then, I'd know what to say.

———

WHILE LEO and Vernita were busy at his office doing debate prep, I made good use of my time. Rather than sit around and think about...things, I distracted myself by replacing the sagging shelves in the living room. I picked up wood from the hardware store in town, Throw a Wrench in It, then sanded and painted them so they matched the bookcase style. The books now stood in a straight line, and shelving no longer gave people a Joker-like smile.

Leo came back sometime in the afternoon, at which

point I was knee-deep in a cable TV marathon of '90s action flicks.

"Wow." He glided a hand over the smooth wood of the shelves.

"No more sagging."

"For starters."

He took a step back to take in the whole project.

"Can you fix my fence next?" he asked, half-jokingly.

"I'll add it to the list."

He chuckled softly and then came the inevitable silence. I looked to him, and he looked to me, and together, we came up with zero words to say. I worried about saying the wrong thing. We were teetering on a cliff, and one wrong move could send our friendship toppling into the metaphorical sea.

I left it to Leo. He was better at words than me.

But he seemed stumped in that department, too.

And then, to my surprise, Leo broke out into a laugh that took over his whole face. His white teeth gleamed, and Adam's apple bobbed with pure, almost silly laughter.

The laughter barreled up my throat and out into the room, getting rid of all the anxious feelings I'd been carrying. The more I watched him lose it, the more I did, too. When was the last time I laughed this much? It really was good for the soul. It turned out to be the perfect response.

"Why are we laughing?" I asked.

Leo held onto the back of an armchair. "I don't know. Better than weird silence."

The laughter pricked pains in my stomach. "We had sex," I said.

The sentence sounded weirder said aloud.

"We had all the sex."

"Us!"

"You had sex with a man."

"Who I've known since the beginning of time." I smacked my head. "I'm sorry, what?"

The laughter pushed out the uncomfortable feelings. We were still friends, no matter what.

"You were like a sex maniac." Leo joined me on the couch. Our knees touched, and despite the laughter and the weirdness, it made me pop a semi. "The second we got inside last night, you were on your knees."

"I was possessed. You weren't Leo. You were a rock god last night, and I was one of your slutty groupies."

Leo massaged my shoulder, one of his thick eyebrows raising. "I liked it."

Those feelings from last night, the ones where I felt us get closer than possible, returned.

Leo wiped tears from his eyes. "I haven't laughed like that in a long time." His hand moved to my neck, brushing through my hair in delicate circles. "We're still friends, right?"

"I built your bookcase, didn't I?"

Leo gazed at the new addition and nodded approvingly. A new kind of quiet came over us. "I wanted to run by myself this morning to clear my head. Last night was a wild, chemical thing. It was incredible. Unbelievable."

I sensed a but.

"But you didn't want it to ruin our friendship," I filled in.

"Exactly. I guess all the stress of the campaign, the joy I've felt having you here all the time, and the nonstop kissing..." He made a turning motion with his hands. We would totally slay charades.

"It all combined to create this perfect storm of sex," I said.

"A triple crown of sex."

"A hat trick of sex."

Going through our old bits brought me much-needed relief.

"Had you ever thought about this before?" I asked. Leo had been gay this whole time. I wondered if there was a sexual attraction I hadn't noticed before. Because now, I saw it all the time.

"You and me? No. No way." He shook his head and turned his attention to wiping away a bit of sawdust off the coffee table. It seemed like an odd time to notice that.

"You're still my best friend. I'm still yours. That's not changing, even if we happen to repeat last night," I found myself filling in, telling him what I knew he wanted to hear. I could make a stump speech like the best of them. "We've been through epic shit over the past twenty years. Losing jobs, losing businesses, losing parents, breakups, divorce, kids, the worst of times, the best of times. I'm not going to toss that history away just because you saw me naked."

I was convincing Leo as well as myself. This wasn't bull-shit. I wasn't going to let us muck up a friendship over sex. Having true friends as you get older was worth more than gold. We were mature men in our forties. I wasn't going to let sex, or the feelings clogging up my chest, muddy the waters.

"You are so right, Dust."

"It's about time I become the one who makes sense for a change."

His eyes crinkled at the edges with a smile, and damn if it didn't take my breath away.

"And now we've gotten it out of our system, we can charge ahead and focus on cruising to victory," Leo said.

Victory. The election. I had to remind myself why I was here.

"I'm gonna go pick up the kids. We can all grab dinner together." Leo kissed me on the lips goodbye. "Really great job with the shelves."

And then he was gone, and silence returned, a deep silence which couldn't be erased with *Double Jeopardy*.

Friends weren't supposed to lie, but I lied. I *hadn't* gotten it out of my system. It was the opposite. My feelings for Leo were taking over my system. That scared me most of all.

Sex didn't have to ruin a friendship. But if Leo found out I was full-on pining after him now, and he still saw me as just a friend, that was the kind of thing friendships couldn't come back from.

19

___

LEO

"What do we think? Red or blue?" I held one tie up to my shirt, then the other. Dusty and the twins studied both choices, and I kept turning around to see for myself in the mirror.

"Red feels aggressive," Lucy said.

"But aggressive can be good," Dusty said. "Like, a mayor that knows how to fight." He did some shadowboxing to underline his point.

"I don't want to seem like I'm beating up Rita. Big bad mayor beating up his sweet little opponent."

"Just because she's a woman doesn't automatically make her a fragile figurine, Dad," Lucy said, making me proud to be raising a feminist daughter.

"Why don't you wear both?" Ari suggested as he chomped on a slice of pizza. "Or wear one around your head like a bandana."

Dusty pointed at my son. "I like that idea."

"Not helping."

The first debate was held at the Arden MacArthur Community Center, which Cal and Mitch had dubbed the

Bea Arthur Center just in case the world didn't already know they were gay. Rita and I would debate on the stage that usually held community theater productions. On the walls of my dressing room were signatures and dates scribbled in by actors of Sourwood community productions past.

I put down the red tie and held the blue up to my neck. "Blue feels warmer, don't you think?"

I looped the blue option around my neck, my hands moving to knot it instinctively. I've put on so many ties in my life I could do it with my eyes closed.

Lucy gave me the thumbs up. Ari followed her lead.

And Dusty?

"I like it."

The way he looked at me made heat rush up my neck. Time stopped, but only for a second because my knuckleheaded kids began cracking up with laughter as they watched us.

Dusty turned away to check his watch. "We should probably leave you to finish preparing. But yeah, the blue tie. That's my vote."

"Mine, too," Lucy said with a knowing smile.

"I vote for bandana."

"Ari." Dusty pointed to the door.

Ari handed me his uneaten crust, which would be my pre-debate meal. Bread was about all I could handle between the debate, Harlen Carruthers showing up, and Dusty continuing to seize my thoughts.

I stopped my son before he left. "Hey buddy, maybe tonight after the debate, I can take another crack at your video game. I think I'm close to beating the second level."

My son's face lit up. I'd had Ari show me his game a few days ago, and while my video gaming skills pretty much sucked and I wanted to put my fist through the screen at all the losing I was doing, I was immensely proud of the creativity on display. Would he go on to be a professional game designer? It was too soon to tell. But seeing that he had the grit to create something so complex gave me the confidence that he'd find success in life, no matter which path he chose.

Lucy and Ari both gave me kisses on the cheeks, and I gobbled them up into a massive hug.

"Good luck, Dad," they said.

"I'll meet you in the audience," Dusty said to them as they left the dressing room. He hung by the door, looking drop-dead sexy in a blue-and-white plaid shirt tucked into gray pants, topped off with a knit navy tie. He was like a college TA who I wanted to bend over the desk.

I'd resisted his charms over the past few days, ever since our sexual combustion. It was hard—er, difficult. Very difficult. (And very hard.) That night between us was one for the history books. It exceeded every dream I ever had about us fucking. But we agreed it was a one-time sexual tension breaker, and I had to stand by that decision.

Even though it was really, really this-can't-be-good-for-my-lower-back hard.

Er, difficult.

"Go kick some Buchanan ass tonight," Dusty said. "I'll be watching."

"You're my good luck charm."

"I haven't done anything except provide you with an alibi." He shrugged off the statement, hands digging into his pockets.

"An alibi? We weren't arrested. Though, I guess that is true in a way."

"I saved you from the spiral of your online hookups."

"You did save me." I gulped back a lump of horniness that always formed when it was the two of us.

Dusty closed the gap between us and planted a kiss on my cheek. "For good luck."

But that wasn't enough. By his tie, I pulled him to my mouth for a kiss I felt in my bones. His hands rested on my hips and pulled me closer.

I felt hazy and dizzy when I stepped back. Had I not cut it off, I would've taken him in my dressing room. Or tried to.

Breath came back to my lungs. "It's showtime."

———

I'D BEEN INVOLVED in many debates in my career, and they all had the same out-of-body quality. Time stopped. I left myself as my brain and mouth worked on auto-pilot to some extent. But I was in the zone, a state of flow as I lobbed and deflected points with Rita. She, to her credit, was bringing her A-game, throwing jabs as hard as I was. Knowing her family, her debate prep team was the best money could buy. The bump she was planning for with The English Patients never materialized.

Oops. My bad.

When the moderator brought up what to do about public park space, things turned even more contentious.

"What Councilwoman Buchanan proposes is taking our beautiful riverfront, where we've taken our families for birthday parties and beach days, and handing it over to a wealthy, select few who can pay her family the most money."

"Mayor McCaslin is unsurprisingly out of the loop of what's going on in his own town."

"Spoken by someone who voted in absentia for half of last year's city council meetings."

"There are several companies who have expressed interest in bringing value to Sourwood, which will make our town more inclusive, not to mention making all of our property values skyrocket."

"Bringing value to who? Your shareholders? Sourwood needs to be careful with who we get in bed with, professionally speaking." The crowd chuckled, more of a tension release valve.

"I could say the same for you," Rita shot back.

"What?" Panic rose in my chest. "What does that mean?"

"It means you brought an aggressive, violent man into our town."

"Dusty?" I asked with a laugh. A big one. "We've all met Dusty. He's a sweetheart."

"Is he? Dusty was fired from his position on the show *Ocean City* for beating up one of the cast members. Adam, the bad boy."

"That's…" Technically, that was true. I wasn't good with outright lies. "That's—what—Dusty isn't the one running for mayor."

The audience murmured amongst themselves. Scandal plus celebrity was like the lifeblood of gossip. I willed myself not to react, not to let her have that. Dusty slunk down in his seat in the front row, hanging his head. He wouldn't meet my eyes.

"If he can't control himself among co-workers, what will he do to residents of Sourwood who dare disagree with him? Is this who you want to associate with, Mayor McCaslin? Violent men who can't hold down a job?"

I shook my head at my opponent, anger like liquid nitrogen scorching my veins. "I'm not going to deflect from the real issues impacting Sourwood to rehash Hollywood gossip. Whatever you heard may or may not have happened, I can assure you that the man I have known for twenty-four years, the man I love, is a good man. A kind man."

In the darkness of the audience, I made out Dusty mouthing I'm sorry at me before the moderator moved to a new topic.

———

"She's getting desperate."

My dressing room had a tenser vibe post-debate. Vernita, Ari, and Lucy sat around in extra chairs, not saying much of anything. Dusty stood in the corner, arms folded, quietest of all.

"The fact she's going after Dusty for an isolated incident that has no bearing on any issue in this race...that is a clear sign of desperation." I wiped off my light stage makeup I wore to avoid getting drowned out under the lights.

"It's a low blow, but it's one that could work," Vernita said. She looked to Dusty. "Is there any information we're missing?"

Dusty remained mum. He was shellshocked.

"Of course, there is!" I said for him. "That actor was sleeping with his girlfriend. Dusty doesn't go around attacking people."

"Is that what we tell people?" she asked with strange doubt in her voice.

"It's the truth."

"It doesn't mesh with our timeline of when you and Dusty got together." Vernita was a master at being the bearer of bad news. "We said that you and Dusty have been together since the summer."

"So we can't have him defending the honor of a girl-friend last month." I smacked my head into the wall, covered with actors signing their names and messages left for future productions. Maybe the drywall had good ideas because I was out.

I heaved out a sigh.

"I am so sorry," Dusty uttered from his corner. I hated seeing him like this, small and meek. How dare Rita do this to him.

I went over and held his head in my hands, stared into him with every fiber of strength I had in me. I would be strong for the two of us.

"You fucking listen to me. You have nothing to be sorry for. You don't owe anyone in this room an apology. I meant what I said up there. You are the best person I know." I planted a kiss on his lips, willing them to curve into a smile. "If things were reversed, I would've beat the crap out of that guy. I mean, we all know I have a better right hook than you."

"That's bullshit. Your pretty hands haven't hit anyone." The edges of his mouth pulled themselves up.

"That's because I prefer to fight with my mouth." I turned back to Vernita with a determination that surged through me like a roller coaster. "What happened happened. What we're going to do is fight back harder. Get back to the actual issues. Hammer Rita on her family's connections, her shoddy track record, her plan to steal the riverfront for her one-percent pals." I laced my fingers with Dusty's, held our hands up for all to see. "We're going to do more events, more rallies, meet with more people. We are a package deal."

"Let's go, Dad!" Lucy yelled. Ari backed her up with a loud WOOOO.

"Bring it in." I held out my hand. Vernita, Lucy, and Ari stacked theirs on top. Dusty remained in the corner. "Dust, you're in this, too. Get in here, hot stuff."

Dusty took one giant leap to the center of the room and smacked his hand on top.

"On the count of three, we say mayor," I ordered. "One, two, three..."

We all screamed mayor, Dusty loudest of all.

20

———

LEO

Over the next three days, Dusty and I brought it. We spent mornings going to every coffee and breakfast place to meet constituents. My volunteers and I worked the phones at night. Fortunately, when we spoke to voters one-on-one, a bunch of them sided with Dusty. Who hadn't wanted to punch out an annoying co-worker? And a contingent of *Ocean City* fans couldn't stand Adam's character. Maybe the damage wasn't as substantial.

I felt a definite turn of the tide when Harlen Carruthers's office got back in touch to schedule a meeting. His endorsement was still on the table.

We met up at a Starbucks one town over for maximum anonymity. Harlen was black, short, and bald but made up for it with his mighty gusto. His speeches were the stuff of legend. He was one of those politicians who pushed past stereotypes of what electable men should look like, breaking down barriers.

As soon as he sat down with his large coffee, he put on his game face.

"I watched a recording of the debate."

"You did?" There was a chance he was going to attend, and I was relieved he'd missed my stumbling performance.

But nope. He caught it.

"That was a great job out there."

I lifted my head, making sure I heard him.

"You're a fighter. I know a fighter when I see one." His hand went to a fist. He was a man who missed the thrill of politics. He was known for his ferocious debates.

"I'm fighting for Sourwood. I want to make sure this town, my hometown, where my family lives, is taken care of."

"That's the spirit. That's what it's about. Too many politicians use office as a power trip. And don't get me wrong, there are definitely perks of the job, but it should first and foremost be about making the people you serve better off."

"And I strove to do that."

"You have succeeded. Every year, I see Sourwood showing up on lists of best places to live. My niece and her husband bought a house on the west side of town. They've heard the most wonderful things about Sourwood. From the activities to the schools. They have two little girls."

"One of my best friends has a son in Sourwood Elementary. It's a great school."

"This small town has grown, but yet you still managed to keep its small-town feel." His wrinkly skin split into a smile. He slurped his coffee. "That's why I have my eye on you for the future."

"The future?" I sat up in my chair and spun my coffee cup in my hand.

"The governor's mansion is up for grabs in four years."

I did a double-take. "What about—"

"She's not going to seek re-election. Term limits."

Harlen's thick, wiry eyebrows leapt up with squirmy excitement, a boy dying to tell a secret. "It's open season."

He was a man who lived for the thrill of politics. We were one and the same.

"I'm always on the hunt for new talent to shepherd." Harlen put down his coffee. "You've been making a name for yourself in Sourwood, Leo. You've done a great job here. But you've got ambition. You want more. I can see it in you. I see that same fire that I had."

"Thank you, Harlen. Coming out in the middle of my first term and weathering a divorce, I felt like I had to fight harder."

"You're an unconventional candidate. I like those," he said as he sipped his coffee. "Is it something you've thought about?"

My heart raced with the possibilities. I loved being mayor of Sourwood. I could see tangible progress in my town, making this community stronger. People had mentioned I should run for a state rep or Congress, but that wasn't my jam. You were stuck in a Capitol building completely disconnected from your constituents except when you needed them to donate or vote. As mayor, my energy could bear direct fruit.

But governor...

Harlen was looking at me, seemingly amused. "I can see the thoughts rolling through your head."

"It's—governor..." I couldn't play it cool. I leaned forward and lowered my voice. "You really think I could be governor?"

"I don't much enjoy blowing smoke up people's asses."

I sat back and let this sink in. Me governor? In charge of New York state, one of the largest states in the country? New

York freaking City would be under my jurisdiction. I could finally get tickets to *Hamilton*.

"You are a rising star in New York politics," he said. "You're young, energetic, well-liked. You've gotten your sex scandal out of the way now."

Milkman. Major cringe. "Will that be a problem?"

"Have you seen the men we've elected governor to New York? And it's all in the past, right?"

"Right." No way was I allowing myself to be exposed to random strangers on the internet. "So, what should I be doing?"

"Keep doing what you're doing. Secure that W."

"Any tips or advice?" Or endorsement you could provide?

Harlen hesitated a moment before answering, something weighing in his eyes. "The main thing is to stay focused. You can't let anything, or anyone, distract you."

I read between the lines. Dusty.

"Rita came out of nowhere with that story. It has nothing to do with the issues."

"Leo, I'm here for coffee, not bullshit. We know how campaigns work." Harlen pressed his fingertips together, thinking through his next question. "Did you vet him before you started dating?"

"Vet him? He's my best friend."

"I was lucky. I met my wife in high school. We knew everything about each other and have been together for fifty years." He cleared his throat. "You've been through a lot, Leo. Marriage, divorce, coming out, a sex scandal. But you're not Teflon. You don't want to take any more chances, especially with greener pastures on the horizon."

Governor.

Could I be governor?

"You asked for my advice. Cut your losses with Dusty."

Get rid of Dusty? My stomach dropped to my shoes. I didn't want to cut Dusty out of anything.

"I can't do that. He's my boyfriend."

"You said that you were friends first. If he is your friend, then he'll understand."

"Understand that I'm dumping him?" Maybe Dusty would understand, but the thought of doing this sent my mind into a nuclear tailspin.

"Politics and romance don't always go together," Harlen said with a wince. He obviously had never watched *The American President*.

I wasn't the guy who believed in magic. You better believe I was the one eyeing magicians closely, looking for the tells behind their tricks. But being with Dusty had been magical. Yeah, I'd call it fucking magical.

"This seems extreme. Harlen, this will all blow over."

"This will, but what about the next thing? I know I'm asking something big of you, but I will make sure the sacrifice is worth it. You'll have my endorsement."

I drank the rest of my coffee and tossed the cup in the trash, sinking a three-pointer. I stood up. "Well, Harlen, I guess I don't have your endorsement then."

His eyes lit up in rage and shock. Nobody said no to Harlen Carruthers. "I'd be careful, Leo. Give this some thought. This is your future we're talking about."

"I have, and the answer is no."

I thanked Harlen for this time and left. I wasn't going to throw Dusty under the bus, no matter how big the prize was. But the hard truth was that our fake relationship was spiraling out of control, my feelings for Dusty were spiraling *way* out of control, and it was up to me to get everything under fucking wraps.

21

DUSTY

Leo knocked on my door at the buttcrack of dawn the next morning. Time for another run. I laced up my sneakers as he opened my door.

"See, I'm up," I said.

"I do see that." His running shirt stretched across his chest, and his tight running shorts did not leave much to the imagination. "Ready to run?"

"Actually, kinda?" I didn't dread running like I did when we started. This had become one of those morning routine things people praised to high heaven that I could never get into. I wasn't one for routines. Fortunately, Leo had enough discipline for both of us.

"Kinda? That's better than the hell no I usually get. Are you enjoying running now?" Leo leaned against the door, his thick hairy arms and legs showing off from his shirt and shorts.

Yeah, there was a reason I was enjoying running, and it wasn't the endorphins.

I gulped back a lump. "I guess I enjoy the company."

I was about to lean in to give him a morning kiss—a

friendly morning kiss—until I saw him stiffen for a moment.

He opened his mouth as if to say something. "Your speed has been picking up. No longer moving at a glacial pace."

That didn't seem like the comment rolling around in his head just now. I was usually a Ph.D.-level expert in reading his mind, but my skills in Leo-ology had gotten murky since we started fake dating and real fucking.

"Hey, it seems like the story about my altercation at *Ocean City* is dying down. I still feel terrible about it."

"Don't. As I said, you have nothing to be sorry for."

His confidence assured me, even though I carried guilt over fucking up the debate. Even with that out of the way, something seemed off between us, like maybe Leo woke up on the wrong side of his humongous bed.

We went down the stairs softly so as not to wake Ari and Lucy. I remembered how I hated being woken up as a teenager. I could sleep for twelve hours at a time if somebody let me.

Outside, we did some quick stretching before taking off. My stretching was never as deep as his because my eyes kept going to Leo's ass when he bent down. Ever since we had sex, I'd been thinking of having more sex with him, even though I told myself it was a one-time thing. That was how addictions worked, right?

"We're already running three miles in the morning, easy," he said, pulling his arm over his chest and showing off his strong triceps. I'd never noticed men's triceps, how they poked out.

"What's your point?"

"A 5k is three point one miles."

I pulled a leg behind me, and the glory of a stretched

quad sang out in my body. "And we're doing conversions to the metric system, why?"

"There's a race this weekend. The Zombie 5k."

"With actual dead people?"

"Yes," he deadpanned. "We've discovered how to bring people back to life specifically for the purpose of a local race."

"When suburbanites set their mind to something, there's no stopping them."

Leo crossed his leg over his other knee and bent down in a figure-four stretch. I followed his lead, and my hips thanked me. I did not realize how stiff I was.

"What's the Zombie 5k?" I asked, playing along. Sourwood really loved its local events.

"It's a regular 5k race people run, but then other people dress up as zombies and pretend to chase the runners. Some will pop out from the sidelines, too."

"And what happens if they catch you? Do they bite?"

"Do you want them to?" Leo cracked a smile, showing off his teeth. He had attractive teeth. I had no idea I could find teeth attractive, especially teeth I'd seen a jillion times before, but he had proven me wrong. "They pretend to chase you, but none of them grab you. It adds a little Halloween flavor."

"Couldn't people just throw candy and condoms at us?"

"Condoms?"

"I once went to a Halloween parade in West Hollywood, and instead of fun-size Reese's, they threw out magnum-sized rubbers."

"That, uh, doesn't happen in Sourwood. Though we are very pro-safe sex." He spread his legs and stretched down to touch the ground between them. He was facing me, so I couldn't ogle his butt. It didn't matter; I was already half-hard around him. Running with a boner would not be fun. I'd rather be chased by zombies.

"So, are you in?" Leo asked.

"For the condomless Zombie 5k?"

"Correct."

I was intrigued by the idea of being chased by zombies. And from what I saw at Applefest, Sourwood knew how to put on events. "Sure."

"As I said, we're already running three miles every morning. At least now, you'll get a medal."

"I'll get a medal?" I couldn't turn down an opportunity for free things. "I guess that's better than getting condoms thrown at my face."

"They weren't used, right?"

We did some final stretches, but my body still felt sore. I shook out my left leg, but tension continued to squeeze my calf and thigh. Perhaps I should have taken his calls for stretching more seriously.

"I told you not to diss stretching," he said.

"Don't rub it in my face." *Unless we're talking about your dick...*

"We're not young bucks anymore, although Harlen did call me kid last night. That was fun." Leo stretched his arm over his head and leaned to the side, exposing a sliver of taut stomach muscle ready for licking.

"How was your meeting last night? You didn't say. Is he on the Leo train?"

"We'll see." Another clenched answer I couldn't interpret. I hoped I didn't fuck things up.

"Get on the ground," he said.

I gulped hard. "Why?"

"We're going to do a deep stretch. Trust me."

I lay on the ground, the cold grass sending shivers up my

skin. Leo got on his knees and hovered over me, his body strong and towering. We were the same height, but being around him made me realize how lanky I was. His body was thick in all the right ways.

More shivers up my skin. I kept my knees up to hide the swelling happening in my exercise shorts.

Leo rested a firm hand on my left knee. "Is this the leg?"

I nodded yes. My love of witty banter suddenly disappeared. My tongue thickened in my mouth.

"Lie back," he instructed. He lifted the leg so it was straight and pushed it up toward my chest. It reminded me of my position on his bed. Perhaps I should have stretched then.

The world was quiet around us, save for the occasional chirping bird and car in the distance. Leo pressed my leg deeper back, opening up soreness in my muscles, bringing a relaxed feeling. His body leaned against my leg, adding more pressure. My ass lifted off the ground and nudged closer to him—part stretch, part demon horniness pushing it closer to him. My erection strained against my underwear, and I prayed he couldn't see it trying to poke through.

"How does that feel?" His voice was a raspy growl as he pressed my leg deeper into the stretch.

"Good," I managed to get out.

His hips leaned against my leg and my ass. A familiar bulge brushed against me, barely missing my hole. Fuck, if he could give me one dry bump, I'd blow my load.

He grunted as he pushed. We kept looking at each other then looking away. I willed myself not to turn this sexual. This was stretching. He was helping me. My leg needed this. Yet all the oxygenated blood circulating in my system traveled to one singular appendage.

"That should open you up," he said.

So could something else.

I grabbed his shirt and pulled him to my lips. The scent of his minty toothpaste and musky Leo-ness filled my nose as our tongues slid between our mouths. I gasped for breath as he thrust against me.

It was over before my mind could process. Leo sat up and hopped to his feet, hand on his hips as he caught his breath. Erection in plain sight. I propped myself up on my elbows, feeling ravaged, my dick still hard.

He turned to me, something between shock and lust splashed across his red face. "Good stretch."

"My leg feels better." I shook it out and stood up. "Let's go."

I took off down the street. Leo chased after me, great practice for the Zombie 5k. When he caught up to me, we got into our normal jog routine, running through the empty downtown. I knew all the stores by heart, their awnings and hopes filling the spirit of Sourwood. We ran in silence into the woods.

It was a tense silence, no doubt brought on by my shameless move earlier. In my defense, the stretch was a very sexual position we were in. And wasn't sex another way of getting endorphins?

We jogged through the path in the woods, surrounded by leaves of all different colors, a cornucopia of fall enveloping us. Running was supposed to clear one's mind; mine only felt more confused. Our one perfect storm of sex didn't feel like enough.

I stopped at our usual spot overlooking the town and the river, the most beautiful spot.

Leo slowed behind me.

"I needed to take a breath. You can keep going if you don't want to stop."

He didn't respond. Instead, he bore into me with his coal dark eyes, his pupils the size of saucers. My heart sped up in my chest, not from running, but because I felt it in the air, the crackle of electricity between us.

I stared right back at him. *You can keep going if you don't want to stop.*

Leo pushed me against a tree. Our lips smashed together, tongues finding each other. His body pressed me into the bark, and this time, I felt a surefire erection in his bulge.

"You drive me fucking wild; you know that?" he growled into my mouth. "Do you know how painful it is running with a hard dick?"

"Yeah. I do." I palmed his crotch, stroking his length through his shorts.

"Fuck. Baby, you feel so fucking good." He rocked his hips to my hand.

Baby. I missed being called baby.

I pulled his rock-hard cock from his shorts. It was hot in my hands. I smeared the drops of precum around his crown and watched Mr. Always-in-Control struggle to maintain that title. His eyes seemed to dare me to keep going. Fortunately, we both knew there weren't other joggers on this route this early in the morning.

I squatted down, feeling the burn in my quads. I took him into my mouth.

"Dusty." Leo moaned and laughed to himself.

He was having a ball. I was having two, tracing them with my tongue, letting the sweat hit my tongue.

The peaceful sounds of nature were interrupted by our moaning and slurping. Leo threaded his fingers through my hair and guided me from his balls to his shaft. He pumped inside me, precum hitting the back of my throat.

"Will we get to do this at the 5k, too?" I asked teasingly, rolling his cock across my bottom lip like I was applying chapstick.

"I don't know what would be worse—getting caught by zombies or the press."

"Both would eat us alive."

"Speaking of eating, put this cock back in your mouth." Leo gripped his thick erection with one hand and dragged down my lip with the other. He shoved himself back inside me and grunted as I took him to the base.

My head bobbed up and down on his cock. I felt him tightening, his body shaking with need. I rubbed myself through my shorts, lust pooling in my belly. Friend, fake, fuckbuddy. I didn't know anymore, and I didn't care. I wanted him so badly I could barely breathe.

"Get up," he ordered. His breath came out in hungry clouds. "I don't have any lube, but I want to fuck you. Maybe we can go back to the house—"

I put my hand over his mouth. If we went back to the house, the moment would be over. "No. I am not leaving this spot until I feel you inside me."

Heat blazed in his eyes. "I want to push you up against this tree and fuck you senseless."

And I wanted that on a fucking Hallmark card. As if I couldn't get any hornier. He was so direct, his voice commanding and confident.

"We can use spit," I said. "Will that work?"

"It's not ideal, but it'll get the job done."

I was in for some pain, but I would take that pain over the serious case of blue balls I'd been carrying this week.

"I don't have a condom either," he said. "Is there a West Hollywood parade nearby?"

I laughed into his chest. I loved that we could joke while being crazed with lust.

"I'm not having sex with anyone else," he said.

"Neither am I." I didn't want to. I couldn't imagine fucking anyone else and enjoying it. "I guess we could run to the high school. They usually have a bowl of condoms, right?"

"Baby, I can't wait that long. If I try to run with this," Leo gripped his cock, fully engorged and leaking on his fat head. "I'm going to pull a muscle."

"True."

Leo kissed me softly. "I promise I won't hurt you. If you feel any pain, we can stop."

Seconds later, Leo yanked my shorts to my knees and leaned me against a tree, my ass hitting the cold air. The beauty of Sourwood provided the perfect backdrop while Leo ate me out. His tongue flicked against my hole, and his fingers opened me up. He took his time getting me slicked up with his spit. I groaned his name into the tree, his mouth doing wonders to me. I wondered if giving all those speeches helped with the dexterity of his tongue.

I shivered with excitement as Leo stood up. His large frame pressed against me. His cold hands held onto my hips, while I pushed my ass out like a good boy, ready to meet him. My body sparked with need as he sank inside me, no layers between us.

I cried out.

"You okay, baby?" His breath danced on my neck.

I nodded. It was the good kind of pain, Leo stretching me out as I remembered how thick he was. I instantly palmed my cock, stroking myself.

The sounds of skin slapping against skin and Leo exhaling huffs of air filled the woods. His arm, slick with sweat, held me across the chest. Precum leaked through my fist as I jerked myself and felt the orgasm build.

"I feel you tightening around me, baby." Leo went faster, hitting me with short thrusts. He stopped to slick himself up with more spit, always the thoughtful partner. The discomfort was minimal, and I soon forgot about it, wrapped up in the thunderous feeling of lovemaking and the orgasm careening through my system.

Leo took his hand and wrapped it around my fist, helping me stroke myself to completion. Come splattered against the tree. Leo brought his hand to my mouth and made me taste myself.

"Fuck, that's so hot, baby," he said with barely contained glee as I sucked his fingers clean. He pulled out, and hot streaks of come coated my ass cheeks.

"Shit." Leo wiped at it with his shirt. "I shouldn't have finished on you since we have another mile to run."

"It's okay. I like it." I was his marked territory. Property of Leo McCaslin. No other guys need apply.

I picked up a few drops with my thumb and tasted him. I'd gone from not into guys to tasting come like I was asking for samples at a Baskin Robbins. Watching how wild it drove Leo, knowing it was something he wanted, filled me with lust and joy. I wanted to make him happy.

We pulled up our shorts; all evidence of what went down vanished. It would be yet another secret held in the woods.

"So that happened," he said with an awkward laugh. "Again."

"It's all your fault." I leaned my arm against the tree to fully catch my breath and steel myself for more running.

"My fault?"

"You attacked me with your mouth."

"Because you ground your ass against me when I was helping you stretch!"

"And they say no good deed goes unpunished."

Leo pulled me into a headlock like we were two kids fighting over action figures.

"Are you seriously doing this right now?" I asked as I tried to maneuver out.

Leo released me. He was laughing so hard tears pricked his eyes. There was a special level of laugh for Leo, where it turned into a monkey-like cackle. I was glad to see him still able to have fun despite the stress of the campaign.

"Do you give all of your pieces of ass post-coital head-locks?" I rubbed my neck, fighting back tears of laughter of my own. "I'm glad to see you smiling. You seemed tense earlier."

"What?"

I tipped my head at him. I was sore and sweaty and not here for bullshit.

"Harlen Carruthers will not be endorsing me."

"Shit. I'm sorry. Is it because..." I put my hand on my chest. Because of my idiocy?

"No. We just didn't see eye-to-eye on certain things."

"You don't need him. You're the rock star mayor!"

"Man, Dust..." His eyes crinkled with a smile that was gone just as fast. He went into serious mode. "Can I ask you a question? What were you planning to do after the election?"

The glow of this wonderful morning quickly dimmed. Our fake relationship had an expiration date, which his question reminded me of. "I—uh, I don't know. I guess go back to LA."

"Yeah. Makes sense." Leo kicked at a patch of dirt. We were like awkward teenagers all over again.

I hated being a teenager then, and I hated it now.

"Leo. Fuck." Did being a preacher's kid score me any last-minute points with the Lord? "I don't want to go back to LA. I want to stay."

"You do?" He looked up at me, suddenly flush with confidence, like he held an ace in this poker game between us.

"Yeah."

I wanted to remember this look he gave me forever, all stubble and smolder and heart.

I pulled him by the shirt into a kiss. His strong arms wrapped around me. "I really like being your fake boyfriend."

"Baby, who's faking?"

22

DUSTY

We were taking things slow. I mean, we were having sex whenever we could find the time to be partially naked, but everything else we were taking slow.

Leo and I were set to go back to Maria Lopez's office at *The Sourwood Gazette* for a follow-up article she promised would be fun. I was hesitant to believe journalism could be fun, especially when I was the subject.

The Sourwood Gazette offices sat in a converted Victorian house amid a strip of restaurants and upscale stores along the river. The house had to be at least a hundred and fifty years old. A creaky *Sourwood Gazette* sign swung on the front lawn.

Leo rested his hand on my lower back as he led us inside, his hot touch burning through my shirt. The "newsroom" of the *Gazette* was about four small desks around the perimeter of what was once a living room, piles of papers and old clippings cluttering every available inch of desk space. Who knew Sourwood had so much news?

Maria got up from her desk in the corner. The wall behind her was covered with a mix of framed clippings and scraggly, colorful drawings from what had to be her son or daughter. "Mr. Mayor, Dusty. Great to see you again."

"Always a pleasure, Maria." Leo shook her hand with a relaxed determination. He was definitely less sweaty and desperate this time around.

"Ditto," I said.

"Thank you for coming in today. I wanted to get your input on a follow-up piece before it went to print tonight."

"You said it was a fun piece," Leo stated with skepticism. "Fun for you, for us, or both?"

Maria laughed off the question. "You're going to love it. It's not a hit piece." She nodded her head, and her ponytail of thick hair followed. "Come with me."

Once again, Leo's hand pressed into my back, and I didn't protest. Maria took us down a narrow hall to a small room that was probably a study way back in the day. Today, it was an archive room, filled with dust as much as articles. Rusty file cabinets and stacks of cartons gobbled up the available standing room. I was dying to introduce the *Gazette* to a scanner.

In the center of the room was a table with pictures scattered. Familiar faces looked back at us. It took me a second to piece it together that it was our younger selves.

"What is this?" Leo asked.

The overlit and faded photographs of late '90s disposable cameras, with their neon orange timestamps in the corners, transported me back to college.

"We had a great response to our original article. People really responded to you. They've loved getting to know you and Dusty," Maria said to me. "They loved the stories about the mayor, and they wanted to learn more. It gave me the idea to track down old pictures of you two."

"Slow news day?" I asked jokingly.

Leo picked up a picture of him squatting and giving two thumbs up in front of the college cafeteria. "What was I doing?"

"You were excited we found the good cafeteria on campus, the one—"

"With the stir-fry station! That was, to this day, the best stir-fry I've ever had." He cleared his throat. "Not including Mr. Chan's on Maple Street. Their food is in a league of their own."

"Nice save," I whispered to him.

"Where did you find these?" Leo stared at his younger self, who had fuller cheeks and shaggier hair but the same wicked grin. How had I never realized how cute he was back then?

"Your friends Mitch and Cal supplied some. And some that weren't suitable for publication."

"Of course, they did," he muttered.

I'd love to see those.

"And then I reached out to people who graduated from college around the same time, found a few who were friends with you. Guys from debate club, from your fraternity."

"Uh-oh. I'm surprised they gave you *any* that were suitable for publication."

"As you can see, they did." She waved a hand over the table, proud of her diligent research. I had to tip my hat to her.

"This is impressive shoe-leather work." I picked up a picture someone took of Leo and me lying out by the water, shirtless and hairless. "Was this the spring you decided to shave your chest?"

Leo looked at Maria, then me. "No comment. I was trying out for the swim team."

"Right. The swim team." That was also the summer he

declared he was trimming his pubes to make certain things look bigger. I could say with certainty he did not keep that habit up—and those things were still big.

"Is it okay if I record some reactions?" Maria took out her phone. "For quotes and video content for our social media channels."

"*The Sourwood Gazette* is getting on TikTok?" Leo asked.

"Trying to stay relevant. My son set up my account last week."

"I've tried enlisting my kids to help me with my social media stuff. They're too busy with their own. Did you know Lucy is making a movie, and Ari created his own video game?" Leo seemed blown away and in awe, his pride as a dad shining through. "I wish I was half as creative as them."

Inspired by Ari's breakthrough with Leo about his love of designing video games, Lucy also came forward with a confession of her own last night: she didn't want to be a brainiac doctor. Instead, she wanted to make movies. It was a secret hobby she'd been tinkering around with in between her regular studies—filming short movies on her phone with friends, writing scripts. To everyone's surprise, including my own, Leo was supportive of his daughter's dream to be the next Sofia Coppola, but still stressed that she had to keep her grades up.

Maria turned on her phone. The white light let us know we were live.

"It's amazing," she said.

"What?" I asked.

"I'm surprised you two didn't get together in the past. You were always making googly eyes at each other."

Leo and I traded a confused look. I was confused, while his face turned white.

"Huh? We were friends," I said. I picked up a picture of

young Leo playing his heart out at a concert in one of the dorm common rooms, sweat dipping from his hair and flushing his youthful face. The room was too small. They were fogging up the windows, so we had to open them in the dead of winter. I probably got a cold, but it was worth it. Leo was electrifying.

"You're doing it now." She smiled and squeezed her shoulders up to her ears.

"Huh?"

"Googly eyes."

I checked myself in a mirror above a filing cabinet, willing my eyes not to get all googly. I flicked over to Leo, who was in his own world of nostalgia, looking just as handsome as he did back then.

"Nothing's changed." Maria handed over another photo from that concert; this one had me in frame in the front row.

It was rare in life to get objective views of ourselves. Maybe more common now with everybody filming shit. But thanks to this random snapshot, I saw myself, twenty years ago, making googly eyes at my best friend. It was undeniable. I stared up at him with awe and inspiration and, most shockingly, want.

"Holy shit," I said.

"Here's another great one." Maria slid a picture over from a frat party.

Leo and I clinked Solo cups, grinning at each other. And maybe we smiled and said something as we toasted or made some joke to whoever took the picture before chugging. But at that moment, in that split second captured forever on film, we were gazing into each other's eyes.

He was giving me hard googly eyes, his bottom lip slightly pouting. And sure, his eyes were laser red thanks to crappy disposable cameras, but they were lasered at me.

Leo swiped the photo from my hands and stared hard.

"Are these bringing back any memories for you two?" Maria asked from behind her phone.

I looked at Leo, but he said nothing. In front of him were the photos he'd been studying before I interrupted.

A group shot of us studying on the quad, Leo gazing at me while I made some dumb-ass face.

A group picture of Leo, me, and his fellow legal interns at a bar in New York, arms around each other in the back of the picture, Leo giving me a knowing grin like the rest of the world didn't exist.

A two-shot of us opening presents with the twins when I visited for Christmas five years ago, me looking up and swooning over him with his new French press machine.

A shot of us laughing while putting on our gladiatorial gear at LeapWorld, a tender expression lancing his face.

Picture after picture.

Year after year.

I tried to meet Leo's eyes; his face flushed of color. Even Maria put down her phone.

"Excuse me," he said and left.

"I'm sorry," Maria said to me. "I'm so sorry. I thought this would be fun."

I chased after Leo, difficult in such tight quarters. Papers fell, as it was their fate.

Fate.

The word tasted different today. My heart pummeled against my chest, begging to be free.

"Leo!"

He darted out of the office. I swung open the front door, and he walked with fierce determination down the steps and past our car. If he wanted a race, he'd get one.

I gave my quads a quick stretch then bolted down the

walkway. I caught up to him on the sidewalk and pulled him back.

"Leo! Where are you going?" I put my hands on his shoulders, begging to see those eyes that had gazed at me for twenty fucking years. "What's wrong? Talk to me."

He seemed out of breath. He was running in his own way.

"I'm fine. I got a big rush of nostalgia and memories. Blast from the past, you know?" He sounded rehearsed like he'd practiced this during his storm out. "Sorry. I need some fresh air."

"That was quite a walk down Memory Lane."

"Dust, I have to tell you something," he said while pacing. The walls around Leo were crumbling, desperate to stay up. My friend was strong, but for the first time, I saw a new kind of fear. His hands were trembling.

Leo sat down beside me, staring across the street into an empty storefront, scraping a rock against the asphalt. "What if I told you that those pictures weren't a surprise?"

"What do you mean?"

"The way I feel about you didn't just happen with our fake relationship." I could feel him muster up strength, the muscles in his back tightening. "Dust, I had a crush on you in college. A major fucking crush. I wanted to be with you, but...I was so confused. I was in the closet. I didn't understand what I was feeling. And you were straight, not interested."

I hissed out a breath, cursing my former douche-headed self.

"And so I tucked those feelings away. I put them in this box inside me and shoved it deep in storage. I wasn't going to let whatever these feelings were ruin our friendship and ruin my future." Leo heaved in a deep breath. I rubbed small circles on his back, kissing his head, letting him know I was here and I wasn't going anywhere. We could talk until the sun went down. I wasn't going anywhere. "I did a pretty good job of it. I married a nice girl, had two wonderful kids, a career. My feelings for you melded into this incredible friendship. But having you here with me…" He did some version of a cough and laugh and cry. The feelings refused to be boxed any longer. "I love you, Dusty. I've always loved you. I am in love with you."

I leaned my forehead against his and peered into his soulful eyes one more time before kissing him, our bodies connected on a different plane. No more lies between us. I pulled him into a hug.

"I thought you weren't into me like that, that you saw this as just a fake relationship," he said. "So I decided I could do that, too."

"Jesus, you really do make everything a competition." I held his hand. I would always hold his hand. "Well, I've been in love with my best friend for twenty fucking years, and I'm only realizing it now."

His gorgeous brown eyes watered up, making them damn near translucent.

"Timing was never my thing. I got frosted tips like two years too late." I wiped away a tear just as it was about to fall.

"You're in love with me?"

I nodded. It was so stupidly obvious in those pictures.

"Ridiculously in love with you. Somewhere along the way, this fake relationship got real for me." I cradled his glorious head in my hands and plucked a sweet kiss on his lips. "I realized that I wasn't kissing you just for show, and I wasn't having sex with you because of a chemical combustion, and I wasn't thinking about you all the time because I was wrapped up in the election." My mind flooded with memories of a friendship that spanned half my lifetime. "Shit. Talking to you at two in the morning was the only reason I stayed awake, and I couldn't wait until we talked the next day."

"But you didn't realize it?"

"Nope." I sat on the curb, arms hanging over my knees. "I did like women, but nothing compared to how I feel about you. Maybe that's why I could never make it work with my long list of exes." With each sentence, more clarity entered my head. The perfect guy had been in front of me this whole time, and I was too stupid and scared not to see it.

I planted soft kisses on his lips and along his cheek.

"Dusty, I love you."

"I know. We've established that."

"I know, but I've waited twenty years to say that. I like the way it sounds."

We cuddled on the curb in the cold wind, surrounded by each other's warmth. Footsteps crunched on the sidewalk. Maria stood above us with a very cringe expression.

"Mr. Mayor, I want to apologize if those pictures brought up bad memories. We don't have to run the story." She chewed at her fingernail.

"Maria, it's all right. Those pictures resurfaced a lot of wonderful memories. Like when I could rock out without throwing my back out." Leo was so damn slick, bringing a smile to her face. He knew how to communicate, how to connect with others. Whoever said he wasn't likable didn't know what they were talking about. (Unless it was Vernita. I'll never second-guess her.)

"Why don't you add one more picture to the collection?"

Leo threw his arm around me and pulled me close, letting my head rest in the nook of his neck.

Maria snapped a picture on her phone, and without looking at it, I knew that Leo was gazing down at me, and I was looking up, giving him the googliest of googly eyes.

23

LEO

I knocked at the door. "Dust, are you ready to run?"

Pre-dawn midnight blue coated the sky outside. I bounced in my running shoes, getting my legs limber while I waited.

I knocked again. "Dust, are you asleep?"

He yanked open the door to the en suite bathroom, naked save for pajama bottoms. His chest and faint six-pack were hot enough to lick. His bedhead crashed like waves across his forehead. A foamed-up toothbrush hung out of his mouth.

"I'm coming," he said. I think. The toothbrush made it tough to decipher.

"We're going to be late."

Dusty spit and washed out his mouth. He flung the toothbrush into the extra holder in my bathroom—our bathroom now—then sidestepped me into the bedroom. He spun on his heel.

"I would've gotten a better night's sleep for this race had someone not poked me awake in the middle of the night." He stared his accusatory eyes right into me.

And I winked back. Guilty as charged.

I pushed him back onto the bed, the same bed where I'd spooned him to sleep, and apparently humped him awake. I dragged a greedy hand over his chest, my lips hovering above his pert mouth.

"If you keep looking at me that way without a shirt on, we may go into round two and miss the race altogether."

Dusty pulled me to his mouth for a hot kiss. "They're zombies. They can wait."

"How did I ever sleep before without you by my side?"

He quirked an eyebrow in consideration. "Lots of pillows?"

"Dusty, Dusty, Dusty."

"What?"

"Nothing. Just like saying your name. While you're under me. Undressed."

He tried to wriggle from my grip. I pulled down his pajama pants and smacked him on his savory, bubbly ass, which was enough to get me officially revved up. I pressed my tongue between his cheeks.

"Shit," he gasped out, wiggling still, but this time to push his ass closer to my mouth.

I opened him up, his pink hole driving me crazy. I flicked my tongue over his opening. My dick hardened in my shorts.

"We're going to be late." His body clenched and quivered with suppressed moans. "Your kids are downstairs eating breakfast."

"I'm having my breakfast, too." I swirled my tongue around his hole, slipping in and out, his heat sending bolts of lust through my veins. I'd wanted Dusty for fucking decades, and now I had him. I was making up for lost time.

"We shouldn't do this," he whispered, his breath husky.

"Do you want me to stop?"

"No."

I pulled down my shorts to my thighs, enough to unleash my leaking steel rod of a dick desperate to plow inside him. I slid a finger inside Dusty while, with my other hand, I reached for the lube in the nightstand.

"Dad, where's the orange juice?" Ari called from downstairs.

"It's in the fridge!" I yelled back as loud as I could, roughly switching to dad mode. "All the way in the back!"

I coated my cock and Dusty's ass. I was already dangerously close to exploding. If I had my way, I'd fuck him so hard he'd have no choice but to scream out his pleasure. But quiet, sneaky fucking also had its charms.

Dusty's ass jutted up like a cannon. He wanted it so bad. Rather than a hard slap, I kissed both cheeks.

"I don't see it!" Ari yelled back.

"It's there!" Fucking kids.

"Oh," he called a few seconds later. "Found it!"

I leaned over Dusty and licked down his neck. "That was close."

"Speaking of being close," Dusty humped against my finger. Goosebumps flashed down his skin. "Your finger's about to get the job done."

I pulled out and replaced it with my thick cock. Dusty balled the comforter in his fist.

"You okay, baby?"

"Fucking great. Just trying to stay quiet."

Me, too. Lord, my body got set on fire as I sank into that warm ass, past his tight ring of muscle. My hands cascaded over his smooth back. I slipped fingers through his soft blond curls, savoring this beautiful man under me. I pulled him by the hair; he arched his back to meet me.

"God. Fuck. Leo." Dusty panted, tiny groans escaping his lips.

My twins didn't need to hear the sounds of skin slapping and grown men grunting. I fucked him slowly, which brought its own form of torturous pleasure. Time slowed down. I felt every inch of me plunging inside him, every jump of his heartbeat.

"Feels so good," he muttered. His ass tightened around me. We'd fucked enough for me to know what that meant.

"Come for me," I growled into his ear. "Stroke yourself."

Dusty balanced on one hand as he jerked his dick, and I resisted the urge to jackhammer him. His hole clenched on my cock as he shot his load into the sheets. I grunted into his hair and filled his ass with my release.

We collapsed onto the bed, laughing and catching our breaths. Dusty's engorged, spent cock hung flopped on his stomach. I gave it a final lick, tasting his final drops.

"Good morning," he said. "Does that count as stretching?"

I was smiling so big I thought my cheeks were going to break off.

"You seem happy." Dusty circled a finger through my chest hair.

"I get to kiss you and have sex with you for the rest of my life. I'm the happiest guy on earth."

I'd wondered if my inability to commit to other guys because of Dusty was a made-up excuse my mind had concocted. It was not. Sex with Dusty was one million percent better than any Milkman hookup.

Dusty pecked me on the lips then pushed me off. "Let's get ready for real. We have some zombies to slay."

"Dad!" Lucy called up. "Ari spilled the orange juice, and we can't find the sponge!"

I sighed. A dad's job was never done. "I'll wash up first."

———

I FINISHED GETTING ready and pinned my race bib to my shirt that said Humans > Zombies. Vernita emailed me the latest polling. I was in a dead heat with Rita. We texted about last-minute ideas to help move the needle, but we both agreed it was going to come down to the final debate on Sunday evening.

I found the kids and Dusty in Lucy's room with Dusty's back turned to her as she drew something on the back of his shirt. Ari painted on his face. Dusty turned, and streaks of fake blood drifted across his shirt and cheeks.

"What's that?" I asked in horror.

"It's for the Zombie 5k," Dusty said. "We were talking, and I wanted to do something fun. Lucy and Ari said people get really into it."

"You're going to be a zombie?"

He shook his head no. "I'm going to look like I was attacked by zombies, so that way the zombies think I'm one of them and leave me alone."

"People get really into it, Dad," Lucy said. "Do you remember last year when that lady ran with a fake arm dangling from her side?"

"Janey Tarberg." The same librarian who flashed me at Applefest back in the day. She had a mighty spirit, that one.

There were some people who really got into the spirit of Halloween. It was the one time of year when they could express their obsession with morbidity out loud—a pride month for blood and guts.

"Oh, can you put some fake blood on my hands?" Dusty asked. "I want it to look like a zombie came up to me, but I punched them and said, 'Drop dead, bitch. Again.'"

I snorted. Leave it to Dusty to bring sass to a zombie apocalypse.

"Do you want anything, Dad?" Ari asked, holding up his thin paintbrush.

"I'll pass. I am proud to be a bloodless survivor for this run." I was still in campaign mode, and I didn't want to show up to the 5k covered in fake blood, lest someone find offense or worse—think I was actually injured. Sometimes, I wished I could turn that part of my brain off and live.

Lucy and Ari wrapped up preparing Dusty, who looked somewhere between human and zombie when they were finished. My heart lifted watching them together. Dusty was a natural and would make a seamless transition from fun uncle to fun stepdad.

I tried to shake the thought out of my head, but I always had my eye on a five-year plan. I let myself relish in its potential a few seconds more.

"Do I look scary enough?" Dusty had streaks of fake blood on his cheeks, and his body looked great in his blood-splattered T-shirt. The red made the blue of his eyes pop, the white of his teeth. I could stare at him all day.

"I'm terrified that this fake blood won't be able to come out in the wash." I ran a finger down a patch on his back before noticing that this was my shirt.

"I don't mind. I'll continue to wear it on our runs, and if people see me, I can give some story like I was attacked by a bear or saved a bus of nuns from a burning building."

"Ha! I doubt that. Do you remember when you tried to put out that trashcan fire by pouring vodka on it?"

"I thought it was water!"

One thing was for sure. There'd never be a dull moment with Dusty.

"We have to get going." I nodded toward the door and made my way there.

"Wait. We should get a picture of you guys," Lucy said. She took out her phone, as did Ari. They were glued to their hands.

Dusty hopped up and stood at my side.

"Should we hold our hands out?" I asked.

"No. You're not zombies." Ari gave me that *are you serious* eyeroll that was very prevalent in teenagers.

"What if I pretended to bite your neck?" I asked, getting into the spirit of the race and Halloween. It was never my holiday, but seeing their excitement spurred me on.

"You're zombies, not vampires," she said. Another eyeroll. They were brutal.

"Man, you will use any excuse to give me a hickey," Dusty said quietly between us. He leaned in closer. "Be a gentleman and save the biting for my inner thighs."

I steeled myself against getting turned on. The last thing I needed was photographic evidence of sprouting wood in my shorts.

"Get closer," Lucy said. Spoken like a true filmmaker.

I put my arm around Dusty and pulled him close. We'd done this so many times, taken so many pictures at events, posed for so many voters. But this time felt more intimate. His warmth made me glow from the inside.

"Smile!"

Dusty rested his head on my shoulder, and that nearly killed me.

"Perfect," Lucy said. She and Ari looked at the pictures on her phone. "You guys are so cute."

"Looking good, Dad! Looking good, Uncle Dusty."

"Kids." Kids? Man, I sounded like such a dad sometimes. "I want to talk to you about something for a second."

I held Dusty's hand as I told them Dusty was sticking around, and we were becoming more than friends. So much more than friends. I explained that we were dating, though I knew that was only a formality. I was already spending my life with Dusty at my side, one way or another.

The twins shared a silent cosmic expression, then turned to us with approving grins.

"Cool," Ari said.

Cool. I would take it.

They ran into the car. Dusty stopped me before we left the house.

"What is it?" Concern flushed over his face.

"Leo, when I was a teenager, I babysat for extra cash, like you do. And one time, when the kids were asleep, I went on the deck and smoked a joint. And this was before marijuana was legal."

"Why are you telling me this?"

He looked out at the kids, arguing over some video on their phone, much like many adults I knew.

"Leo, being with you means being with your kids. I love these kids like they're my own. They are so frickin talented and smart and kind."

"Then why do you look pained?"

"Because I am a few steps away from being their stepdad, and I need you to know that I smoked pot when I was babysitting."

I rolled the sentence over in my head. "I don't see how that's relevant."

"Do you want me around your kids permanently? I don't know how to parent. Being a parent means being in charge of people's lives. I can barely manage my own. I'll be like the mom in *Home Alone*, except that will happen *all the time*."

I barked out a laugh. I wanted to tell Dusty how adorable he was being, but that'd only frustrate him more.

"I'm glad the wellbeing of your children is so hysterical."

I stroked his arm and came away with smudges of fake blood. "First of all, they're teenagers who will be getting their driver's licenses soon, so it's okay if they're in the house alone."

Only four years until their driver's licenses? Fuck, where did the time go?

"Are you sure you want me as their parent?"

"Yes."

"How can you be so sure?"

"Because you're not."

Dusty raised an eyebrow. "I don't follow."

"Dusty, you're concerned about their wellbeing. You're full of doubts about your competence. You're constantly afraid you're going to fuck up." I paused. "You are a parent."

Relief flooded his being. If I wasn't so puppy dog in love with him, I would've made him sweat it out a bit more. Just because we were in love and a couple didn't mean we had to stop messing with each other.

"Let's race."

24

DUSTY

Goodbye apples. Hello, gore!

The cutesy, festive fall spirit of Downtown Sourwood I experienced with Applefest was replaced by the haunted merriment of the Zombie 5k. Across the intersection of Maple and Hudson Streets was a huge, inflatable sign that said Sourwood Zombie 5k—START. Runners, many of whom were dressed up like me, congregated at the start, a sea of bib numbers. The street was abuzz with zombies and those cheering them on. Local shop owners set up tents to feed and support those participating. "The Monster Mash" and Michael Jackson's "Thriller" played on loop.

Lucy took more pictures and filmed the general mayhem of the event. Leo and I found an empty light pole to lean against while stretching. My heart pounded with anticipation. I'd run 5k's every morning with Leo, but those felt like a rehearsal for the live show of today. The streets were thronged with people coming up to wish us good luck. I was one of them, a part of this town's beating heart.

"You ready?" Leo whispered in my ear, his grabby hands at my sides.

"Ready to leave you in the dust."

"Pun intended?"

I *just* got that.

An old lady in a skeleton costume and a hat that said Zombie Breakfast went to the podium at the start. Leo informed me she was the oldest person in Sourwood. "Runners, are you ready?"

The crowd cheered back. I got hit with a boost of adrenaline, a contact high from the crowd.

We took our spot in line for kickoff. Hundreds of runners in assorted ghoulish gear surrounded us. Some were decked out in normal clothes, some had fake blood, some wore orange and black for general Halloween. The theme of this race was definitely elastic. I appreciated the verve of Sourwood, the excitement of people. It made me proud to serve such a festive group.

My eyes scanned the crowd, taking in the spirit and energy. They found a familiar face off to the side on the sidewalk: Rita.

Next to her was an old man with a thin mustache and malevolent eyes laser-focused on me. He flashed a creepy smile that sent a bitter taste to the back of my throat.

"Who's that guy next to Rita?"

"The puppeteer. Rita's dad. Gus Buchanan." Leo rolled his eyes, then waved at Rita with every burst of faux small town neighborliness he could muster.

"He's like the evil twin brother of the Monopoly man."

Before I could make heard or tails of it, the old lady rang a bell, and we got to running. Ominous theme music from a horror movie played out on speakers on the route.

I pushed creepy old Monopoly man out of my mind. I

had a race to finish. The people of Sourwood loved me. I couldn't disappoint them by falling flat on my face.

"So when do the zombies come out?" I asked.

"You'll see," Leo said with a sly smile.

"You're going to make me suffer in a state of anxiety while I run?"

"You bet."

We ran out of Maple Street, down a side street that would take us to a field to finish the race. That was where the zombies would come out to play, I figured. More space. Leo said the race had originally taken place only through downtown, but we'd had people get injured. Too many things that pop up when you're getting chased. A zombie broke his foot when he banged into a parking meter. Another smashed into a mailbox. Fields were much easier.

"They can pop out at any moment. Even from the manholes." Leo pointed down.

"Are you serious?"

Leo laughed, giving himself away. I smacked his arm.

"Having zombies grab for runners' feet seems like a lawsuit waiting to happen. You're getting in my head, aren't you?"

Just for that, I was determined to leave him in the dust. At some points, he struggled to keep up with me for a few seconds.

Other runners waved at us as they passed. It was like one big party with friends. Leo hi-fived people who passed and encouraged everyone along the way, keeping in the spirit of these races.

When we left downtown and entered a path in the woods, the mood changed. A chill went up my spine.

"Watch out!" I threw a protective arm across Leo as two

zombies jumped out from behind the trees making groaning sounds. I recognized one of them as the mailman.

I made a quick dart to the left to evade capture.

"Shit. That was scary." I would think twice before entrusting him with my letters.

"And that's only the beginning. That was a slow zombie. Some of the younger kids who take part prefer being the fast, running zombie."

"Are you fucking kidding me?"

"Welcome to the Zombie 5k!"

"What happens if one of them gets me?"

"You keep moving forward. They won't chase. They have lots of people to scare. For most people, it's a way to participate without having to actually run."

We cleared the brush into an expansive field with green grass, surrounded by mostly-bare trees. Dark branches twisted into the gloomy gray sky, a perfect setting for a Halloween-themed run. We followed the crowd of runners.

"Watch out! Behind you!" Leo grabbed my arm and pulled me away from a pair of zombies emerging from the trees.

"There's no way I'd ever survive a real zombie apocalypse," I said, huffing and puffing. The scares pulled at my energy. "Even though I wouldn't have the ability to think, I'd try not to bite you if I saw you."

"You can bite me." Leo threaded his fingers through mine. "I'm in it for the long haul."

Leave it to Leo to turn a zombie scenario into a quasi-marriage proposal.

One of the zombies lunged for my singlet and caught it in his fingers as he did the zombie moan, the stench of his breath getting too close for comfort.

I shrugged out of his grasp, and he flashed me a quaint smile of enjoyment. I snuck him a thumbs up.

A woman behind us gasped as a zombie jumped up from behind a bush. Two teenagers strolled across the path with arms outstretched, gleefully blocking traffic. We darted around them.

"Why couldn't we do a normal, leisurely race? Something where I could listen to a podcast while I ran." I gestured around us. "Instead, you make us survive an undead uprising."

A pack of zombies ran down from the hill above. We'd have to outrun them to not be cut off.

An inflated archway with FINISH scrawled across was in sight. I grabbed Leo's hand, and we ran toward it together, avoiding a battalion of zombies pretending to push through the barriers that flanked the path. But eventually, they cleared, and it was all people cheering and waving signs for runners as we barreled through the finish line. Ari and Lucy screamed and shouted from the sidelines, along with the rest of the Single Dad's Club. The announcer called out each racer's name.

"And here comes our fearless mayor, Leo McCaslin, and his boyfriend, Dusty Michaelson."

As we barreled to the finish line, the cheers died down. I thought it'd be the opposite. An eerie quiet descended on the scene, and I clocked a few scowls. But before I could second-guess myself, Leo grabbed my hand, and we finished together. For the second time today...

My breath came back to me, and the pain of running returned to my legs. The post-finish line was a whirr of different people handing us medals, water, bananas, and a bag of potato chips. Holding the banana in my hand, of all things, it hit me that I ran a race.

"We just did that," I said to Leo, to myself, to the world around us. I had no idea where I was going in the sea of people. Music played from a DJ stand, the familiar strands of "Thriller" reminding me that we came full circle. Leo directed us to a tree for a post-run stretch.

"How do you feel?" he asked while pulling his leg into a quad stretch.

"Euphoric. And a little sore. Kinda like sex."

My joke fell on distracted ears. Leo scanned the area, something changing in his expression.

The twins and Single Dads Club met up with us, but their ecstatic reactions were replaced with the same concerned look creasing Leo's face.

And I finally saw what he saw. People looking at us. Staring.

My throat went dry. Not even the celebratory water could quench it.

"What's going on?" I asked.

"Yeah, what's going on?" Leo asked, much more pressing.

The nice old lady who fired off the gun to start the race narrowed her eyes at me, going from sweet to scary. What did I do?

Was this part of the Zombie 5k? Was the twist that we were the zombies?

"Who has my phone?" Leo held out hand. He decided not to run with his phone lest it get damaged during the race.

Mitch and Cal traded a concerned expression.

"Can we go somewhere and talk for a second, buddy?" Cal asked, his face pinched. A crushing sight considering his face was always so buoyant and happy.

"What? Why?" Leo asked.

"What's going on?" I asked, surprised at how hard it was to get an answer.

"You're disgusting!" A zombified man yelled at us as he walked by, getting the attention of more onlookers. Leo and I were used to being the center of things, but not in this way.

"I'm not going anywhere until somebody tells me what the hell happened," Leo said, barely containing the yell he no doubt wanted to unleash. He threw his chips and water to the ground.

"Hey guys," Cal turned to the twins, and their terrified faces were daggers in my heart. "Russ is with the boys at the kiddie race. Why don't you go meet up with him?"

"We can stay here," Lucy said.

"Kids. Go," I said, more tired than mad.

"I'll go with them," Cal said quietly. He turned to Mitch and gave him a "you're up" look.

Mitch handed Leo and me our phones. "I'm sorry, guys. It was posted while you were running. They probably timed it that way."

"Mitch, what the fuck is going on?" Leo hissed through a gritted fake smile. As soon as his fingers made contact with his phone, he began swooping and swiping and typing like he was a conductor leading the shitstorm symphony.

A mother in yoga pants and bib with her daughter came up to us and shook her head. "You really had me fooled," she said to me, angry and hurt. "You had us all fooled."

Fooled? A rock of dread plunked in my stomach, rippling out through me.

"Shit," Leo said. "How did they..."

"You were hacked," Mitch said, as he said all things— matter-of-factly. I could've used a dash of sugar-coating in this circumstance.

"Oh, my God," Leo muttered that prayer over and over. Not in the good way like he did during sex, though.

"What are we looking at?" I asked. I didn't know what app to turn on or email to check. I was a little kid lost in a store, parents nowhere to be found.

Leo looked up; that strong face he put on so well was starting to crumble, and he was giving all this strength to keep it up. *Don't let them see you sweat.*

"So they hacked your phone and found more sexy photos. Not the end of the world, especially when you look good." I hoped like hell my attempt would land.

It did not.

"I wish it were pictures they leaked." Leo sighed. "They found text messages where we talked about our fake relationship to help me boost my polling. It's all out there."

I glanced at this phone. A headline in bold, black letters was plastered on the screen. "The Mayor's Lie."

"Everyone here knows."

All the scowls and comments clicked into place.

"They know we lied," he said. He gripped his zombie medal in his hands and gave it a passing smile. "It's all over, Dust."

25

LEO

I spent the day in sweaty clothes and smeared zombie makeup doing whatever damage control was possible—calling donors and influential voters, who chewed me out for lying and for having multiple scandals now. Meeting with my volunteers and staff, some of whom claimed they felt betrayed. Reading social media comments and then instantly regretting it.

It was Saturday, and the election was on Tuesday. There was no way to come back from this so quickly. This was quite the October surprise. I'd rather have a kick in the nuts.

Straight from the 5k, I went to my office to make more calls and scroll through the endless social media posts about this bombshell. People were shocked that Leo & Dusty was a lie engineered to get their vote, calling me untrustworthy. Others darkly joked that this meant love was dead.

"Don't you think people are being a tad melodramatic?" I asked Vernita as I paced in my office. My post-run stench made her keep her distance.

She shrugged, giving credence to these reactions.

"Seriously?"

"People are hurt. They don't like being lied to."

"You were the one who said I needed a boyfriend to win this thing."

I looked up at the ceiling and laughed. The universe sure had a sense of humor. "The irony is that I'm actually in love with Dusty. We're a real couple now. Can we put that in a press release?" I ask wryly.

When I left Dusty to go with Mitch and Cal, I assured him that despite how awful this turn of events was, it didn't change how I felt about him. And he assured me he was still madly in love with me. That was the saving grace of this debacle. But why couldn't I have love *and* my career?

Vernita sighed warmly, sympathetic to my plight. "They're upset because they believed you. You guys were the last to figure out how meant-to-be you were. This whole town figured it out before you."

I leaned against my desk chair, making sure to keep my odorous distance. Vernita took a polite step backward.

"What do I do, Vernita?"

"I'm not sure. You can deny the story, which will destroy your credibility. You can go on the attack and make the focus that you were hacked, but that won't change the facts. You can come clean, but doing so forces you to admit that you were in a fake relationship and pulling one over on your constituents. People don't like being lied to."

She let out a whole body shrug. She thrived on having the answers and figuring out a strategy. This development was killing her. In terms of political scandals, it was an oddity.

"Do I have the power to declare war?" I cracked a half-smile, hoping to elevate her spirit.

Smell be damned, I walked over to her. "I'm sorry."

She nodded, years of unspoken friendship between us. "None of this changes what a profound mayor you've been, how you've transformed and preserved Sourwood, all the good you've done. This horseshit gossip is temporary. What you've done, that will live on. I'm proud to be on your team, and I'm happy that you finally found someone to spend your life with."

I put my hand over my heart, then pointed at her.

She was more than a staff member, more than a colleague. I would miss working with her. She grabbed papers off my desk and strolled to the door. "It's not over yet. The fat lady has not sung."

"She's warming up."

"Leo." She crossed her arms, her stern game face back on. "You are many things. Uptight, smart, a pain in my ass. But you're also a fighter." A smile escaped her lips. "So fight."

———

AFTER GOING HOME, showering, and changing, I met the guys at Stone's Throw Tavern for a badly-needed drink. I walked in on Dusty clinking glasses with Mitch, Cal, and Russ. On the one hand, I loved seeing my guy meshing so well with my friends. But on the other hand, after today, what was worth celebrating?

"Hey, it's the guy who's in a not-fake fake relationship!" Cal held up his pint glass to me, and I was very close to saluting him with the middle finger.

Mitch got to work pouring me a beer. I sat on the free bar stool next to Dusty. He spun in his chair and kissed me, giving me something positive today. He brushed a thumb over my chin, his warm touch a balm I badly needed.

"What's with all the merriment?" I asked the guys.

Dusty looked over his shoulder at the Single Dads Club. "Cal and Russ and the boys are all moving in together."

I did a double-take, but Cal raised his glass in confirmation.

"Not immediately," Russ said. "This winter."

"Who's moving in with who?" I asked.

"They're coming to my house." A knowing smile flitted across Russ's lips that I wasn't the only one to catch.

"You say that like it's obvious." Cal put down his beer and stared loving daggers at his boyfriend.

Russ tipped his head. "Isn't it?"

Cal could use some pointers on cleanliness, and Russ was a neat freak. This was either a wonderful idea or would end in bloodshed.

Cal rolled his eyes and turned back to me. "We're going to put my house up for sale this spring."

"The Hogan House. Time to say goodbye." Mitch wiped down the counter.

Mitch and I used to hang out with Cal's older brother Derek in high school at his house pretending to study, which mostly entailed raiding the fridge and shit-talking classmates. When his parents passed, Cal inherited the house and moved back in with Josh.

"I'm excited for you guys." I went over and clapped Russ and Cal on the shoulder. They were a ridiculously cute couple. Though, Dusty and I might be giving them competition. "I'll help you move out, Cal."

"You will?"

I nodded yes.

"Thanks, buddy!"

Perhaps it was the emotions of today that overwhelmed my common sense. I'd probably regret offering, but I was grateful to have these guys in my life, and if that meant a little manual labor from time to time, it was well worth it.

"I'll have plenty of time next year." I sat on my stool, refusing to look at the pity glances my friends were probably giving me.

I drank a healthy, needed gulp of beer, and when I put down my glass, I didn't find looks of pity. My friends had stony faces of determination as if we were in a football huddle.

"You guys look a little scary," I said.

"What's the plan?" Dusty asked.

"Still figuring that out. Taking a brief hiatus to drink." Another gulp of beer went down my gullet.

"We can figure it out together," Dusty said. "We can reach out to Maria Lopez at the *Gazette*, do an exclusive interview rebutting the story. It's no longer true because we're actually in love."

Hearing Dusty say he loved me continued to send bolts down my spine.

"She's not answering me or Vernita's calls. She tweeted it was time to stop believing in fairy tales. She feels lied to." Maria was so excited about the old pictures and seeing us together. She, and the rest of the town, thought we gave an Oscar-worthy performance.

"You can have a rally," suggested Cal.

"You can push the things you've done to help Sourwood, do a massive nonstop campaign tour," said Russ.

"I can hold an event here," offered Mitch. "Reinforce your talking points and remind them they like you."

"Thanks, guys. I was with Dusty to improve my likability, which I've now shot in the foot." I wasn't being negative, I told myself. I was being realistic. I never did well playing the likability game, and it backfired on me.

Dusty was unusually quiet. His forehead scrunched tight in thought. I was intrigued, and a smidge turned on. Amazing how my dick could find a way to get hard no matter the situation.

"What's on your mind, Dust?"

"You're thinking about this all wrong," he said, getting my attention. "This isn't about talking points or the campaign. Sourwood is like a boyfriend you've wronged. You need to win him back."

"I don't think I follow…"

"Ever since I got here and agreed to this, I've heard how you had a likability issue, but you don't, Leo. I've seen how you are when you meet constituents out and about. You're warm and thoughtful. You show them the sides of you that made me want to be your friend and made me fall in love with you. You care deeply, but you encase it behind this professional sheen and this wall of sharp-tongued comments."

Dusty combed his hair back, his eyes alive and bright. "Your polling didn't climb because of me. They climbed because you let voters in. You were genuine. You weren't trying to project this image of the perfect politician. I helped show that side of you, and people want to see it."

"I had to project that image." I felt like I've always been trying to win people over, convince them I was worthy of the position.

"They want to see the real you."

This sounded nuts. I tried to turn away, but Dusty swiveled my seat to face him. The other guys were clustered around, listening intently.

"For years, you've been referencing your favorite movie, *The American President,* in our texts and calls. What does

Michael Douglas do at the end? He pours his heart out to the American people."

I didn't start this fake relationship to deceive. I did it so I could continue serving them. But from their point of view, I began to see how cruel that seemed.

"This town has trusted you for eight years. Isn't it time to trust them back?" Dusty had the sweetest grin on his face as if he had found all the answers to the universe.

"You're down, but you're not out. You still have one more big event," Mitch said.

The debate.

I looked back at Dusty, my North Star. He kissed me. "Sourwood is a relationship worth fighting for."

"The best ones are," I said back. "I'm a fighter. So I'm gonna fight."

26

LEO

"We're ready, Mr. Mayor."

I had a silent heart-to-heart with myself in the dressing room mirror. Wished myself luck, then told myself I didn't need luck. I could do this on my own. I did one final check of my hair, one last smile to ensure no food was in there.

It was go time.

The auditorium was packed with Sourwood residents, more full than the last debate. I wondered how many were people hoping for a trainwreck, a continuation of this current news cycle against me. I chose to view it as people engaged in local politics.

I received a healthy, polite round of applause when I stepped onstage and took my place at the podium. I straightened out my suit jacket and gave the crowd a wave.

When we shook hands, Rita flashed me a plastered-on smile, a vicious warrior behind those eyes.

"It's been nice working with you, Mr. Mayor."

"Don't count your chickens just yet."

The moderator was Maria Lopez, who'd moderated

debates in the past and who I appreciated as being very prepared and fair, even if I was on her shit list.

Rita and I got a small bit of applause as we walked to our podiums. In the crowd, I spotted all my favorite people silently cheering me on.

"Welcome, everyone, to the debate." Maria's voice echoed across the room. "I'd like to try something different tonight. We're going to start by giving each candidate one minute to introduce themselves and give a final summation on why they're running for mayor. Mr. Mayor, we will start with you."

It was showtime—no going back. But I didn't want to go back, not back to my old life alone. I straightened my tie—picked out by my kids—and cleared my throat.

"Good evening, Sourwood. I am your current mayor and have been so for the past eight years. I've lived in Sourwood my whole life and live here now with my two children, Ari and Lucy. Lucy is looking for extras for her film she wrote and directed, so if you're interested, let me know."

The crowd politely chuckled. I found Lucy in the second row and beamed a smile at her, then at Ari, and then at Dusty. I held on him a second, soaked in his spirit before moving on.

"So I know I have a minute to explain why I want to continue to be your mayor. And I do—more than anything. But serving a town, serving people, is about being honest with them. I know, honesty from a politician. What a concept. I've always striven to be honest with you, but recently, I've failed. I've been lying to you."

Murmurs rose up from the crowd, as expected.

"By now, most of you have probably read the articles or spoken to others. Sourwood may be experiencing record growth, but this is still a small town. "

I got some soft chuckles. Whoever they were, I'd take it.

"Dusty is a close friend of mine since college. I asked him to fly out here and pretend to be my boyfriend. My campaign manager and I determined that I needed a boyfriend to be more likable. We've been pretending for a lot of the time, playing it up for articles and social media. But a funny thing happened on the way to re-election."

My body clenched with nerves and excitement. Was I really spilling my guts to a room full of people? I guess I was.

"This fake relationship with Dusty...well, it stopped being fake. Somewhere in there, I fell in love with my best friend. Or rather, the feelings I once had for him, feelings anyone in here who'd once crushed on a friend knew well, came rushing back." Through the darkness, I caught a head nod here and there. "And it turned out I was the luckiest schmuck in existence because Dusty felt the same way."

I gave him a wink in the crowd. He nodded his head at me, full of pride and admiration in his eyes like when I played at Applefest. There was no fear.

"Now that the truth is out there, I need to apologize to you, all of you." I removed the microphone from its holster and walked to the foot of the stage. "I would not be the man I am today without the support of this town. Through growing up, making the leap from lawyer to mayor, becoming a father, divorce, coming out, you've been there for me, whether we've met or not. I've shopped at your stores, eaten at your restaurants, participated in bake sales, and run zombie 5k's with you. You've contributed to the fabric of what makes this little town of ours special. And I went and lied to you. For votes. So I could present this image I thought you wanted. For that, I'm sorry."

The pin-drop silence of the room reverberated in my

head. Maria Lopez looked up at me, eyes full of hope, hanging on my words.

"I should've had more faith in you, faith that you would've continued to accept me as your mayor no matter my relationship status." I heaved out a breath. "So why do I want to be your mayor? Because Sourwood is my home. It is my heart. Because it's one of the few places left that feels like a real community. We may not know everyone's name, but we're still going to wave when they walk by."

Another small chuckle. A few more smiles through the darkness.

"It's a special place that doesn't deserve to be sold to the highest bidder. It doesn't deserve to be turned into a mini-mall filled with impersonal national chains that force our businesses to go under, or a haven for the ultra-rich who want riverfront property." I cut my eyes to my competition. "I have countless memories of my life here, and I want to cultivate a town where those memories can flourish for new generations. It's because of you that Sourwood is listed as one of the best places to live. Thank you for trusting me these past eight years. I don't take that responsibility lightly. My name is Leo McCaslin, and I want to continue to be your mayor."

Clapping spread through the room, becoming louder and louder, morphing into cheering. The volume got so high I thought I was going to blow out an eardrum.

I smiled as I choked back tears, as a town of people beamed at me. I turned to go back to my podium and took a second with my back turned to make sure I wasn't going to cry. I dabbed at my eyes and composed myself. In the wings, Vernita was full-blown crying, not even trying to compose herself as she clapped. When I returned to my place on the podium, I found Dusty again, and my heart swelled accordingly. I wanted to keep looking at him always.

I blew him a kiss.

"I cede the rest of my time to the moderator," I said, back to business as the applause died down.

At that moment, I stopped worrying about the polls. I stopped worrying about the election. I had the man I loved, the best kids in the world, great friends, and life in the best town. Whatever happened, I already won.

AT THE DEBATE INTERMISSION, Dusty charged into my dressing room.

"Leo! You were incredible." He pushed me against the wall and planted a huge kiss on my lips, quite literally taking my breath away.

Vernita cleared her throat to remind him we weren't alone.

"Oh, sorry." Dusty stepped back and smoothed out the wrinkles he'd created on my suit. "But Vernita, you have to admit, he's been on fire tonight."

"His head is already big enough," she snarked with a smile. "But objectively, Mr. Mayor, this is the best debate I've ever seen of yours."

"Same here. Better than any of your OG ones," Dusty said of my college debates.

"We've got Rita on the ropes. When we get back out here, I'm going for the knockout." I demolished her talking points and shot back questions that left her stumbling, exposing her for the blatant, clueless corporate shill that she was. If I were her, I'd sneak out of the Bea Arthur Center and hitchhike out of town.

"The crowd is loving it. I lost count of all the times they clapped at what you said." Dusty was practically bouncing.

I took a sip of water, but what my mouth really wanted was more of him.

"As long as you keep doing what you're doing, I think we're in this," Vernita said.

"You told me to fight, so…"

"Modesty was never your strong suit." She patted me on the back. "I'll see you back out there."

She clicked the door shut on her way out. I twisted the lock shut.

Dusty got the message and licked his lips. I loved that I could openly gawk at this hot piece. Even better, I could have him.

"Seeing you up there, taking charge, has been quite a turn-on." Dusty dragged his fingers down my suit jacket lapels until they hovered over my belt. "I can help relieve some of the mid-debate tension." His fingers circled the belt buckle, dipping down to my quickly hardening dick.

"You could." I placed my hand over his. "But I have a better idea."

I moved it away. I walked to the closet in the corner of the room.

"You see, as I was crushing the debate, I'd sometimes look out at you in the crowd and think about what I wanted to do to you. I wanted to know what you wanted me to do."

"Was I wrecking your concentration?"

"Not at all. The opposite, actually." I pulled my briefcase from the closet and reached inside, unzipping a secret compartment.

"If you're pulling out an engagement ring, then we need to have a conversation because that is way too–"

It wasn't a ring I held in my hand. It was a black butt

plug, something I'd wanted to use in the past but never had the nerve to try with anyone. I wasn't sure what prompted me to bring a butt plug to my most important debate.

I needed a good luck charm?

Even though Dusty was new to the world of gay sex, he seemed to pick up on its use without trouble. His pupils went wide.

"What are you doing with that?" he asked, his voice raspy with lust. "Is that a leftover prop from an old production of *Oklahoma*?"

I shook my head no. My tongue was heavy and thick in my mouth. "I want to put this inside you now, and after the debate, I'm going to replace it with my cock. When I look out into the crowd, and I see you squirming in your seat, stretching yourself for me, I'll know what you're thinking."

"Dirty mayor," he growled and readjusted himself. "Putting the ass in assessments. Looking to put your signature in my legislation."

"The intermission is ending soon. Enough with the terrible puns. Bend over."

Dusty undid his pants and bent over the vanity, staring at me through the mirror. I shoved his jeans and his boxers to the floor, savoring the sight of his ass in the air. I thwacked the plug against his cheeks, watching them bounce in response. Were these walls thicker, I'd have given them a hearty slap.

I got on my knees and licked a stripe down his crack, then spread him wide and flicked my tongue over his pink hole. He quaked under my touch, letting out stifled, short groans that he muffled into his arm.

"You taste so good, Dust."

"Give it to me," he breathed out.

I had lube in my briefcase, but I couldn't let this faceful

of ass go to waste. I swirled my tongue around his hole and pressed inside the tight ring of muscle, pressure and passion exploding between us.

Someone knocked at the door. "Two minutes, Mr. Mayor."

"Thank you!" I called back before sucking my index finger and plunging it into his hole.

Dusty arched his back, pushing his ass closer to me. I alternated between finger and tongue. I was tempted to stroke myself, but if I so much as brushed a finger over my dick, I'd be compelled to forgo the plug and fuck him here and now. And I sure as hell wanted more than two minutes to do that.

I darted my tongue in and out, cradling his balls in my hands but careful not to do anything more, lest I cause him to come. No, we'd both have to be adults and wait.

I coated the plug with lube and slid it in place. Fuck, I couldn't wait to really have my way with his ass later tonight. A moan cracked out of him, but fortunately, the hubbub backstage drowned out the noise.

I kissed up his lower back as I stood up, desperate to rip off his clothes and keep going. But I had a debate to win, and for the moment, my competitiveness beat out my horniness.

Dusty pulled up his pants, his eyes drunk with pleasure. "Feel okay?"

"Yeah," he said with a mumbly laugh like he was high.

This was going to be fun.

I patted his ass, which clenched under my hand. "To be continued."

DUSTY

Leo's butt plug gave new meaning to being on the edge of one's seat. While he crushed the second half of the debate, I squirmed and shuffled and bit back the raging lust piling inside me. Ari asked me if I had to go to the bathroom. Leo was forceful, on fire, and I kept imagining what he'd do to me afterward.

And those times when he'd shoot me a sly smile from the stage? I nearly blew my load.

Leo received a line of well-wishers congratulating him on his wonderful performance and vowing their support. Yeah, that was all well and good, but I was getting impatient. Once the crowds departed and the twins went with their mom, Leo and I had to take a quick detour to his office to pick up something, and then we'd go home and replace this plug with the real thing.

The city council building was empty and dark, the custodians long gone. It was a quaint, old building that maintained its charm. We walked past displays of past events in Sourwood history and rows of pictures of important people in ugly suits. His office was the double doors at the end of the hall.

"What's so important that you have to get it now?" I asked, my cheeks clenched with the desire to be ravaged.

Leo made a cocky stroll to his desk, his ass bouncing under his pants. He sat on his desk and flashed me a sly, sexy smile.

"Come here." His growl carried across the room.

Every bead of my skin prickled with want. My dick pushed against my jeans. I rubbed my ass against the door, letting the plug apply its kinky pleasure for a few more precious seconds.

I did as ordered and stood between his legs. He pulled me to his chest and devoured me in a heady kiss.

"How are you feeling?" he slapped my ass. "Ready for the real thing?"

"You took me all the way to your office so that you could fuck me on your desk?"

"I've been in public office for eight years, and I've never so much as kissed someone in this room."

"Well, that needs to change, obviously."

Flames of heat licked in me. I had never wanted to sully a piece of furniture so badly in my life.

I wrapped my arms around his neck. Our lips met in a kiss that was soft at first but thundered with passion under the surface. We were ready. My heart felt as full as...well, my asshole. I wanted to give my best friend all of me, over and over again.

"Are you going to do the motion where you sweep everything off your desk?" I asked as heat built inside me.

"Everything except the computer. Nikolai, our IT guy, will give me shit if I drop another laptop."

"You don't want to be wasting taxpayer money."

Leo grumbled, eyes a forest fire of need. "Why are we still bantering? Get on your knees."

I dropped to the floor like it was my civic duty. My ass stuck out, plug finding new nerve endings to tickle. I bit my lip, fighting the urge to go faster. I undid Leo's belt and fly, while above me, he unbuttoned his shirt.

And then the mayor was naked, thick cock sticking out. I raked my eyes over this beautiful specimen of man, his hairy pecs and belly, ropey, defined arms, smoldering smile sending me love and lust in equal measure. I still wasn't sure how gay I was. It wasn't like I was checking out other guys. And I mostly watched gay porn to get ideas for the bedroom.

I threaded my fingers in his bush, then took his cock in my mouth, letting its salty taste hit my throat. He massaged a hand through my hair and gently pushed me toward him. As if I wasn't headed that way. For a guy who spent forty years not sucking dick, judging by the moans coming from above, I'd say I had a natural gift. But who was bragging?

My lips and tongue slid over his thick head and disappeared his entire cock into my mouth, taking him to the base.

"You are like a blow job savant." He pumped inside me, fucking my face with steady thrusts.

"Would you say I'm better than you?"

"This is one competition I'm willing to lose."

"Let's call it a tie." I tongued his balls and flicked down his taint as his heat and scent made me dizzy with desire. He cried out in pleasure.

"You're wearing too many fucking clothes." He grabbed me by the back of the head and thrust three more times into my mouth, pre-come coating my throat. "Get up."

As soon as I stood up, I was naked, Leo tearing my shirt

from my chest and shoving my pants to the floor. I did not expect to be in my birthday suit in the mayor's office, but the power he wielded was its own aphrodisiac. How many important meetings had been held here? How many important people had sat where I'm sitting now, Leo's head bobbing between my legs?

He glanced up at me with a wicked smile as he sucked on my dick, his firm fist applying pressure as he crammed it into his mouth. His eyes glimmered in the darkness, a sliver of moonlight slashing across his face, silence in the building except for the slurping sounds of sex. I threw my head back and thrust into his mouth.

One of Leo's devious hands found its way to my balls, then my taint, then the promised land.

I yelled out a moan that ripped through me, not realizing I could hit that volume. Ecstasy cracked me open as he brushed his fingers against the plug. He twisted it lightly in my ass like he was fiddling with a combination lock.

"Fuck!" Pins and needles swarmed my body. My cock dribbled pre-come into the mayor's mouth.

"You like that?" Leo asked with bewildered curiosity thrown into his usual dark voice.

"I do. I really really, really fucking do. Yes, I—"

Another twist. Another number in the combination that could unlock me. My fingers dug into the chair arms nearly scratching out the fabric. I wanted to moan for the entire fucking town to hear.

"Do you want to keep this in, or do you want my dick?" he asked, having way too much fun at the exquisite torture he was giving me.

"Dick. Fuck. Dick." I was speaking in tongues; my brain scrambled with new pleasure centers being unearthed. My dick was rock hard and leaking like the world's worst faucet.

"Get on the desk." Leo stood up and, after carefully removing his laptop and lamp, swept his forearm across the desk. Knickknacks and folders and pens and papers careened to the floor. Hunger burned in his eyes. His usually slicked back hair had become loose, strands falling in his eyes.

He was beautiful—a beautiful sex god of a best friend.

I lay down on the desk and threw my legs in the air like a man who knew what he wanted.

A guttural groan escaped my gritted teeth as his fingers made contact with the plug and pulled, ever so slowly, dragging out the heat and bliss until I was empty, a cavernous hole desperate to be filled all over again. I was shaking, absolutely wild with need. This was multi-hour foreplay. My rocks very badly needed to get off.

Leo's thumb circled my stretched hole.

"You are all ready for me," he said. "Unless you've had enough."

"You can fuck right the hell off with that."

"Language. We're going to have to get you better media training."

I flipped him the bird. He flipped it back to me, then took that bird and slid it into my ass.

I cried out as he fingerfucked me fast, my lungs not filling fast enough with air.

"You are so fucking gorgeous." Tenderness splashed across his face, warming his eyes and slightly tugging at his lips. Years of trust had bonded us.

When he finally entered me properly, with his dick like a gentleman, we entered a new plane. We felt in sync in a way I'd never felt with another person. Our connection crossed worlds and time. He humped me in soft, steady moves at first, making sure I was comfortable, checking with me as he went a little bit faster, then a little bit faster. His eyes never left mine. The wood desk was cold against my back. I gleamed at Leo between my legs, his swimmers build chest glistening with sweat.

My cock remained hard as ever, pre-come pooling on my stomach. Leo put a knee on the desk, giving him leverage to lean right on top of me, chest to chest, nose to nose, lips finding each other between sweaty, husky breaths. He plunged deeper inside my opening, building up the fire at the precipice of exploding. My balls tightened with the pull of orgasm.

"I love you," he whispered through tight breaths.

I wanted to say it back, but my mouth couldn't function. The orgasm ripped through every cell, making me sensitive and numb at the same time. Leo's furry abs rubbing against my cock was enough to push me over the edge, seed spilling onto both of our pecs.

"Come inside me," I said, borderline begging.

The idea seemed to turn him on, his black pupils widening into hockey pucks. Above me, my powerful, confident lover shook and thrust wildly; the sound of his hips making contact with my ass echoed. A high-pitched, almost childlike groan cracked out of him as he filled my hole with hot warmth.

"Holy shit." He heaved in air and kissed down my neck.

We lay down on the floor, on top of a fleece blanket he'd been given as a gift once. My back ached with repercussions of not having sex on a supportive mattress, but it would heal. The pleasure was worth the pain.

"So we're doing this, huh?" I asked, the darkness and quiet outside a stark contrast to the nonstop noise of Venice Beach.

"Guess so."

"Boyfriends." It had a nice ring to it. After years of horrible relationships, I was in the strong arms of someone not afraid to love me back. "Will I be the First Gentleman of Sourwood?"

"I hadn't given it much thought." Leo tried to smooth his hair back, but I stopped him. I wanted my floppy-haired Leo.

"First Gentleman sounds too formal."

"We don't have titles for mayoral spouses. This isn't the presidency," he said, but it was too late. My mind was already thinking of possibilities.

"What about First Dude?"

"I guarantee nobody will ever call you that," he deadpanned.

"Grand Duke? Oh, can you knight me?"

"I should've put the butt plug in your mouth." Leo shook his head and laughed despite himself.

I burst out in hysterical chuckling, and soon the quiet city council building was alive with riotous laughter, laughter that had echoed over two a.m. phone calls and meals at the college dining hall. We might've been naked and covered in each other's come, but our relationship was as rock-solid as ever. It hadn't changed. It had evolved into something stronger and more wonderful than I had ever imagined.

Friends.

Lovers.

Mayor and Grand Duke.

These were merely words. The real magic between us couldn't be contained by a label.

28

LEO

I once read that the weather can influence elections. If it's rainy or cold or even merely cloudy, that can affect turnout and tip the election one way or another.

When I looked out the window on Election Day, I saw a few scattered clouds amid the blue sky, which I hoped bode well for me. But after a second, I drew my attention to something more important than the forecast: the guy sleeping next to me.

Dusty stretched and leaned against me, sending electricity into my core. He wiggled his butt into my crotch, turning my morning wood into an erection with intent. I wrapped my arms around him, curled up in the comforter like he was swallowed up by clouds.

"Good morning," he purred, eyes still closed.

I kissed his cheek. "Morning. Today's the day."

"It's finally here." He turned to face me, his sleepy eyes and dopey grin warming my heart. "You nervous?"

"I think we're in a good position."

"Whatever happens, you tried your best."

I snorted. "There are no participation trophies for elections." I brushed the hair out of his eyes and caressed a thumb through the mature lines in his forehead. "At least I can count on your vote."

"No. You can't."

"I can't?"

He shook his head no. "I can't vote for you."

I leaned back, curious how much of this was actually a bit. "Do you not like my positions?"

"I think we could stand to do doggie style less, but that's a conversation for another day."

My cock got even more pokey. I dipped my hand under the blankets and traveled down to his stiff dick. "Well, what do I need to do to win your vote?"

"I won't be swayed by sex."

I pulled my hand back. "Wait, I can't tell if you're being serious."

"I am. I can't vote for you." His weak half-smile was playing games with me. Was this a bit or not?

"That's your choice. Democracy and all that. But can I ask why?" The politician in me stirred awake, ready to persuade.

"Well, unfortunately, amidst all our fake relationship-ping, I never changed my address. I'm technically not a resident of Sourwood. Thus..."

"You can't vote in our election."

"I'm sorry." He shrugged. His hands were tied. Not in the good way. "But I'll still pull your lever."

"Thank you for the offer. If I lose by one vote, Dusty..."

"Then you are allowed to punish me."

My mind reeled with the possibilities at the mention. He'd be a great troublemaker to get in line.

Dusty sat up. "You should probably go vote. Isn't that a

thing? Reporters following candidates to the voting booth to watch them vote for themselves?"

I nodded my head yes. "Maria Lopez is meeting me at my precinct this morning. Then don't forget we have the results party at Mitch's." Mitch was setting up extra televisions so we could watch the local news as results trickled in.

Dusty climbed on top of me, his sleepy eyes sparking to life. He leaned down to whisper close. "And then after the party, I'll take you where you really want to celebrate."

I let out a guttural groan.

Dusty licked his lips and wiggled his eyebrows.

"Applebee's," we said at the same time.

"MITCH, YOU'VE TRULY OUTDONE YOURSELF!" Stone's Throw Tavern was decked out head-to-toe with campaign gear and posters and red-white-and-blue everything. Two tables were laid out with a buffet of appetizers. People stood around small cocktail tables watching the TV as results started to come in from elections across the county.

Mitch walked me around the restaurant showing me everything he and his staff had done to get it ready.

"I am truly impressed. Thank you." I clapped him on the shoulder, then pulled him into a hug. "Thanks for everything."

"I'm proud of you, Leo. I knew when you were the annoying kid, you had a life of politics in your future."

"Thank you for thinking so highly of me."

"Just calling them as I see 'em."

Cal raced up the stairs and flashed his "I Voted" sticker on his chest. "I voted. I just made it."

"The polls have been open since seven in the morning," Mitch said.

"Mitch, I had a day. Josh would not wake up this morning, and we were almost late to school. And I forgot to make him his lunch because I was recording until late last night."

"What about Russ? Where was he in all of this?" I asked.

"Russ had to work late on end-of-year corporate spreadsheet-y stuff. I told him I would handle getting the boys up and to school in the morning since he's having a busy week."

"And Russ actually agreed to that?" Mitch asked, eyebrows arching. "He has met you, right? He knows that's basically like asking you to do rocket science."

"First of all, fuck you. Second of all, just kidding, I love you. Third of all, I have been able to raise a child on my own. And fourth of all, fuck you again." Cal exhaled a deep breath. "Mitch, you remember what having kids is like."

"It's been a long while for Mitch," I said, getting a kick out of how opposite these guys could be.

"Please. My staff are teens and twentysomethings. I'm always parenting." He rubbed his forehead and let out a sigh. People filtered around us and kept interrupting to congratulate me. But I couldn't focus on them, not when my friend was obviously dealing with something.

Cal and I directed him to a corner.

"Mitch, what's going on?" I asked.

He always had on a game face. He never let anything get to him, at least that others could see.

"One of my busboys called in sick, and I had to let a bartender go today. I caught him stealing. I hate firing people. I fucking hate it." He rested his head against the wall.

I couldn't imagine how tough it was to manage a staff like that, of people who didn't see this as a long-term gig.

I've had to let people go and ask for resignations. It's never fun.

"So begins the hunt for another bartender. I may be pulling double duty tonight."

Cal stepped forward. "When I was living in Manhattan doing the acting thing in my twenties, I went to this course and got certified to be a bartender. I keep my license active just in case I needed a job between voiceover gigs. I can step in and help tonight."

"So can I," I said.

"It's your party!" he said to me.

"Then that means I can do what I want to, and I want to help."

"I can't let you do that."

"As mayor, I will institute martial law on the restaurant."

Mitch cocked an eyebrow at me, but he knew that I wasn't backing down. "Okay."

Cal and I followed him to the employee area. I took off my suit jacket and rolled up my sleeves. Not for a photo op or to show the populace I was one of them. I was doing it for a real cause, a friend in need. He handed me a black apron and put me on busboy duty. Cal went behind the bar to work his alleged magic.

"What are you doing?" Dusty asked when he saw me pick up a stack of used dishes from a cocktail table. "Aren't you supposed to be mingling?"

"I'm helping out my friend."

He watched me in silence. "Can I help, too?"

We flitted around the restaurant, cleaning up tables, bringing dirty dishes and glasses into the kitchen, going back and forth. I was still able to mingle with everyone there, but with a crate of dirty dishes between us. In fact, I liked it better than usual parties because I wasn't standing around. I got to stay on my feet and stay busy. Mitch shook his head whenever I brought a new crate into the kitchen, but that was Mitch—always being modest. We had enough history that I could tell he was grateful.

"You really don't have to do this. Especially tonight," he said each time we crossed paths.

"I know," I answered back every time.

As I was picking up a stack of dishes and clumps of cocktail napkins from a table by the window, Vernita approached with a photographer.

A perfect photo op. The mayor who wasn't afraid to get his hands dirty.

I held out my hand to block the shot.

"Nope," I said, shutting it down. "No pictures."

"Are you sure? This would be a great picture for tomorrow if you win."

What would it look like if Mitch's restaurant was so understaffed that he needed the guest of honor to run cleanup? It might've made me look good, but Mitch would be mortified. His pride would be shot.

"Nope. I'm not doing this for a photo op. No pictures," I said firmly. "The only thing people need to know tomorrow is that we held our viewing party at Mitch's restaurant, and it was a great time. Great food, great atmosphere."

Mitch flitted around the restaurant like he was a wind-up toy. He was moving so fast, checking on food, bringing out more, checking on how people were doing. I wondered for a second if he was cloned. How he managed this place day in and day out for damn near twenty-five years blew my mind. *Did* he clone himself? Compared to owning a restaurant, being mayor was a piece of cake. Mitch was one in a million. I hoped he found dependable staff soon. He ran a tight ship, and it wasn't for everyone, but the right people could learn a lot from him.

I also hoped he found a boyfriend, too, but that was another point for another day.

I came up to the bar to collect pint glasses and wine glasses that had been left there. Cal poured two women glasses of white wine. He had the dishtowel over his shoulder in full Sam Malone-mode and made small talk with them.

"How's it going?" I asked him.

"I haven't messed up anyone's drinks yet. Mitch hasn't removed me from my perch."

"Congrats on not wildly fucking up."

"Thank you, Leo. I appreciate that." He wiped down the bar, then flipped the dishtowel back in place. "Did you want a drink?"

"I'll take an old-fashioned."

An old-fashioned was my favorite, but also one of the more complicated drinks.

Cal shot me a look of death.

"Beer it is."

He cracked a beer for me. I surveyed the room of those here to celebrate. No matter how the results came in, I was incredibly lucky to be surrounded by supportive, loving people in my life. Across the room, I made eye contact with Dusty, who was talking with campaign volunteers. He tipped his head to me, and it was a thunderbolt to my heart.

Man, I was totally one of those suckers now, wasn't I?

Dusty ran over, flanked by the twins, interrupting my train of thought. "You have to come see what's on TV."

Lucy turned on her iPhone to record reactions from tonight to use as social media content for future campaigns.

She'd pitched me ideas for campaign ads for the future, and I was impressed by her creativity. I had really awesome kids.

I took Dusty's hand and walked to one of the TVs hoisted over the bar. There was my face side by side with Rita's. Because of the close race and my scandals, our mayoral race was one of the more high-profile local elections in the area.

"We have some updates as more precincts come in," the newscaster said. "In the hotly contested local mayoral race in Sourwood, with seventy percent of precincts reporting, we can project that Leo McCaslin will win re-election."

A huge green checkmark appeared next to my name. Whatever the newscaster said next was drowned out by the cheers that erupted. I became enveloped in a circle of hugs and backslaps and, most importantly, kisses from Dusty. It was like being carried off the field. I couldn't see outside the swarm of well-wishers. I couldn't hear anything but cheers and applause. It was sensory overload, a greater feeling than my previous victories.

Mitch broke in and took the busboy crate from me. "You're off the clock. Go celebrate." His voice was firm. No room for negotiation here. "Congratulations, buddy."

The rest of the night was a blur of people congratulating me and donors looking to get plans back on track for things they wanted. I shook so many hands that my palms were sore by the end. That was the thing about being a politician. You were always campaigning, always working a room. It was a good thing I enjoyed people.

I stepped onto the balcony to catch my breath despite the cold. The night air refreshed me.

"You need some alone time?" Dusty asked at the door. Perfect timing. He was a perpetual sight for sore eyes.

"Never." I nodded for him to join me. He curled against my side as I wrapped my arm around him. We took in the soft sounds of the river, the crisp night air. It was the cherry on top of an incredible night.

"How does it feel to be mayor...again?"

"Feels like the first time." I kissed the top of his head, smelled his shampoo, which was actually mine. It made me think of home all the same.

"When do you start your campaign for governor?"

"You're getting ahead of yourself."

"I know how politics works. I've learned a thing or two being your fake boyfriend."

Yesterday, Harlen Carruthers came out endorsing me for mayor. He wanted to resume talks about having me run for governor in four years, with Dusty at my side.

"Right now, I'm focused on leading Sourwood. And then we'll see." I had a feeling the next morning, Vernita would be at our house devising a strategy for statewide office. Then donors across the state would get word and come forward. More planning, more hobnobbing. It was a lot to prepare for, and I started to get nervous.

Seeming to sense this, Dusty gave my hand a squeeze, putting me at ease. All at once, anything felt possible.

29

DUSTY

A FEW WEEKS LATER

Christmas on the East Coast is vastly superior to a West Coast Christmas. I forgot how magical this time of year could be when it actually looked like a winter wonderland outside. Sure, I didn't have an ocean view, and it was getting a lot harder to wake up for a freezing cold morning run, but a snow-covered Sourwood was a sight that consistently took my breath away. I was turning into one of those holiday obsessives. Give me all the cheesy Christmas movies, all the candy, and all the songs.

Oh, and give me Leo dressed up as Santa Claus.

It was an annual Sourwood tradition. On Christmas Eve, the mayor would dress up as Santa for the kids who visited city hall to sit on his lap. Leo really got into it, decked out in a thick white beard and using a Kris Kringle chortle. I hung off to the side and watched from a distance. And developed a Santa fetish in real time.

Alas, I was too old to participate. That was okay. I didn't need anything from the North Pole. I had everything I needed. Life was good. And besides, it would be difficult to sit on his lap while wearing a butt plug anyway.

I clenched my butt cheeks. Had to get the chimney ready for Santa.

"Dusty!" A sturdy hand clamped on my shoulder, jolting me out of my Leo fantasies.

Bud Hawkins, a rough-looking blue-collar guy with a heart of gold, maintained the facilities at the Bea Arthur Center and always had a smile on his face.

"Hiya, Bud."

"I love that bookcase you built for the Center's gift shop. We get compliments on it at least once a week. When will two and three be done?"

"Let's say mid-January. Business has been unexpectedly booming."

"It's well-deserved. You do good work."

Apparently, I did. Since I was staying put in Sourwood, I needed to find a job. While I began my job hunt, I started with doing odd fix-up jobs and building the sets for the children's theater group's Holiday Pageant. Word got out that I was good at making things, and requests rolled in for custom built-in shelves, tables, you-name-it. Come spring, I was going to be very busy with building wedding trellises and outdoor decks. For the first time, I didn't feel stuck in a job. I had ownership over my career. I was building a business. And on top of that, I was enmeshing myself into the fabric of Sourwood. I felt like a part of the community and happy to contribute something back.

My sexy Santa Claus sidled up to us. He shook Bud's hand and asked about the Center and how things were going. He might've been wearing a big red suit and fake beard, but he knew how to turn on the mayoral charm.

After Bud left to file forms with the county clerk, Leo and I walked back to his office. Holding hands, of course. It still sent a bolt of energy up to my heart.

Leo ripped off his Santa suit. There was a regular suit underneath. My Superman.

"What's this article for?" I sank onto the loveseat against the wall. It was too small for two grown men, but in certain positions, we made it work for us.

"Just a few questions about how we're spending the holidays, our hopes for the new year." Leo checked his hair in a magnet mirror stuck to his file cabinet, getting rid of stray fibers from his Santa suit.

"Is she going to ask about the investigation?"

"Probably not. This is a light, fun piece. But you never know." Leo put the mirror in his desk drawer. "It's still fresh.

"I can't believe it." My stomach turned with the memory of first finding out.

"Neither can I. It's definitely going down in the annals of Sourwood history."

Maria stopped by a little bit later, where we were back to all smiles. As Leo predicted, she asked about our holiday plans. Leo talked about his famous roast chicken he makes for Christmas. He ran down a high-level agenda of goals for the coming year and stayed mum on plans for running for governor. It was a decision he was in the process of mulling.

I chimed in with how excited I was to have a white Christmas for the first time in decades.

Maria positioned her phone to make sure she was capturing the audio before moving the next item in her notepad. "Mr. Mayor, does Christmas feel any different after the arrest of Rita and Gus Buchanan two weeks ago?"

"I'm not going to let that ruin our holiday." Leo had a rehearsed answer. I knew he would. But he was still processing the reality of what happened. "It's horrible, but I'm relieved justice is being served."

"We're all shaken up by it. How did you realize that they were behind hacking your phone?"

"Dusty." Leo put a hand on my knee and squeezed, telling me everything he couldn't say.

"Gus gave me this really strange, kinda threatening look at the Zombie 5K. It stuck in my head. I brought it up to Leo after the election when Rita refused to acknowledge his victory, demanded a recount, and wouldn't even look at him during city council meetings."

"So we investigated," Leo said.

"And that's how you found out one of your aides was working for her," Maria said, shaking her head in disbelief. "The police said that the aide hacked your computer and grabbed your text messages."

Leo nodded yes. "I'll never sync my phone and computer again."

"I know Leo may've had some scandals, but you have to admit an online hookup and fake boyfriend pales to computer hacking and information theft. That's a real scandal," I said, eager to get this point across. Leo didn't have scandals. He just had a weird dating life.

Maria nodded in agreement. "Dusty, what are you most looking forward to for your first Sourwood Christmas?"

"I've loved being here for the holidays. Everyone is so festive and cheerful. Maybe I'll get Leo to read me *The Night Before Christmas* tonight."

The kids were with their mom for Christmas Eve. We had the house to ourselves to enjoy our long winter's nap. Except without the napping.

———

LEO HAD the whole Single Dad's Club contingent over for a Christmas day feast. A thick dusting of snow had covered Sourwood anew with white beauty overnight. The kitchen was all abuzz with roasted chicken, rosemary garlic potatoes, and sauteed green beans while Christmas pop hits played out from my phone. It was a very "God bless us, every one" vibe.

Leo treated meal prep as a plank in his platform, rolling out a whole plan for Christmas meal perfection. The only thing thwarting his efficiency was his co-cook, who kept hugging him and kissing him and pinching his cute butt whenever they crossed paths in the kitchen.

Sorry, very not sorry.

"Kids, have you set the table yet?" Leo called out.

No response.

I put my hand over Leo's chest to stop him from going into the living room. "I'll handle this."

It was another step forward in my mission to be more dad-like. The un-fun part of being a father. Lucy and Ari already saw me as an uncle, so I wasn't coming to this cold.

I pushed through the swinging door to the dining room, where an empty dining table sat, then onto the living room, where the kids were sitting next to the Christmas tree playing with their luxurious Christmas toys. Lucy had gotten a camera while Ari was in the zone, thanks to his noise-canceling headphones. When I was their age, I got a Monopoly game board for Christmas that my parents had picked up from Goodwill. Leo explained that he and his ex-wife had both chipped in for one big gift each for the kids.

"Hey," I said to two kids very much in the zone.

It took them a few seconds to realize I was in the room and talking to them. Ari pulled off his headphones sheepishly.

"Your dad asked you to set the table."

"We will," Lucy said.

"What's stopping you from doing it now?" Leo told me to hold my ground. Especially at this age, kids were like expert cross-examiners, ready and eager to break down your logical argument.

"People aren't coming for a little while. We'll do it, Dusty. We promise." Lucy gave me a teacher's pet smile, which nearly threw me off my fledgling game.

"Your dad—*we* would like you to do it now. Get it out of the way rather than rush later."

"It won't take that long," Ari said.

"So you can do it now." I sat on the couch arm and decided to take the good cop approach. "I'm trying to look out for you. If your dad goes into the dining room and sees the table not set, he's gonna go ballistic. I know that it's not Christmas unless someone ends up in tears, but I don't want it to be you two."

They looked to each other, their twin minds communicating in some advanced way, before giving me the green light head nod. They got up and went into the dining room.

Another parenting challenge aced. Well, B-plussed. I'd get better about putting my foot down in the future. Promise.

———

MITCH WAS the first guest to arrive with his daughter, Ellie, and her boyfriend, Tim, in tow.

Or rather, fiancée.

"Holy diamond ring, Batman!" I said to the rock on his daughter's finger.

"Tim proposed this morning," she squealed. Ellie was a

big, professional lawyer, but never underestimate the power of love and jewelry to reduce grown adults to little kids.

"Congratulations!" I squealed back. I didn't know much about jewelry, but I knew that diamond could be seen from space. Well done, Tim.

"Mitch." Leo clapped his friend on the back.

"Ellie's getting married." Mitch's usually stoic face couldn't withstand the emotion. It crumbled into a giddy smile. "My girl's getting married."

"I remember when she learned how to ride a bike," Leo said. "Do you remember that, Ellie? We were at that lake house we rented one summer."

"I was so excited I couldn't stop and almost biked into the lake. Thank goodness you were there to stop me."

"Mayor McCaslin, looking out for all constituents at all times," I said.

"That was pre-mayor," he corrected with a smarmy half-smile that managed to make my stomach do a flip. "Come in, come in. I have a bottle of champagne we can crack open."

Cal and Russ came a little bit later with the boys. Russ apologized for getting here on time rather than ten minutes early. He cut his eyes to Cal, who kissed away his frustration. They brought more sides. Josh and Quentin ran upstairs with the twins to play, their laughter and happy yelling filling the house with warmth.

Right before we were set to eat, fresh off a plane from Seattle, came the elusive fourth member of the Single Dad's Club: Buzz, his boyfriend Shane, and their toddler Anne.

"Buzz! Shane! I finally get to meet you!" I pulled them into hugs. They smelled great. The most unique cologne I'd ever sniffed. "And baby Anne! You are cuter in person." I bopped her on the nose.

"The famous Dusty." Buzz was tall and lanky with floppy blonde hair and a boyish smile. He was the cheeriest-looking bigshot corporate guy I'd ever met.

"It's so nice to learn you're not actual floating heads." All I'd seen of them were small FaceTime headshots.

Shane took off his coat, revealing a tight polo that showed off armfuls of tattoos. I did not see those on FaceTime.

"Shane—you've got ink!"

He glanced at his arms, amused. "That I do."

A flicker of fire burned in Buzz's eyes as he glimpsed his boyfriend's muscled, inked arms while Shane flashed him an intimate smile back. It was good to see that a baby hadn't depleted their heat for each other.

I took their coats and hung them up. Dang, Shane was more gorgeous in person. He was much younger, with close-cropped hair and a smolder that in some alternate universe would've made him a perfect model. They were an odd pairing, the businessman and the tattooed hottie, but their love shined through.

"How was the flight?"

"Good, for the most part," Buzz said.

"We were doing great until somewhere over Cleveland, Anne had a little meltdown." Shane cradled her in his arms and made an exaggerated face at her. "Yes, you did!"

"I don't blame you, Anne," I said. "Nobody likes Cleveland."

I walked with them into the living room, where the rest of the Single Dad's Club greeted them like they were the Beatles. They swallowed Buzz and Shane in huge embraces and passed Anne around for kisses and cuddles. The fireplace crackled in the background. I wanted to pinch myself at how I wound up here.

Last Christmas, I was alone, strolling down the beach, sidestepping homeless people and kids trying to sell me drugs. My ex-girlfriend, Audrey, had flown to Atlanta to shoot a movie over the holidays. On Christmas Day, I went to the movies, then ate a grocery store sandwich on the beach, silently wishing that next Christmas would be different.

A lot can happen in a year, I told myself.

I took my rightful place on the couch arm, facing Shane in the armchair with Anne wiggling to get off his lap. "So, Leo tells me you and Buzz met because you worked for him?"

"I was his manny."

"For how long?"

"Three days."

I leaned in closer. "Three days? Is that what you said?"

"Yeah." Shane cracked a knowing smile. "We moved a little fast."

I couldn't find a dentist in three days, and Buzz and Shane found soulmates. Time was a funny son of a bitch.

"It was a wild three days." Shane's eyes widened as he reflected back on them, and he was a guy who didn't seem to get blown away often. "But it was the best thing to happen to me."

"How's life in Seattle?"

"It rains a lot. Doesn't get cold like it does here, though. I would've dressed warmer," Shane said of his polo. "But we love it. Buzz is heading new eco-friendly fragrance designs at his company. Everyone he works with is super chill and really welcoming. They threw us a big party when we arrived. And apart from that, we've been able to go on hikes with this little lady. The only thing that's missing is all of you."

"We'll have to plan a big trip out there next year. I want to see the Space Needle, and I'm sure Leo will want to visit the original Starbucks and worship at their altar."

"It's literally just a Starbucks. There's nothing special about it. But there's an incredible mac and cheese place next door that you must check out."

"And I don't drink Starbucks." Leo put his hands on my shoulders. I leaned back, and he dipped down to kiss me, his face hot from all the cooking. "Only in a pinch."

"You'll fit right in. Nobody in Seattle likes Starbucks," Shane said.

———

DINNER WAS INCREDIBLE. I barely helped. I mostly measured out ingredients and then put them away in the proper cabinets. But I still happily took credit for the delicious food. Leo and I had been friends for-freaking-ever, and how was I only now discovering he could cook? It made me more excited about our relationship. We knew each other front to back, yet there was more to learn. There were volumes of the Leo World Book Encyclopedia I hadn't cracked open yet.

The dining table was a hotbed of activity: plates being piled with food, dishes passed around, drinks being poured, candles aglow in the center. Leo and I sat at opposite ends of the table, but how I wished we were next to each other. I wanted to hold his hand and plant kisses on his cheek, and let him know how happy I was. He kept looking at me, face soft in the candlelight, that cocky, warm smile filling me with all good things.

"It's crazy how our group has expanded in the last year," Cal said. "Everyone's pairing off."

Around the table were couples: me and Leo, Cal and

Russ, Buzz and Shane, Ellie and Tim. Mitch could feel the unintentional eyes on him.

"I didn't mean—what I meant..." Cal stammered before deciding to shut himself up with a forkful of mashed potatoes. Russ chuckled and rubbed his hand.

"I'm happy for everyone here," Mitch said, and I thought I detected a hint of longing, but with him, it was hard to tell. He covered it well. "And kudos to Dusty. I never thought there was anyone out there who could put up with Leo."

The resulting laughter drowned out the awkwardness of before. Leo blew his friend a kiss filled with equal parts contempt and love.

I tapped my knife on my glass. "Excuse me."

Leo eyed me over the candles.

"Leo isn't the only one in this relationship who likes to make speeches." I held up my glass. "I wanted to make a toast. To friends, and family, and the friends who become family."

We clinked glasses with those nearby, and a few enterprising guests reached across the table to clink.

"Leo, anything you wanted to add?" I asked, knowing that Leo couldn't resist having the last word and giving the best speech.

He shook his head no, to my surprise. "You said it perfectly, Dust."

———

Thank you for reading!

Can Mitch find his happily ever after when he hires a new bartender...his daughter's ex-boyfriend? Find out when he takes center stage in *The Barkeep and the Bro,* an age gap, boss/employee, grumpy/sunshine romance.

To read about how Buzz and Shane got together, join my mailing list *The Outsiders* and receive the free story, *Three Nights with the Manny.* It's filled with humor, heat, heart, and creative uses for baby oil. www.ajtruman.com/outsiders

Please consider leaving a review on the book's Amazon page or on Goodreads. Reviews are crucial in helping other readers find new books.

Join the party in my Facebook Group and Instagram. Follow me on Amazon and Bookbub to be alerted to new releases.

And then there's email. I love hearing from readers! Send me a note anytime at info@ajtruman.com. I always respond.

ALSO BY A.J. TRUMAN

South Rock High

Ancient History

Drama!

Romance Languages

Advanced Chemistry

Single Dads Club

The Falcon and the Foe

The Mayor and the Mystery Man

The Barkeep and the Bro

The Fireman and the Flirt

Browerton University Series

Out in the Open

Out on a Limb

Out of My Mind

Out for the Night

Out of This World

Outside Looking In

Out of Bounds

Seasonal Novellas

Fall for You

You Got Scrooged

Hot Mall Santa

Only One Coffin

ABOUT THE AUTHOR

A.J. Truman is a gay man living in Indiana with his husband, son, and fur-babies. He writes books with **humor, heart, and hot guys.** What else does a story need? He loves spending time with his family and occasionally sneaking off for an afternoon movie.

www.ajtruman.com
info@ajtruman.com
The Outsiders - Facebook Group

www.ingramcontent.com/pod-product-compliance
Lightning Source LLC
Chambersburg PA
CBHW022117310726
48972CB00007B/2083